De...

thank you.

Help Wanted

Peace,

3-24-06

a novel
by Shawan Lewis

FIRST EDITION

Edited by: Leslie German
Cover Design by: Brandon Reevey
Book Design by: Brian Holscher

Acknowledgments

Last year was a trip. When storms knocked me on my ass, the sun rained down so I could see my way through. Thanks to the Father who knew the dream before I believed. For everything under the sun, there is a season. For every disappointment, there is a reason. Finally, it's harvest time.

Sevalyn, a mother beyond measure. When I fall short, you pick me up. I cannot thank you enough for all you've done. You are the true meaning of grace. Paul, thank you for the calm moments. Nia Amel, my adorable daughter whose energy keeps bags under my eyes. Never change because you are the reason I strive. Thanks for making me feel, Golden. Wanna sing? Nana, thank you for being a wonderful grandmother. Granddaddy's gone, but I remember his story because of you.

David and Sandra, thanks for being there from the beginning and reminding me not to sweat the stupid stuff. Peace and love from your little sis. Godsons Allen and Ian, I blinked and you two weren't babies anymore. Keep making me proud. Shawnda, a true sister. A friendship built from ivy leaves will grow infinitely. Love ya, Schmoo.

Godmother Rebecca, your little chicken has come along way, huh? I look forward to spending more time with you. Family and friends, thanks for your love and prayers.

Azarel, you have definitely been an angel to me. You are an example of how God puts the right people together at the right time. Life Changing Books, Inc., thanks for letting the world know about me. Leslie German, you made sure every voice in the story got a fair chance to be heard. Thank you for straightening out my mess.

Tina McElroy Ansa, thank you for your encouragement and pearls of wisdom. Sapelo Island is a wonderful place to fall in love with words.

Annika Young, I give you credit for putting this project in good hands. If you had not introduced me to Azarel, I would still be sitting on my butt, wallowing over rejection postcards from literary agencies. Benita Paschall, thanks for the advice and the jokes during our mad dash through the airport. Most importantly, thanks for believing in me. The radio show was an awesome experience. Yahya Muhammad and R. Khalil Muhammad, thanks for being supportive and patient during my first radio interview. You all were wonderful hosts.

To the readers and proprietors who have supported my debut novel, my success is because of you.

To the new writers on this winding road with me, stay encouraged. Your heart will make it happen.

For Walter C. Hill, my guardian angel.

Prologue

Bad Eve

I thought a burglar had broken into my home when I felt the hard slap to my face. My sleepy eyes fluttered as I tried to see the man straddled on top of me. His face was hard to recognize in the dark, but when two calloused hands encircled my neck, I knew my husband was trying to kill me.

Gabriel was the culprit who left a stinging scratch on my breast as he hurled me out of bed. I cried out in fear as my body hit the cold wooden floor. I was dumbfounded as I held the torn fabric from my powder blue eyelet nightgown. It was the wedding anniversary gift he'd given me a year ago on Christmas Eve.

His voice echoed off the bedroom walls. "Anela, that's the last time you'll sleep in that bed!" he yelled. "A whore when I married you, and been one ever since!"

I flinched when he spit on me. "Gabe, stop it!" I cried.

Tightfisted as he kneeled down to my face, I quickly shielded my head from the next assault. "You didn't think I'd catch you and the preacher together yesterday, did you?" he asked. "I knew that jackass was a ladies man, but fooling around with my own wife!"

"Gabriel, I'm not seeing Pastor Michaels," I said in a labored whisper. "I talked to him about your drinking problem to see if he could help."

"I don't wanna hear your lies, Anela! My mother told me not to marry no spoiled woman. I should've listened."

I shook my head as my husband bound me by the feet and hands, using the same rope he had nailed up in the basement to hang wet laundry. I wondered why he pulled the rope so hard around my ankles. I was stricken with multiple sclerosis at the age of thirty, so I couldn't go too far. Maybe he thought the miracle I'd prayed for all these years would show up in the nick of time. He doubled the rope around my legs.

A blistery night of high winds did not prevent Gabriel from dragging me out of the house. He put me in his rusty pick-up truck and drove to the construction yard where he used to work. My husband was my caretaker. Mama used to say, "Be grateful to a man who takes care of his own." Those were her words of wisdom when she placed pearls around my neck the eve of my wedding. She forgot to tell me that there's a difference between being taken care of and being cared for. Pearls felt like rope when pulled too tight.

Gabriel and I were in the midst of abandoned forklifts. Henson's Contracting employed quite a few folk here in York, Pennsylvania. You could make decent money and work your way up. Gabriel made it all the way to Foreman. We were doing all right until last month. His boss let him go. Layoff was what Gabe told me. Alcohol on his breath was what I knew.

"I ain't had nothin' but bad luck since I been with you!" he shouted. "I lost my job and the bank denied my loan. I dedicated twenty-five years of my life to you, and you blushin' in some other man's face."

"Gabriel Grace, it's the dead of winter," I said. "You got me out here half naked, and tied up. I can't waste breath convincing you of who I am because either the freezing weather, or that gun in your hand gonna cut my time short. Pastor Michaels did hug and kiss me on the cheek, after he told me he was leaving York. I guess you saw us out in the gazebo, because that's where I asked him to take me. I'd been in the house all day, and I wanted to go out for a minute to get some fresh air. I could tell Pastor was worried about something. He told me the sins he laid down at the altar were falling back on him." I took my eyes off of the gun and stared at Gabriel. "Pastor said he was sick from loving too many women—and men."

Gabriel's brow twitched from the single line of perspiration bleeding from his scalp. He grabbed the rope on my wrists and raised me off of the wet ground. I shivered from soaked undergarments as he pulled me close to him. The vapors from his breathing burned my skin. My bare feet were numb from being covered with muddy snow. Gabriel's caramel colored eyes, the ones I admired, were now black as coal. "What did he say to you!" Gabriel shouted with his chest heaving.

I closed my eyes as I prepared to speak. "He said he was sorry, Gabriel. He asked for forgiveness when I told him I was gonna leave you."

"That son of a bitch!" Gabriel cried as he aimed the gun to his head. Suddenly, he removed the gun from his jaw and bent down to get me. I was pulled a few feet in front of a ditch wide enough to catch anything thrown its way. Gabriel put his right arm around my waist, balancing the revolver in his left hand. He pointed the steel piece at my womb. An empty space where previously two babies never survived beyond the first three months. I shed tears for all of us.

Then, I visualized a final moment being peaceful. I looked at my husband and saw Cyrus, my first love; the one who spoiled me. Cyrus Williams was a traveling jazz musician who never got sick of the love poems I wrote for him. He filled the silent places of my poems with music. Cyrus made love to my words with his guitar. A bus accident killed him. I stopped writing love poems because the silent places made me miserable.

I blinked and saw Gabriel again. At fifty years old we were both at the crossroads. He had lived a secret life, and I had never gotten over the loss of Cyrus. Now, husband and wife were face to face, waiting for fate to decide how to fix broken hearts.

I managed to grab the bottom of Gabriel's denim shirt. I tugged it to get his attention. He stared at me, but his mind was a million miles away. "Gabe, I found out yesterday about your father," I said. "I'm so sorry he did those terrible things to you. I wish you would have told me, but it don't matter now. I just want you to know that you matter to me. I can't erase the demons beating you from the past, but I can tell you it's gonna be all right. Love doesn't have to end this way. We can find someone who can help."

Gabriel choked on the tears that ran between his lips. "No, Anela. I can't." I felt him nuzzle the gun into me.

"Gabriel, please don't. Please!" I screamed. "I'm begging you."

His ashen hand removed the bobby pins from my bun, allowing freshly colored auburn hair to fall to my lean shoulders. My hairdresser Mae said the color complimented the honey tones in my skin. A new hair color to spice up my look didn't mean much, right now. Tears clouded my eyes, and everything in my life got blurry.

Gabriel tried to kiss my cheek, but I turned away. There was no love in what he was about to do. I looked down at the necklace resting around my neck. I should have gotten rid of my mother's pearls a long time ago. "Until we meet again, Anela," he said.

"God be with you Gabriel because we will not meet again," I said, out of breath.

"Bang!" was all I heard. Suddenly, a white light erased the darkness. I felt a warm breeze under my feet. Next thing I knew, I was walking along a beautiful beach. A tender hand held mine as a miracle guided me, each step of the way.

Do not neglect to show hospitality to strangers,
for thereby some have entertained angels unawares.
Hebrews 13:2

Rainmaker
2003

Damn Phone

The voice mail messages sent chills down my spine. Her screams, fresh in my mind, as I sped down the Jones Falls Expressway. I was petrified as I glanced at the radiant sunbeams reflecting in my rear view mirror. Last night's fallen snow would not survive this sudden heat. Disappointed by the crimson light, I drove out of the city, praying for rain.

Pashen, a derivative of passion. Misspelled on purpose. The meaning—love. Whatever the fuck that meant. Pashen, my mother—a heat seeker. Pain was her plight. Rain—her only solution. I hoped that one day, when the sun met the rain, the devil would stop beating the shit out of her.

❖ ❖ ❖ ❖ ❖

This morning when my cell vibrated, I ignored it. I wanted to relax as Jonathan made love to me, but I couldn't. He stroked gently, attentive to the fact that he was the first. So *fine*, I thought as I brushed the dreadlocks away from his eyes. The cognac colored dreads were a perfect match for his sandalwood skin. He tried so hard to please me. When I moved the locks away from his face, he looked concerned. I smiled at him, but he seemed unconvinced. "Baby, you want me to stop?" he asked.

"I'm fine," I muffled. I crushed a mound of the bed sheet in my hand as I stifled a painful moan. I couldn't relax my stomach muscles, which made his thrusts unbearable.

"Then why are you crying?" he asked. He stopped moving. His warm fingertips swept my wet face. "I don't get satisfaction from hurting you. I'm not that type of man."

"I know you're not," I said. "I'm nervous, that's all."

"What can I do to stop those tears? Tell me what you want."

"I want you." My hands slid down his smooth skin, massaging the small crevice in his back. He moved again. I paced my hips to his rhythm, trying to block out the shit that was heavy on my mind.

Jonathan intensified his thrusts inside of me. His muscular hands caressed my back. He enjoyed what I had to offer. Vibrations. Moans. Passion. I looked at the phone on the nightstand. Vibrations. Moans. Pashen. I felt a new sensation. There was no more burning between my legs. Jonathan had found my spot. I felt intense pressure down there. Pressure I didn't want to stop. I closed my eyes and held Jonathan close, feeling him go deeper and deeper. The phone vibrated on the nightstand, moving closer and closer to the edge. I lost it.

"Jonathan!"

"You like that?"

"No!"

He frowned. "What? What's wrong?"

I wriggled from under his pelvis, breathless. He looked down as his dick was ejected by my movement. "Look," I said pointing at the floor. "My phone fell. It vibrated off the nightstand."

"You're joking, right?" he said. "You stopped me because of a fuckin' cell phone!"

I rolled my eyes and snatched the sheet from over him. "Jonathan, you don't have to get loud," I said as I reached to pick up the phone.

He shook his head. "Hailee, I've already seen what you got." He kissed me. "I'm sorry for getting upset," he said. "I was caught up in my zone and lost my head."

My seductive stare at his chiseled torso made him smile. "Looks like you still doin' all right to me," I said.

Jonathan stood up and pulled the slick latex off his thick, erect flesh. "Why don't we wash up and get something to eat?" he asked. "We could hit IHOP and talk about what's on your mind?"

I stood on my tiptoes to kiss his freckled nose. "I need a rain check. Pashen called twice. I gotta get home because I think she's in trouble."

He hugged me. "Maybe I should go with you to make sure she's okay."

"Thanks Jonathan, but this is something I have to do on my own," I said. I grabbed my clothes and headed for the bathroom.

"Call me as soon as you can," he yelled out to me. "Let me know everything's cool. I won't leave my room. I'll probably order a pizza and crack open that MCAT study guide."

I came back into the bedroom fully dressed. Jonathan threw on his sweat pants. He kissed my forehead. "Good luck studying," I said as I zipped up my Old Navy fleece hoodie.

"Thanks," he said shaking his head. "Undergrad at Johns Hopkins is tearing my ass up, so you know med school gonna kill a brotha."

"You'll be fine." I looked down at the floor. "I'm sorry I ruined our day."

He raised my chin. "You didn't ruin our day, Hailee. This morning was beautiful."

"Thanks for everything, Jonathan." I caressed his face before I let him go.

"Call me," he said as he followed me into the living room.

Trying to fight my emotions, I nodded *yes* and walked out his front door.

I cried leaving the apartment building, because I knew I would never see Jonathan again. Not in this way, at least. Trouble don't dissolve in a day. It would take time to handle family business. Pashen had my heart.

What's Up With That

Last night I waited at Starbucks for Jonathan to get out of class when I received a strange text message. The message read, *Do you like trains? Your Mama does.* I immediately called Pashen. She answered on the third ring. "What's up?" she said, nonchalant.

"Pashen, you all right?"

"Yeah, why?"

I sighed. "I got this message on my phone, and it scared me."

"What was the message?" she asked.

"I can barely hear you. Why you whisperin'?"

"Look, I'm busy. I'll catch up with you later."

"Where are you?" I asked.

Pashen sucked her teeth. "I'm where I wanna be. Worry about me when I don't answer the phone."

"I was just concerned that's all," I said.

"I gotta go. Peace." She hung up.

"Yeah, okay," I said as I snapped my phone shut. Ain't no peace in lies. I knew I'd have to face Pashen's truth sooner than later.

All I did was chase after Pashen. I'm the only person who tolerated her trifling ass. There were only fifteen years between us, because I wasn't planned. I was four pounds when I was born, probably due to the girdle she wore under her clothes to hide me from her mother, Geraldine. When Pashen went into labor Geraldine put her in a cab, slammed the door, and didn't think twice about moving back to North Carolina.

Pashen had me in the back of a cab during a rainstorm. She said the wind raged, moving the car from side to side. She thought God was punishing her for lying with a guy who left her so quick, his sperm hadn't even dried from around her pussy. Pashen was alone, yelling to the top of her lungs until I gushed out.

The rain had turned into hail by the time the cab reached the hospital entrance. I was cuddled in my mother's arms, wrapped in her gray sweatshirt. When Pashen was lifted out of the car by the paramedic, she covered me with her body, protecting me from the storm. She named me Hailee because she said I must've been strong to survive that night.

Twenty years later, we fought like cats and dogs—more like sisters than mother and daughter. I was the pretty, high achiever. Pashen, the phat mami, always looking for trouble. She handed out more business cards to thugs, than arrest warrants, when she was a cop. I loved her, though. She was all I had, and in this cold ass world, being a part of her drama was better than being alone.

❖❖❖❖❖

"Why the fuck did I waste money on this earpiece!" I shouted as I yanked the connector out of my cell phone. "Piece of shit never stays in my ear." I sighed in frustration as I got off the expressway at Northern Parkway to get some gas. I put ten dollars in the tank, then dialed Pashen's cell phone number when I was back on the road. I could tell by her *hello* that she was in deep shit.

"Pashen, where are you?" I asked frantically.

"What the hell is wrong with you, Hailee? Didn't you get my pages!" she yelled.

I gripped the steering wheel tighter. "I got 'em," I said. "I was in East Baltimore. I'm on I-83 now."

She didn't respond, but I heard her moaning in pain. "Ma, talk to me. You paged me 911. Tell me what happened."

She coughed in the phone. "Hail . . . Hailee I'm so cold."

"Where are you?" I asked.

"I don't know where I am. Them niggas pulled me out of

the truck and threw me into the woods. Punk ass bitches. Lucas asked me to deliver some Coke. I ain't think twice, because that powder was gonna have me paid. Somebody besides Lucas must've known about the Benjamins involved on my run, and decided to mess me up."

I held my head with one hand and kept the steering wheel straight with the other. "Pashen, you're outside in the damn cold? Where's Lucas?"

"Lookin' for my ass, probably. Hailee, you gonna have to talk to him for me. Try to get him to calm down. He said he gonna cut my throat. I know that shit's real. I fucked up, Boo. I fucked up real bad."

"Ma, calm down," I said. "Let me figure out where you are, then we can talk about Lucas, okay?"

"Hailee, hurry up. Lucas could be in these woods right now with a scope on me."

"You gonna be fine, just listen to me," I said. "Where were you before those guys forced you into the car?"

"I was at a party with Remy, a guy Lucas used to roll with when he lived in New York," she said. "Earlier this morning, Lucas and I went over the run I had set at this doctor's house in Guilford. He told me to meet Remy at a row house in Bolton Hill, to give him money for a job he did last night."

I switched the phone to my other ear and turned the volume down on the car radio. "You ever dealt with Remy before?" I asked.

"Naw, last night was the first time we met." She sneezed. "When I got to the party, I had a Hennessey and hollered at this guy I knew. Remy walked over and introduced himself. He acted all familiar and shit, talking 'bout I was good people, and how he wanted to hook up on a future deal. I told him *no*, 'cause I don't even flow like that. I don't let nobody roll shotgun on my dime unless it's Lucas. When I gave Remy the envelope, that midget looked at me like I was short. Oh shit!"

"What? Pashen!"

"Damn deer ran across and scared the crap out of me."

"Please be careful," I said. "Try to find a place that has

people around. You see any houses?"

"I'm walking, but I don't see nothing but snow and trees," she said. "Anyway, I was still at the party when Lucas called. I told him his boy was shady, but he said he was cool. I rolled a blunt and relaxed for a minute. I went to my car for some Motrin, because my head was pounding, and these two men stepped out of a Tahoe. One grabbed my arm. I pulled my gun, but I got hit with something. I woke up in their truck with bruises on me and a knot on the back of my head. I tried to fight the big ass dude in the back seat with me, but my 125 pounds was no match for him. He opened the door and threw me out."

"Pashen, I'll call Jeff," I said paying close attention to my speedometer when I saw a car ahead hydroplane from the slushy roadway. "Jeff will know what to do."

"Hailee, don't bother. I already called. He brushed me off."

"I'll call you right back," I said.

"Hailee, wait a minute. If by chance you don't reach me, I want you to know I love you."

"Pashen, I got you. Don't worry."

❖ ❖ ❖ ❖ ❖

Sweat beading on my nose from anger, I dialed Jeff's number. "Lieutenant Brooks speaking," he said with an attitude.

"I need a favor," I snapped.

"Who is this?" the lieutenant asked.

"You were almost my stepfather. You forgot my voice already?"

He didn't say anything for a few seconds, then he finally mumbled, "Hailee."

"That was messed up what you did to Pashen, but I don't have time to get into that. I need you to trace her cell phone and go get her ASAP."

"Look, I'm en route to an assignment," he said.

"No, you're en route to find my mother. You're a lieutenant. Delegate that other shit to someone else. Pashen needs you!" I yelled.

"I can't quit working every time your mother has a crisis.

Pashen always needs something."

"Well damn, when did cops stop responding to crisis situations?" I asked. "Oh, I see. Y'all too busy stealing money from the city and beatin' on women. Switchin' police chiefs like I switch dirty underwear. Baltimore's finest. No wonder Pashen quit."

"Your mother got fired," he reminded.

"No, Pashen was placed on medical leave and she resigned. Now I'm asking you to be about my mother for a minute. Back in the day, you had time for her, your wife, and my best friend."

He breathed heavily into the phone. "I swear I fuckin' don't need this today," he said.

"Jermaine turned three last week," I said. "Name sounds familiar? Maybe you forgot you had a beautiful little boy, because Tiffani said you ain't dropped dollars in over a year. I bet Fox Channel 45 would love to get wind of a cop scandal: *Upstanding Lieutenant, moonlighting as a security guard for Legacy strip club, fathers a child with dancer who was a minor at the time. . . .*"

"What!" he hollered. "How dare you threaten to blackmail me, you ungrateful. . . ."

"Ungrateful!" I shouted. "You got some nerve. Pashen saved your job, despite being hurt by you crawling into her bed with your broken promises. You fucked Tiffani like she was some prostitute, leaving her with a kid to raise. She could've had your ass locked up. You need to be grateful, not me."

He sighed. "I'll do the trace and call you once I locate her," he said.

"I thought so," I replied. I clicked him off and called Pashen to let her know that help was coming.

❖❖❖❖❖

Jeff called to let me know he'd found Pashen at a pub in Carroll County, nodding off in a booth. The owner was about to call the police when he arrived. Jeff took her to the Holiday Inn in Westminster where he thought she'd be safe. I got off the elevator and saw him walking down the hall. His dark brown face looked tired. The natural curls on his head were tussled, and his muscular shoulders were slumped. "Room 403," he said handing me the key.

"How is she?" I asked.

"As well as Pashen can be right now. I offered to get her something to eat, but she said she just wanted to take a shower and rest."

I hugged him. "Jeff, I know I got upset earlier, but I do appreciate you finding her."

He pulled away and gave me a stern look. "Hailee, when are you gonna wake up? It gets to a point where you have to stop saving a person who doesn't want to be saved. All Pashen cares about is sweatin' dope. Are you gonna spend the rest of your life bailing her out?"

I folded my arms. "How I deal with Pashen is my damn business," I said. "It's not about saving her, it's about me loving her. She needs to know I'm there when other people like yourself leave her assed out."

He threw up his hands in desperation. "I tried to get her help," he said. "She refused treatment. How do you think I felt seeing her get hooked on heroin? She was one of the best cops in the city—street smart and savvy. Fifteen years in law enforcement gone, because of some punk who threw her some money under the table."

"Lucas ain't got shit to do with what you did," I said. "I hate that bastard, but I loved you, and you left us." I didn't want to cry in front of Jeff, so I ran down the hall, ignoring him as he called my name.

Jeff and Pashen were partners, and when she made lieutenant, she fought for him to get promoted. Pashen was his confidante when he separated from his wife, Connie. My mother even saved his job by not reporting his situation with Tiffani. Jeff and Pashen fell in love and talked about marriage. When Connie developed breast cancer, their affair ended. Jeff felt like he had to move back home. He and Connie had been together since high school. He told Pashen he didn't want to divorce Connie while she was battling a disease. Pashen was devastated.

"Hailee, wait," Jeff said catching up with me.

Jeff hugged me as I wiped my tears. "How could you leave someone you loved, to go back to a marriage you wanted to end?" I asked. "I'm sorry Connie got sick, but that shouldn't of changed what you had with my mother. Connie's cancer is in remission. Pashen is sick now. Who runs back to her? Nobody but me." I broke away from his embrace. He was silent as I walked to Pashen's room.

"Hailee. Hailee, stop for a second," he said. I turned his direction. "I got a man outside on surveillance, and you can call if you need me to come back. Lucas is a dead man if he tries anything stupid."

I stared at the ceiling, aggravated at Jeff's offer. "Yeah, whatever," I said. "You wastin' overtime with one man. Lucas ain't never been that soft. He got eyes everywhere."

I placed the key into the lock on Pashen's door. Jeff touched my shoulder. "Hailee, listen. Pashen didn't want me to say anything, but she was in bad shape when I got to her. She wouldn't let me take her to the hospital. Her pantsuit had blood on the back. I think she was raped." I quickly opened the door, shutting it in Jeff's face.

❖❖❖❖❖

Pashen sat on the edge of the bed. There was a white towel wrapped tightly around her body. When she saw me, she smiled. I kissed her cheek and sat down. We didn't say anything, just hugged and rocked for a while.

"You came through Boo, just like I knew you would," she said. "Thanks for having my back."

"Ma, you worry me to death," I said.

She pinched my cheeks like she used to when I was a chubby eight year old. "I know I do, but if you didn't have me, your life would be boring now wouldn't it, Miss Brainy Act." She laughed.

"You're not funny," I said, bothered.

"Well, today had too much drama so humor me, dammit." She got a smile out of me. "That's better," she said. "I forgot you had a date with your friend this weekend. I guess my shit blocked you gettin' that swerve on, huh?"

I just shook my head. "I can't believe you even thinking about that."

"What? Hailee, I'm just playin' with you."

I frowned. "Stop playing and start telling me the truth, Pashen. I wanna know what happened to you, so we can put those guys behind bars."

She sighed and twisted a damp strand of hair between her fingers. "Jeff told you."

"Pashen, you should've told me," I said.

"How easy do you think it is to tell your daughter you've been raped?" she asked. "I'm the one that tells you to be careful around roughnecks. Dudes don't normally get over on me, but those bamas represented. I didn't think they were ever gonna stop pounding me." She wrung her hands in her lap. "Shit got so bad, I couldn't feel nothing down there after a while."

I bolted to the bathroom, throwing up repeatedly from hearing Pashen's ordeal. Once my stomach settled, I put a wet towel to my face. My mother's cries resonated outside the door. I exhaled and pulled another fresh towel from the rack. I walked out of the bathroom. Pashen's hands covered her face. Water dripped from her hair down to her arms. I draped the towel around her shoulders and kneeled in front of her.

"You gotta tell me everything that happened, Ma," I pleaded. I bit my bottom lip. "The text message I got on my phone yesterday, was it from them?"

She got up and walked over to the other side of the room to turn up the thermostat. "Hailee, there are some things you don't need to know," she said.

I stomped over to her. "You want me to convince Lucas not to kill you?" I shouted. "I'm in the dark on what went down. That doesn't help me, or you!"

She retreated, leaning against the window ledge. "All right, I figured Remy was the one who planned the attack outside the party," she said. "He was in the Tahoe with those other two dudes. When I woke up from being whacked over the head, I was downtown in a suite at the Hyatt."

I placed my hands on my hips. "Did they say anything about Lucas, or the deal you were supposed to handle in Guilford?"

She nodded *yes*. "When you got that text message, one guy had a nine to my head," she said. "Another one pulled my clothes off. I knew I was either gonna get fucked, killed, or both. Remy wanted in on my deal with the doctor. I told him he'd have to get clearance from Lucas, but he said, "No." He wanted a cut of my share. I told him he might as well do me, 'cause that was the only cut he was gettin'. That job was six figures. I knew the deal was squashed anyway, because by the time they stopped harassing me, it was morning. I got dumped in the sticks."

"I can't believe this, Ma." I held my head back to prevent tears from falling. Pashen was telling me the truth, but my heart couldn't take much more.

Pashen walked over to the desk and took a rubber band off some stationery. "They kept my piece, but threw my purse and cell phone out the window when they rolled off," she said as she put her hair in a ponytail. "Remy had seen Lucas's number three times on my phone, so he probably figured he was gonna kill me for missing the run." She came back over to the window. "I called Lucas to let him know what happened. He didn't answer, so I left him a voice mail. He called back in like five minutes, but he wasn't trying to hear no explanations. In the middle of him cursing me stank, he told me that Remy was hit by bullets, and I was next."

Pashen broke down. My arms held her close as I tried to remain strong. "Jeff played me," she said. "By the time you called, I was damn near frozen." She rubbed her arm. "Sugar was my only solution to get warm." Tears fell hard down my face. Pashen lifted my chin. I looked at the brown slashes on the inside of her arm that crossed over her veins. Tracks leading to nowhere.

I grabbed her arm. "Ain't nothing sweet about this, Pashen!" I yelled. "You hear me?"

She yanked her arm away and sat down on the bed, cursing me under her breath. "Don't start on that, I'm not in the mood," she said.

I sat next to her. "Pashen, you want Lucas to spare your life, but you're killing yourself," I said.

"My shit is under control," she said. "I don't even hit while I'm working, and Lucas knows that. That's why he trusted me with this doctor. I'd dealt with him before. All of my jobs were tight. I got set up last night. Now I'm hiding out from my own nigga."

"You were raped last night!" I yelled. "Is the money really worth all that?"

"Last night could have been worse," she said in a smug tone. "I showered and got over it. Ain't nothin' a little water can't heal." She took the edge of the towel to wipe her face. "Besides, I have you to take care of me. You my rainmaker, right?"

Pashen noticed from my serious expression that there was no way to downplay her torment. I stood up from the bed. "You need something before I go to Lucas's house?" I asked.

"Bring me some clothes and food in case I gotta lay low for a while," she said.

My hand massaged my forehead. "Pashen, what do you want me to say to Lucas?"

She gently grabbed my wrist. "Whatever it takes to keep me with you."

Make Me Wanna Holla

The fact that I had to talk to Lucas made me nauseated again. A drug dealer originally from Harlem, Lucas Blacke presently hustled in Baltimore. He did a good job keeping guys on the corner, and keeping funeral homes busy. I can't stand his ass now, but when he and my mother hooked up at a jazz concert three years ago, I didn't have a problem with him. He was laid back and had this Barry White voice. Not bad lookin' for a guy pushing fifty. Lucas was a tall, clean cut man whose tailored suits gave him the appearance of a respectable businessman instead of a hard core criminal. His skin tone matched mine—medium mocha. I imagined if Lucas resembled my dad. Pashen only dated dark skinned brothas, 'cause she was fair skinned. She said she didn't want no vanilla babies looking like her. When I was little we used to watch the movie *Sparkle* all the time. I told her she looked just like Sister—beautiful.

When Lucas came into the picture, we were about to lose our house. Pashen and Jeff had bought this brand new townhouse in Randallstown with upgrades galore. She used most of her savings on that house, because she figured with two salaries, things would work out. Then Jeff left Pashen to go back to Connie, and money became tight. I got a job dancing at Legacy. I knew Pashen couldn't balance her bills and my tuition. She struggled to pay a big house note on one salary. The bank sent Pashen a foreclosure notice. Lucas told her to tear it up. He paid the mortgage and took care of all the bills, including my tuition at The University of Maryland Baltimore County.

It wasn't long before Lucas asked us to move into his six

bedroom, brick house in Owings Mills. I swam daily in the indoor Olympic size swimming pool. Pashen frequently enjoyed her spa showers after a long day on the force. We chowed down on fried chicken, barbequed ribs, baked maca-roni, and other soul food dishes that Lucas's chef prepared in the custom kitchen. Pashen didn't think twice about putting her house on the market.

Once we got settled at his house, things started to change. Pashen worked for Lucas on the side. She had connections to make sure his shipments arrived safely at the Sparrows Point dock, near Baltimore's Inner Harbor. She was good with his upscale clients, and the money piled up. Pashen treated herself to a BMW, and bought a RAV-4 for me. It was nice to have some ice and designer clothes. A far cry from living out of her run down, '76 Chevy Caprice when I was a toddler.

Life was hard back then, but at least it was honest. After a year of living with Lucas, I realized there was nothing kindred about being kept. Pashen started feigning dope. Lucas ain't do shit about it, 'cause she brought him business, even after she left the police force. That's when I lost respect for him. He was another man using my mother. I knew it was time to bounce the day he came into the media room while I watched a movie and said he wanted to fuck me. I never told Pashen. I moved on campus to get away from him. Now I'm faced with the dilem-ma of trying to resolve a bad situation with a man who only has murder on his mind. I gotta do whatever it takes to save Pashen's life, even if it means giving Lucas what he wanted from me six months ago.

❖ ❖ ❖ ❖ ❖

I drove onto the circular driveway of Lucas's estate. His bodyguard came out, holding a gun by his side. He smirked as I got out of the car. "Is Mr. Blacke expecting you?" he asked.

"No," I whispered.

"Then why are you here, Hailee?"

"I need to talk to Lucas. It's urgent."

"I bet it is. Wait right here." He slammed the door in my face.

I waited for about five minutes before the door opened. There was no one in the doorway. "Come in" was all I heard. I walked onto the white marble foyer, taken aback by the coldness of the room. I bit down hard on my bottom lip, knowing his presence was eminent. Two men seemed to come out of nowhere to frisk me as Lucas stood staring from the top of the winding stairwell.

"I hope this is important," Lucas said coming down the stairs. "You interrupted an important phone conversation."

"Lucas, I appreciate you seeing me on such short notice," I said.

"Oh, you appreciate me now?" he said. "When did that start?" I didn't say anything. "I know you don't like me, so you have five minutes to say what you have to say before I kick you out."

"Can I talk to you in private?" I asked.

He scowled. "Why? I trust my crew up in here. They ain't like your junkie ass mother."

"Please, don't talk about Pashen that way," I said.

"I can talk any way I damn well please."

"I thought you cared for her?"

"That's what you get for thinking. What do you want? Stop wasting my time," he said, irritated.

I sighed. "I know Pashen messed up, but. . . ."

Lucas waved his finger at me. "No, see messing up my money is along the lines of a few grand," he said. "That bitch messed up my business when she botched that delivery. That one client was worth over a half a mil a year, easily. Don't stand here and give me some sob story about your mother. My mind is made up. She ain't foolin' nobody with her little runaway routine. I know where she is."

I pulled his sleeve. "Don't hurt her, Lucas," I cried.

Lucas brushed my hand away. "Don't worry. Pashen won't suffer. Her death will be fast and easy. Now why don't you take those crocodile tears somewhere else? Save them for your mother's funeral."

"Please, Lucas. Let me make up for her mistake," I pleaded. "Let me work for you."

He looked at his bodyguard then smiled at me. He pointed to the library. "Step into my office."

"Lucas?" his guard said.

"I'm straight, Trevor," Lucas said. "I'll be out in a few." He closed the mahogany door. "So, you wanna work for me?"

I glanced down at the floor. "Yes," I said.

He crossed his arms. "Doing what?" he asked.

"Sellin'."

"Selling what, Girl Scout Cookies? You too naïve to deal dope."

I shrugged. "I can learn," I said.

"Yeah, that's what your mother said," he huffed.

"Lucas, if there's anything I can do to make up for Pashen's mistake, I'm willing to do it. Anything."

"You can't make up for a half a mil," he said. He leaned against the desk with his hands folded.

I walked up close to him, gently placing my hand on his chest. "Isn't there something I can do?" I asked.

He laughed at me. "So, it's like that now?" he asked.

"If you want it to be. If it will mean saving Pashen's life."

Lucas began to twirl my hair, giving me a sinful smile. "When can you start?"

"Immediately," I assured him.

"You're fine, so I'm gonna let your mother live, for now. Here's the thing, though, you are now my trick. When I call, you jump. Is that understood?"

"Understood."

He kissed me as I looked at him, hating myself for selling my body and soul. His tongue tried to enter, but my mouth refused it. He frowned at me. "You got job experience?" he asked.

"Yes," I mumbled.

"Then you better kiss me like you got some sense," he said as he pressed his lips hard against mine.

❖❖❖❖❖

Pashen and Lucas were together again. I moved back in his

house, forced to deal with bullshit. Drugs made Pashen a crazy woman. Most of the time I didn't want to be around her, which depressed the hell out of me because we used to be so close. Lucas told her to stop shooting up in the house. She slapped him and he broke her nose. I was in the middle of all this mess, suffering alone. I couldn't tell Pashen what was going on with Lucas, because I didn't know if she'd feel like I'd betrayed her for sleeping with her man. That's how unpredictable her state of mind was. I couldn't refuse Lucas, because I knew he would take Pashen out for costing him his best client. I stayed out of the house as much as I could, and I didn't deal with Lucas or Pashen unless I had to.

I had just run a mile at UMBC's indoor track and I was exhausted. All I wanted to do was shower and crash into the bed. When I walked into the living room, I tried to ignore my mother givin' head to Lucas. He spotted me first and had the nerve to wink. He tapped Pashen on the shoulder. "We got company," he groaned.

Pashen rose up, high as a kite. "Hi baby," she slurred.

I fought back the tears as I ran to my bedroom.

I was awakened by a hand reaching inside my panties. I didn't turn around. I didn't have to. I knew it was the devil visiting again. I pushed his hand away. "Stop it Lucas," I said. "I'm not feeling well, and I'm not interested in your nonsense. Go back to bed with Pashen. She's your woman, remember?"

"No, she's my whore. You're the real woman, Hailee. You ain't been picked over like your mother." He reached under my T-shirt and fondled my breasts. "Who you savin' all that good lovin' for?"

"Get off!" I grunted.

"Did you forget our little agreement?" he asked. "That hit can drop at anytime."

My silence was his cue to pull my panties down by my ankles. He didn't even remove them. He just pulled my left leg out and rolled me on my belly to assume his favorite position. I closed my eyes and squeezed the pillow edges tight as I heard him pull his boxers off. He repulsed every inch of me, so I knew I had to brace myself for his entry. He never made it smooth and easy. Truth be told, I'm glad he never did foreplay. I didn't want him to ever get the impression that I enjoyed him violating me.

Lucas forced himself in, which forced me to place my hand over my mouth to prevent Pashen from hearing my agony.

Start counting Hailee, I thought. *100, 99. This shit hurts so bad. Breathe Hailee*, I repeated in my mind, trying to coax myself through his thrusts. *Keep your eyes shut . . . Don't let him see you cry.* More hard thrusts. By count 75, Lucas had his chest on my back. He wrapped his arm around the base of my neck to hold onto my shoulder. I felt his hot breath inside my ear, as he moaned obscenities about how I pleased him.

"Damn, you tight girl," he said panting. "Definitely better than that wide load your mama got."

My eyelids were heavy from holding tears. I wanted to scream, but I thought that would only prolong my pain. Instead I exhaled, hoping he would come before I reached number 10.

"Hurry up, Lucas," I said. By 13, he had buried his head in my pillow to muffle the scream of God's name in vain. He came. I groaned from being pummeled. Lucas kissed my pierced navel and glided his rough tongue farther down to my vagina. He licked sore tissue and my hands swung at his face. He smirked as he eased up from the bed and strutted out of the bedroom. I curled into a fetal position and closed my eyes to think of a better way to save my mother's life.

New Year, Same Shit

Lucas and Pashen decided to throw a New Year's Eve party and insisted that I come. What a wonderful way to bring in the new year—making small talk with thugs. I sat on the staircase with my arms crossed. Pashen came towards me. "Hailee, stop pouting. We have guests," she said placing her hair behind her ear.

I toyed with the diamond stud in my ear. "No, you and Lucas have guests. I told y'all I didn't want to be here," I said. "I got a paper to write."

Pashen was on one of her high horses. She pointed her index finger. "Hailee, you act like an old lady."

"Somebody's got to act their age."

She sucked her teeth. "Why don't you get a drink?" she asked. "Loosen up."

"I had a drink already," I said. "It didn't work."

She snapped her fingers. "Well, get up. I got somebody I want you to meet."

I sighed as I got up. "Pashen, I'm not trying to meet nobody right now."

"Come on," she said. She grabbed my arm and sashayed past the guests. Her nails dug into my skin. I grimaced as I tried to free my arm from her grip. The silver sequined gown she wore was bustin' at the seams. It would have been pretty if she had purchased the correct size; but the weed I smelled on her breath had her delusional, in a size two gown. Lucas was in the great room, flirting with some other woman, so I guess Pashen decided to work my nerves.

We walked downstairs to the game room. "I think you'll hit it off with this young man," she said. "He's a nice guy."

"Does he work for Lucas?" I asked.

She pursed her lips. "Yes."

"Then he ain't nice," I said, agitated as I looked at my watch.

"Stop being so critical," she said. "I'm tryin' to get you a life."

"That makes the two us," I said as we approached a scrawny dude standing near the pool table. He looked like he had been smoking more crack than he sold.

"Bam, this is my daughter, Hailee." She spun me around like a Las Vegas show piece. He extended his hand for mine. I almost gagged when I saw three silver teeth in the front of his mouth. Platinum or not, that shit was ugly.

"Your name is Bam?" I asked.

"Yeah," he said with pride.

"Uh . . . Nice to meet you," I said, trying to keep a straight face as we shook hands.

Before I knew it, Pashen had gone back upstairs and closed the door. *Sugar Hill* played on the plasma television screen. *How appropriate*, I thought.

"You wanna sit down and watch the movie?" he asked.

"Naw," I said. "I've seen this movie one time too many."

He moved closer to me, wrapping his arm around my waist. His teeth lit up the dark room. "What you wanna do, then?" he asked. He had the nerve to give me a kiss on the neck, like I was supposed to get a rush from those sandpaper lips.

I pushed his ass away. "Bam, you don't know me like that," I said. "If I want your lips on me, I'll let you know."

He frowned. "Why you so uptight? Pashen said you want-ed to be down with me."

"Pashen doesn't speak for me," I said. I rolled my eyes at him and looked over at the TV screen.

"You sure ain't like your mother," he mumbled as he went up the steps.

I never even looked back at him. "You're right, Bam," I

said. "I'm not like my mother."

Spring semester started and I signed up for the Advanced Painting class. I entered only to find a tall, lean brotha standing so fine in front of the class. He seemed too young to be teaching college students. He gave the class a syllabus and supply list for upcoming projects. Then he reviewed the student roster and dismissed class. My name wasn't called, so I approached his desk. "Professor Graham?" I said.

"Yes," he said as he put some papers in his briefcase.

"Hi, I'm Hailee Shaw. My name wasn't called, but I'm enrolled in this class. I did late registration yesterday."

"And just think, the school spends thousands of dollars on new computer equipment that still screws up attendance records," he said. "I printed out the class roster this morning."

"Job security for the guys in registration, I guess," I said.

"I guess you're right." He peered in his briefcase and pulled out his grade book. "Give me the spelling of your name and social. I'll take care of the rest."

His dimpled smile gave me butterflies. I told him my information and left. I knew for sure I wouldn't be cutting any of Isaac Graham's classes.

As my foot hit the top step to the upstairs hallway, I was frightened by the screams that drowned the classical music playing from the intercom. My right fist nearly caved in the bathroom door. "Pashen!" I yelled. "What's going on in there?"

"Open the door, Hailee!" she hollered.

I opened the door and Pashen was naked from the waist down, curled up in pain on the tile floor. The blond highlights in her long hair were darkened from sweat. "Ma, what's wrong?" I got on my knees beside her. She gripped her stomach with one hand, practically pulling out her hair with the other. "Pashen, what's happening! Tell me what to do."

"Get me some towels out of there," she moaned. I quickly got up and opened the closet to get the towels. "I think I'm having a miscarriage, Hailee."

"Oh my God!" I said in total shock. My mother showed no signs of pregnancy. I handed her the towels. "How far along are you?"

"I'm not certain. Four months maybe," she said.

"Pashen, I'm scared. You need a doctor."

She winced as she rubbed her stomach. "No, I need you to follow my instructions. Go to my bedroom and check the top drawer of my nightstand. There's a large switch blade in there, bring it to me."

"For what, Pashen!" I cried. Pashen didn't need another child, but she didn't need to suffer like this, either. A miscarriage was one thing, but the thought of a self-inflicted abortion was sickening. She didn't say anything, just stared at me. I thought she was in shock when I witnessed blood trickling from her vagina. She snapped out of her trance.

"Get me the knife, dammit!" she shouted.

I cursed her in protest, but still followed her orders. "Pashen, I gotta get you some help!" I screamed as I ran back into the bathroom. I carefully handed her the knife. "I'll call 911." I turned to walk out of the bathroom.

"No! Hailee, come here!" she shouted.

I ignored her, but she jumped up in a frenzy. Blood gushed all over the floor. She grabbed my arm, and stared into my eyes like a demon. "Bitch, you better not pick up that phone, you hear?"

I backed into the corner, terrified by her stare. "You need to go to the hospital," I said.

Pashen pointed the knife at me. "You ain't calling nobody," she snarled. "I can handle this."

I clasped my hands and tried to reason with her. "Please, Pashen. At least let me call Lucas."

She frowned. "Hell no. He can't know about this."

"Why?" I asked.

Pashen slowly put the knife to her side and bent over, taking deep breaths to ease her pain. "This ain't his," she groaned. "He got fixed a few years back."

I put my hands on top of my head as I tried to think of what to do next. "Well, we need to call somebody," I said, exasperated. "You might hemorrhage and die!"

"Then, I'll just die!" She pushed me into the bathroom mirror and wrapped her hand around my neck. Pashen looked completely insane as she placed the knife at my throat. "You'll die with me if you don't keep your mouth shut!"

We both shivered. The knife cut me as I pushed her away and ran out of the bathroom, fearing for my life. Pashen screamed and slammed the door. I applied pressure to my neck and went into my bedroom, locking the door behind me. A few minutes passed, and no more screams or curses filled the air.

I stood at my dresser, holding a T-shirt firm at my neck. I removed it to check my wound in the mirror. The wound was not too deep. My T-shirt was stained, but my bleeding had stopped. A flush of the toilet let me know that Pashen's bleeding had stopped as well.

Around midnight, I heard a tap on the door. "Hailee? Hailee, can we talk?" Pashen asked.

"No," I said lying in my bed. "Not until you come off of that shit. I can never talk to you when you're high."

"Fine, be like that. Just remember, you didn't see nothing, right?" she said.

"Whatever you say, Pashen."

Not Him Again

It was a month before Spring Break, and I was alone in the art lab working on an oil painting. I preferred oil media, because it seemed more dimensional than watercolor. More vivid and textured. Professor liked my first oil on canvass so much, he displayed it in the student gallery. I thought I'd done a pretty good job. It was entitled: *Deliverance.* The work depicted a woman giving birth. Sweat covered her tan skin. Her stomach was translucent and it contained a beautiful fetus. The woman had a flower in her hair. Exposed from the waist down, her face was contorted as she pushed to deliver the baby. A black hand emerged from her vagina. It was a man's hand, grasping a shattered crack pipe. I won a summer internship at The Maryland Institute of Art because of my portrayal.

My latest project was an oil painting that depicted Pashen as an angel. I stopped painting when I saw Professor Graham come over to my easel.

"I must say you certainly have a flair for oils," he said. "Very nice imagery here. Your usage of blue hues is spectacular."

"Thanks," I said. "Blue is my favorite color. Blue sorta mimics my life. Light shades for when I'm happy. Dark tones for when I'm down."

"I noticed you used the same woman depicted in the painting displayed at the gallery." He smiled. "She resembles you."

I looked down at my paint tray. "I know, but it's not me," I said. "It's my mother. We're having issues right now. Sometimes I feel like we don't even know each other anymore. So, I try to understand her through my art. I express my love for her best on canvass."

"I'm sure she'd be proud if she saw your work," he said.

"Maybe."

"You should invite her to the student showcase next week."

"I already have," I said. "I don't know if she'll show up. She's real preoccupied."

"I'm sure she'll make it. Have faith," he said with a tap to my shoulder. "Please turn off the lights and check the door before you leave."

"I will Professor," I said. "Thanks for letting me stay in the lab a little longer. I want to get this project finished."

"No problem," he said. "Just make sure you come back to visit when you make it big." He winked at me as he put on his wool jacket. "Don't forget about us starving artists."

I blushed. "I won't forget you." He waved goodbye and walked out.

I put the final touches on my painting, when I heard footsteps. Distracted by the loud sound, I turned, only to find my worst nightmare. "Hey stranger," Lucas said with a sinister grin.

I sucked my teeth. Dreams of my gorgeous professor had been interrupted by the jerk standing behind me. I laid my brush on the easel and lowered my head. "Lucas, my curfew is not until later, so why are you here?" In spite of my fear, my voice stayed leveled. "Is my mother okay?"

He moved in closer. "Your mother's fine. Who said anything about a curfew?"

I realized I had set myself up by asking that question. "Well, I'm usually at home by now," I said re-shifting myself on the stool. "I know you like to get your entrée with Pashen before midnight, and then get your dessert with me, so I try to accommodate you as much as possible."

"Funny girl," he said grabbing his crotch. "You should be a comedian."

"I should," I said. "Maybe get some regular gigs at *The Comedy Connection* in Laurel. Then I could make money faster to pay your ass back, so you can leave me alone." I got up and walked to the back of the room to wash my hands. Lucas was right on my heels. He massaged my shoulders as I waited for the water at the sink to get warm.

"You hate me don't you?" he asked.

My arms stiffened from his touch. "Everybody hates you, even God," I said as I rubbed soap on my fingers.

"Is that right?" he said as he strolled over to some of my work displayed on the back wall.

"That's a fact." I gave him a cold stare as I dried my hands. He looked over his shoulder as if he felt the piercing hatred I had in my heart for him.

He raised a brow. "These your paintings?" he asked pointing to the wall.

I removed the bandana from my head. "Yeah," I said.

"Damn, you do have skills. I thought my money was going towards some jive ass watercolors, but this shit is deep."

I rolled my eyes to the ceiling. "I appreciate your support. I'm sure you know that." "How come you don't bring any of these home?" he asked.

"Why?" I said. "So they can be sold for drugs before I get a chance to hang them over the mantle?"

He tightened his jaw. "You got a bad attitude."

I folded my arms. "And you got a bad heart."

"Who's your mother pulling out of the flames in this one?" he asked nodding to the first picture on the wall. "The arm looks familiar."

"What makes you think she's pulling you *out* of the flames?" I said with my hands on my hips.

"Watch it," he said as he turned the collar up on his trench coat. His scornful expression made me hold my tongue to prevent a future beat down. Lucas came close to me, and firmly cupped my face with his hands. He kissed the top of my head. "I'm sure it requires a lot of time to create these masterpieces, so stay out as long as you like," he whispered in my ear. "Just remember who you belong to." He walked briskly towards the front of the studio and exited, without saying another word. I held my stomach as I breathed a sigh of relief, happy that Lucas was out of my sight.

Pashen was in my room in the mirror, trying on different pairs of earrings. She and Lucas were going to see Jill Scott in concert. "Do these match my outfit," she asked holding a pair to her ears. I sat on the edge of the bed shaking my head.

"No?" she said.

"They match," I said. "I was shaking my head for another reason."

"What now, Hailee? I don't have time for your mess. Lucas will be back home in five minutes."

I crossed my legs. "Why are you putting up with Lucas?"

"Because he changed my life," she said checking her profile in the mirror.

"Yes, but his wealth has made your health and our relationship deteriorate."

She adjusted the earrings in her ears. "He's good to me."

I stood up and walked over to her. "If he's so good, why won't he pay for you to go to a good rehab program?"

She abruptly turned towards me. "Hailee, go to hell."

"That ain't nothing but a short walk," I said. The sting from her slap to my face got the best of me. I held my head down and cried.

"That's just what your ass needed to bring you down a peg or two," she said. "Your sassin' has been gettin' on my last damn nerve, you hear? No matter what you think of me, I am still your mother!"

"Really? Well, if slapping my ass will get you to act more like a mother, then I'll keep talking trash!" I shouted. "Do you like what you've become? Do you like what we've become?"

"Girl, wise up. This is the real world. Ain't nobody got time to wait for Uncle Charlie to pay us what he thinks is fair. I'm a survivor. If I wasn't, your ass wouldn't be here. We may not be livin' legit by your uppity standards, but we livin' right. Don't think for a minute them blue eyed bastards you go to school with are any different. Most of them got parents that are doctors, lawyers and politicians who thirst for prostitute fucks, and sweat thugs like Lucas for narcotics. Shit, that classmate who did the art show with you last year? His ass is always making purchases. He drives down Lafayette Avenue so much, you'd think he was in a parade."

I pulled a tissue from the box on my dresser and blew my nose. "Who are you talking about?"

"The white guy with the ponytail," Pashen said as she turned her back to me to look in the mirror. She fluffed her silky curls with her fingers and sprayed hair spritz to hold her style in place.

"Evan?" I asked as I fanned the spray mist away from my face.

"I don't know what his name is, and I don't care," she said reaching for lipstick out of her cosmetic case. "He's strung out just like half the folks in this world. Everybody's addicted to something. Some just try to sugar coat sins to suit their taste. There ain't a soul on this earth that's better than me, so I'll live the way I wanna live. Do what I gotta do to get mine."

"Even if it means putting your life in the hands of a felon?" I asked.

She placed her hand on her hip as she glanced back at me. "Hailee, I don't know where you come off being so high and mighty. I didn't raise you like that."

I plopped down on the bed. "No, you raised me to stay out of trouble, and to study hard in school. You taught me to respect those in authority. Was all of that hot air you were talking?"

Pashen smacked her lips at me then looked back in the mirror to apply her berry gloss. I kicked off my shoes and picked up the latest edition of *Essence* magazine; her antics had pissed me off. "I'm tired of this discussion," she said walking towards the door. "You're grown now. I've done my part." She shrugged. "If you don't like the good life that Lucas has given us, then you can pack your shit and leave."

I looked up from my magazine. "Are you kicking me out, Pashen?"

She walked out, leaving my question unanswered.

Redwood Trust was the right spot to get my party on tonight. My friend Tiffani Banks and I chilled by the bar as the pulsating house music helped us to unwind. I met Tiffani four years ago while dancing at Legacy. The manager didn't care that we were underage, so we got paid. Shakin' ass wasn't a big deal when things were kept in perspective. We both wanted to go to college because a degree was a step above lettin' fools feel you up, and drool at you greasin' a pole. A year after starting at Legacy, Tiff got pregnant. At first, she didn't know who the father was because she was fucking a doctor in order to get the medication her mom needed for free. Her mom Janice had AIDS, and health insurance didn't cover a lot of the treatment.

One night at work, Tiffani and this girl Roxanne fought because Tiffani thought she'd stolen money from her locker. Roxanne pulled out a knife and when I got ready to represent for my girl, Jeff busted in the dressing room. He saved Tiffani and me, 'cause that dike would've jacked us up with that blade. From then on, he made sure Tiffani was all right. He even drove her to work, because his brother lived a block down from her house on McCullough Street.

Tiff told me when she and Jeff had sex. His wife went on some writers retreat and he called my girl over. When she found out about the baby, she was gonna get rid of it. The night before her appointment, Janice died. She made Tiffani promise to keep the baby. Tiffani had never told her mom she was pregnant but somehow, she knew.

Jermaine Elijah Brooks came into this world with a mother headed for law school and a father hiding behind a badge. A DNA test revealed Jeff was the daddy, but even after that he stayed in denial. Pashen was the one who got him to face his responsibility. She and Jeff were just squad partners at the time, but they had a close friendship. He started seeing the baby and giving Tiff money, when she asked. After a while Tiff didn't trip on Jeff. Janice had a life insurance policy at McCormick where she'd worked. Tiffani got the money, left her past in Baltimore, and moved to D.C. To attend Howard University. I quit dancing when Tiffani left because I didn't want to get trapped into a lifestyle of loving fast money and sugar.

"It's packed in here, huh?" Tiffani shouted against the music.

"Yeah, niggas are definitely deep up in this camp," I said looking around.

She picked up some pretzels from the tray at the bar. "Well, hopefully the niggas that are supposed to be here are here."

I took a sip of my lemon water. "Who are you talking about?" I asked.

"Kenny. The FedEx guy I met a few weeks ago," she said. "I told him to meet me here, and to bring a friend for you."

I got off my stool and started dancing to the beat. "Girl, I don't need no handouts. I told you about setting me up."

Tiffani stuffed her mouth with more pretzels. "I'm tired of you messing with Lucas. His ass needs to get a life."

"Unless you want Pashen to lose her life, I'ma have to deal with him until he feels he's paid in full," I said. She drank some of my water and got up. I rolled my eyes at her. "Thanks for polluting my water."

"No problem," she said shaking her hips. "Let's forget about that Nino Brown wanna be and have a good time."

"Bet. You think Tyrone can hook us up with some drinks?" I asked.

"Yeah, but not at the bar. He told me to get a table and flag down his girl Iris when we were ready. He doesn't want to take any chances with Undercovers carding us."

"Let's find a table then," I said. "I could use a *Sex On The Beach*."

"That's my drink," she said.

We found a small corner table and sat down. Tiffani wore caramel suede pants with three inch boots to match. A shimmering vanilla poncho complimented the golden suede crop top she sported. She was definitely hot tonight, but still falling second to my black DKNY pinstripe pantsuit that revealed a hint of my black satin push up bra from Victoria's Secret.

Tiffani looked out at the dance floor. "Aw shit, here come

my nigga."

"Who are you looking at?" I asked.

Two nice looking guys walked our way. My face brightened up. She grinned. "I did good, didn't I?"

"Damn right," I said.

"Well, don't stare at the one with the cornrows too much," she said. "That's my ride."

"Cool. I'm feelin' the wavy haired cutie, anyway."

"Yeah, he got it goin' on," she said.

"Stocky, just like I like 'em," I whispered.

The guy with the cornrows said, "Good evening ladies." He sat down in the empty seat beside Tiffani.

"Hey Kenny," she said as she leaned back to receive his kiss. They were tonguing down.

I scrunched my face up. "Y'all need a room?" I asked. They released their lips and smiled at me.

"I was thinking the same thing," the other guy said sitting in the chair next to me. "Hi sweetheart, I'm Maxwell. Max for short."

"Nice to meet you Max," I said shaking his hand. "I'm Hailee."

He leaned over and kissed my cheek. "A pretty name for a very pretty lady."

I giggled. "Thanks."

"Hailee, would you mind if we got our own table?" Max asked. "I'd like to talk to you."

"That's a good idea," I said. "I think we're disturbing Kenny and Tiffani's groove." Those two were locked at the lips again. I poked Tiffani on the shoulder. "Tiff . . . Tiffani!"

She slowly stopped kissing Kenny and looked at me, annoyed. "Girl, what?"

"I want to thank you for properly introducing me to your friends," I said.

She pouted as Kenny laughed. "Kenny, this is my girl Hailee," she said.

"Nice to meet you Kenny," I said shaking his hand. "Max and I will leave you two alone."

"See ya," Tiffani said as she got back up in Kenny's face. I shook my head as Max and I left to search for our own table.

I led the way as Max held a secure hand on my back, trying not to get separated in the midst of buzzed club patrons. Unsuccessful at finding our own table, we decided to find a spot on the dance floor. We started slow dancing to Floetry's song, *Say Yes*.

Max licked his lips. "So, do you come here often?" he asked.

I locked my arms around his waist. "Naw," I said. "I felt in the mood to hang out a bit. My life is hectic right now, so I figured a night out would give me temporary relief."

"I heard you were an artist?" he said gliding his finger over my diamond cross pendant.

His light touch to my chest aroused me. "I'm trying to be," I said with a seductive smile. "What do you do?"

"I work delivery at FedEx, like Kenny. I'm also a bounty hunter, part-time."

I jerked my head back. "Bounty hunter? Sounds dangerous."

"It's never boring. That's what I like about it," he said. He kissed my earlobe. "Are you seeing anyone?" He blew warm breaths of air over my neck. My foot stumbled from the tickling sensation, causing us to dance offbeat. He laughed.

"It's your fault," I said pinching his side.

He put his hands up. "What?" he said with a sly grin.

"Your turning me on, that's what." I held him again.

"Answer my question," he said.

"No, I'm not seeing anyone," I said. "How about you?"

He shook his head. "There's no one special in my life. I mean, I flow from time to time, but I'm not serious about one particular lady." He surveyed my body. "Seeing you though, I don't know. You might have what it takes to make a brotha break bad habits."

He slowly moved his palms down the curve of my ass. I liked the way he grinded his pelvis into me, and I wanted to feel more. I moaned as I inhaled the Lagerfeld scent he wore; the sweet musk mixed with his sweat drove me sensually crazy.

"You all right, Hailee?" he asked.

"Fine Max. Just fine," I hummed.

Then I heard Tiffani's voice in my ear. "Hailee, listen to me." She tapped my shoulder and I opened my eyes. "*Men In Black* are here," she said looking cautiously around the dance floor.

"Shit," I said letting go of Maxwell.

He frowned. "What's up?"

I rubbed his back. "Max, I'm sorry. I need to talk to Tiffani in private for a minute."

He grabbed my hand and squeezed it. "Okay, I'll be at the bar. Come by there when you're done."

"I will," I said.

"Don't leave me hanging," he said as he smiled and walked away.

I nodded and quickly walked with Tiffani to the Ladies Room. Inside of the lounge area, I sat down on the sofa with my head in my hands.

"Hailee, I'm sorry, but I had to give you heads up," Tiffani said. "You never know what Lucas and his boys are gonna do. Especially when it comes to their women."

I slanted my eyes at her. "I'm not his woman," I said.

"Well, whatever," she said, running her hand through her hair. "Let me just say he wasn't pleased, seeing you hugged up with Max on the dance floor."

"Where is he now?" I asked.

She sighed. "I don't know. He saw me walk over to you, and he and his boys went upstairs to the pool hall."

"Tiff, I don't mean to spoil your night, but I gotta get out here. I don't want Lucas causing a scene up in here."

"I told Kenny that I probably would have to take you home," she said. "He's straight, so let's go."

"Okay."

Tiff pushed the door open to find Lucas directly in front of us, leaning against the wall. I couldn't move. Tiffani got in front of me. "Leave her alone, Lucas," she hissed.

"You need to check your girl," he said looking over at me.

I knew he was serious, so I moved from behind Tiffani. "It's okay," I said touching her shoulder. "Let me talk to Lucas. Why don't you go back to your date?"

She folded her arms. "Huh?" she said.

"Tiff, please. I'll call you as soon as I can."

"I better hear from you tonight," she said hugging me.

Lucas grabbed my elbow. "Let's go." He pulled me away from Tiffani. I yanked my arm from him and headed towards the exit. I heard his laughter behind me. When I got outside to the parking lot, I looked around for his truck. He smacked my backside.

"Did you have fun?" he snickered.

"Where's the Hummer?" I said moving away from him.

"No truck tonight. I came in the limo." He turned to his boys who were leaning against a black Mercedes. "I'll see you guys back at Trevor's, around three."

"All right," they said and got into the car.

"Limo's around the corner," he said.

We walked to the car. The driver let us in. The privacy glass rolled up as Lucas kicked off his black alligator loafers. He smiled and put his nasty hands on my hair. I flinched when he kissed my bra.

"Was that my competition I saw you dancing with?" he asked.

"No, I'd just met him, Lucas," I said. "It was nothing."

He puffed out his cheeks. "Into fat boys, huh?"

I looked out the window. "Don't talk to me."

"Good, I'm not in the mood to talk, anyway." He started to unbutton my jacket. I looked up at the ceiling, wondering how long I was gonna have to do this.

I shooed his hand away. "Can't you at least wait until we get to your house?"

He slapped me hard on my thigh. "Shut up!" he shouted. "You don't feel like talking, remember?"

I shook my head at him as he got up from the seat and laid down on the floor. "Come down here," he said. I laid down with him, putting my mind on autopilot to block out the shit he was about to do.

Too Blue

The stress at home had me fucking up at school. I blew off assignments in several of my classes, and honestly, I didn't care. I made sure I did enough to pass for the year. I was about to leave Professor Graham's class when he called me.

"Miss Shaw, may I see you for a moment?" he asked. He sat on the edge of his desk. I sighed and walked over to him. I knew what this discussion would be about.

"I was grading the last assignment, and I didn't come across yours in my file," he said. "I thought maybe I'd overlooked it. Did you place it in the student gallery?"

I looked down. "No, I didn't do the last assignment," I said.

He ran his hand down the length of his paisley tie. "Oh? I was hoping that wasn't the case. Well, I must admit that disturbs me. I was looking forward to seeing your work. You're one of my best students. May I ask why you didn't do the assignment?"

I shrugged. "I'm just not into nude male still life that's all."

"I'm surprised, since you've done quite a few nude subjects."

"I don't look at those subjects in my other works as being nude, just pure," I said. "I'm not a big fan of naked men right now. I can't immortalize something I don't respect."

"You don't respect the male gender?" he asked adjusting his position on the desk.

"I respect the male gender, just not the men I know," I said. I walked away from him over to the newsletter corkboard on the wall. "They tend to be mean motherfuckers. Besides, I'm an artist. I should be able to express myself freely, and not be confined to a certain category. That doesn't seem fair."

I felt his presence behind me. "Miss Shaw, life isn't always fair," he said putting his hand on my shoulder.

I turned to stare at him. "Looks like it's been fair enough to you," I said eyeing his flawless skin all the way down to his Timberland boots.

"Meaning?" he asked with a confused look.

I shook my head. "Never mind," I said as I adjusted my backpack on my shoulder.

"Sometimes we have to do things we don't want to do, including uninteresting school assignments," he said.

I leaned my hip against his desk. "I'm doing too much of nothing right now, so I decided not to take on anything else that is of no interest. I'm fully aware of the consequences of not turning in work. Unless I get to do the type of assignment I wanna do, I don't see the point of continuing this conversation."

He raised a brow then sat down at his desk. "I see. Well, the assignment has not changed," he said as he flicked a pencil between his fingers. "If you change your mind, I'll accept it late. I'll have to deduct points for not adhering to the original deadline, but you can still turn it in prior to Spring Break."

I walked towards the exit door. "No thanks. I appreciate the second chance, but I'm going to audit this class."

He stood up. "But you're an art major?"

"Not anymore," I said putting my hands in my jean pockets. "I've decided to go into another field."

"What field?" he asked as he took a sip of tea from his mug.

"Law enforcement," I said in low voice.

"A cop?" he said.

I frowned. "Hell no. One cop in the family was enough. I want to go to law school and become a prosecutor. Try to rid the streets of criminals who hurt people and break up families."

He put his mug on the desk. "There's always room for creativity. You're too talented to give up your painting for good."

I rocked nervously on my heels. "I'm not gonna give it up," I said. "I'll just put it on the back burner while I try to shake the devil off."

"I don't understand," he said folding his arms.

I put my hands on my hips. "My life is real complicated right now, Professor Graham. I have a lot of personal problems. You're a great teacher, and I've learned a lot from you, but my priorities are elsewhere. I'm late for my Black Literature class. I'll see you next week." I opened the door.

"Miss Shaw," he said as he quickly moved to the door.

"You can call me Hailee," I said adjusting the flower clip on the side of my hair.

He showed that perfect smile. "I've been commissioned to do a mural at The Baltimore Convention Center," he said. "My assistant backed out. I really admire your work. I'd like for you to assist me. It's a paid position."

"I don't know," I said trying to sound uninterested. "I'll have to think about it."

"Well, I start this weekend," he said. "They've given me flexibility with the time frame. I could work around your class schedule?"

I bit my lip. "When do you need my decision?" I asked.

He held up his hands. "No rush. Just show up. If you don't, then I'll figure you turned me down , and get someone else."

"Thanks for thinking of me," I said extending my hand for a handshake. "I'll give it some thought."

"I hope so," he said. He smiled and slowly wrapped his fingers around my hand, like he was protecting it from the cold.

❖ ❖ ❖ ❖ ❖

I walked down the Convention Center corridor where the professor was located. He stopped tracing the mural outline when he saw me.

"So, you made it after all," he said shaking up a spray can.

"Yes, sorry I'm late," I said removing my backpack.

"I'm just glad you showed up." He looked down the corridor. "As you can see, I got a lot of wall to cover. I welcome your help."

I took my handkerchief from the pocket of my overalls and tied it over my head. "Well, tell me what you need me to do."

"Why don't you glance at the sketches I have on the ladder over there," he said pointing to his left. "You can start painting the areas that I've outlined down the hall. I brought an extra mask for you."

"Okay." I walked over to the ladder and picked up the mask. As I pulled up my sleeves, he came over to me.

"I was sorry to see your name removed from my class roster yesterday," he said wiping his forehead.

I unclipped the fasteners to my overalls for more comfort. When the denim straps fell below my belly, exposing my diamond loop, I caught him taking notice. I cleared my throat.

"Yeah," I said in a husky voice. "I decided to drop the class. No offense to your teaching."

He smiled. "No offense taken. I see it as a bittersweet departure."

"What do you mean?" I asked.

He stepped close to me, leaving only inches between us. "Well, I'll miss you as a student, but perhaps I can get to know you better as a fellow artist," he said with a sexy stare. I got butterflies again.

Damn, I need to keep it together in front of this man, I thought. I looked over at his boom box. "I see you got that new Angie Stone CD playing."

"I like her style," he said. "Good music for working."

"I like her too," I said.

He toggled a spray can in his hands. "Hailee, how old are you?"

"Does it matter?"

"I . . . uh. I just wanted to know," he said looking away for a moment.

"Professor Graham, how old are you?" I asked.

He closed his eyes for a second. "Call me Isaac, please."

I licked my bottom lip. "All right, Isaac. Answer my question."

"I'm twenty-seven," he said as he rubbed his goatee.

"Well, don't worry," I said with a wink. "I'm old enough to work with a twenty-seven year old man."

Isaac had asked me to sit for a portrait. I gladly obliged. "Your studio is nice," I said admiring the spacious and eclectic feel to the room.

"Thanks," he said. "It needs some work, but I think it has potential."

"When do you think you'll be opening?"

"In about sixty days. I gotta paint and get an electrical contractor in here. I'd like to re-finish the wood floors as well."

"You're not gonna paint the walls, are you?" I asked feeling the textured brick.

"No," he said as he mixed some oil colors on his work desk. "That's what I love about this place."

"Do you have all your pieces lined up that you're gonna sell?"

"I have a few, but I need more." He smiled. "I was hoping you'd grace the place with some of your pieces."

I took my leather jacket off and draped it over the sofa. "Please," I said. "My stuff isn't good enough to sell."

"Says who?" he said. "I would've never asked you to work on the mural if I didn't think you were a good artist. You shouldn't doubt yourself."

"Are you going to sell the portrait you're doing of me?" I asked.

He shrugged. "Depends on how it turns out," he said. "I may have to keep it for my private collection."

I smiled. "Well, where can I change?" I asked.

He glanced behind him. "There's a bathroom straight back."

I stood beside him. "I'll only be a few minutes," I said. "You didn't specify what I should wear, so I brought my favorite slip. Is that acceptable?"

"Perfect," he said.

"I'll be right back."

I changed my clothes, put on some sandals and walked back out into the studio. Even at five foot five, I felt like a model. I sauntered closer to Isaac. He caught a glimpse of my outfit as he steadied his easel.

"Simply gorgeous," he said, gazing at the three raindrops

tattooed on my inner thigh. I sat on the stool and crossed my legs. I raised the edge of the slip to reveal more of my well defined leg. The smile that ran across his smooth lips let me know he enjoyed the view.

"Thanks for the compliment, Isaac," I said. "I thought azure blue would be a good color for a portrait. I like the name Azure. If I have a baby girl one day, I think I'll name her that."

"Nice name," he said. He stared at my chest as he clumsily dropped some of his paint brushes on the ground. I chuckled. His bronze face got flushed as he bent over to pick them up.

I looked down at myself. "You'll have to excuse these," I said patting my nipples. "They have a mind of their own."

"Are you cold?" he said adjusting the height of his stool.

"No, they stay perky."

His almond shaped eyes narrowed seductively. "I assure you, they are a pleasant distraction."

I straddled the stool like I was getting ready for a striptease act. "Well, do you want me naked like Rose from *Titanic*?" I asked.

"Not unless you feel it's necessary," he said pulling the tail of his tank top out of his khaki's. He was obviously heated from my body language. "Hailee, I don't need your clothes off to see your beauty." He swallowed hard and scooted behind the easel, out of my view.

I frowned as I drew my legs in and stopped moving on the stool. "Can I ask you something?" I said.

"Sure," he said.

"Are you gay?" I asked.

He peered around the easel, then moved to face me. "Why would you think I'm gay?" he said. "I know you don't think that because I'm an artist."

"Of course not," I said resting my hands on my lap. "You don't carry yourself like you're soft, but you're different. Like not wanting me to take my clothes off. Most men would have been down for me removing my panties. Remember at the Convention Center when you stood behind me on the ladder as we painted?"

"I remember," he said.

"You were so close, I could feel your breath on my back. You didn't try to kiss or feel on me. Nothing like that."

He raised a brow. "Was that what you expected from me, or is that what you wanted?"

He made me speechless. I looked at him and smiled. He put his brush down.

"First, let me say that I am a heterosexual man," he said. "Second, I have a mother and a daughter. When I interact with a woman I'm interested in, I tend to keep the two of them in mind. I'm certainly not a saint, but I try to respect a woman's space. Let her get comfortable with me. And technically, I never said I didn't want you to take off your clothes. I just said it wasn't necessary."

"I stand corrected, Professor," I said.

"Ex-professor for you," he said. "If you were still my student, we would not be doing this portrait, or engaging in this conversation. Are you ready, Hailee?"

"Yep."

"All right, give me good posture. That's nice. Now, turn your stool more towards me. You can cross your hands on your lap."

"Okay, Picasso. You want me to smile?"

"No, just be natural," he said. "Look directly at me, so I can see those beautiful hazel eyes." He began painting.

"Since I have to be still, you need to talk," I said.

"What do you want me to talk about?" he asked.

I noticed what appeared to be a birthmark showing from above his tank T-shirt. "What's that on your chest?" I asked.

He stopped tracing and looked down for a second. "Oh, that's my fraternity brand. I'm an Omega." He signaled for me to lift my chin. "Are you interested in pledging?" he asked.

I straightened my posture. "No. My theory is that if we're trying to uplift our people, we don't need to be divided into cliques," I said. "I'd prefer being a member of an organization like the NAACP, support my man Kwesi."

"Too bad you're not down with the sororities," he said. "You'd look real good in some pink and green."

"You have a thing for AKA's?" I asked.

"I used to," he said. "My best friend was an AKA."

"Isn't she still an AKA?"

"She's an Ivy Beyond The Wall, now," he said. I looked at him, confused. He stopped sketching and bit his lip. "She was my wife. She's dead."

I suddenly regretted asking him to talk to me. "I'm so sorry, Isaac," I said.

"Me too. She died of leukemia a year and a half after our daughter Lena was born. That was three years ago." We were silent for a few seconds. Isaac resumed work on the portrait. "You remind me of her," he said.

"I do?" I said.

He slid his stool directly in front of me, tracing the outline of my face with his fingertip. "Yes, you have shimmering, coffee brown skin like she did. She was slim, with a hint of baby fat in all the right places . . . Like you." He softly kissed my cheek. "You have stunning high cheekbones." I stared dreamily into his eyes. He smiled. "You also remind me of Irene Cara. Has anyone ever told you that?"

"Yeah, once or twice," I said. "What happened to her? It's like she fell off the face of the earth."

"I know," he said gliding back to his easel.

I glanced at myself in the mirror behind Isaac's work desk. "I think she's prettier than me."

"I disagree," he said painting. "I know you must have brothas begging you for a date."

I puckered my lips like I'd eaten something sour. "Nope. Just one bat I can't seem to exterminate."

"What's his name?" he asked.

I looked at my manicured fingernails. "I'd rather not say."

He moved within my sight again. "So, you are involved with someone?"

I shook my head. "I used to be, but not anymore," I said. "A word of advice. Never get involved with your landlord."

"I'll keep that in mind," he said. "Listen, I'm not getting much done. It's dinner time. You feel like taking a break to get something to eat?"

"That's fine with me," I said.

"You like burgers?" he asked.

"Uh huh."

"I'll treat you to a burger at the *Double T Diner* on Route 40."

I smiled. "Great, I'll get dressed."

❖ ❖ ❖ ❖ ❖

Isaac and I ate at the diner then headed back to the studio. We were in his Ford Explorer.

"Thanks for dinner, Isaac." I said.

"Thank you," he said. "I had a good meal and good conversation from a nice lady."

I nudged him. "How do you know I'm nice?"

He turned down the radio. "I don't know for sure, but I picked up some energy from the way you paint. Your work can be abstract, yet delicate at the same time. Your art captures life in its most bare and innocent form. I like the way you create."

I smiled and looked away from him. "You think I got skills, huh?"

"Definitely," he said. "You're still a little rough around the edges, but I can help with that."

"Oh yeah?" I said.

"Yes," he said. "If you'll let me spend more time with you, I might be able to show you some tricks of the trade."

"Well, since I'm not trying to make a career out of making art, I wouldn't want to bother you," I said.

We were at a stop light. He had a serious expression as he brushed his hand over mine.

"I know you have other aspirations Hailee, but don't stop painting," he said. "Don't let that talent go to waste." He sighed as he gripped the steering wheel. "Maybe I want you to continue to be an artist, because I know if you don't, I'll run the risk of not seeing you. Art is our common link."

He was silent as he continued driving. I touched his shoulder. "I'd still be able to help you out if you want, Isaac," I said. "Any upcoming projects where you need an assistant, just let me know."

After he pulled into the driveway of his studio, he took my hand. "I appreciate the offer, but I want you to be more than my assistant," he said. He kissed my palm. "I want you to be in my life. I know you have personal matters you're dealing with, but I'd like you to know I'm here for you."

I held my head. "Isaac, I got major baggage."

"Do you want to make changes in your life?"

"Yes, but change doesn't happen overnight."

"I know, and I'm not in a rush," he said lifting my chin. "I'd like to see what could happen between us. So, I'll be patient."

I squeezed his hand. "I want to be in your life, Isaac. I'd like that very much. We have to take it slow, though."

"Slow is good."

"And I want to meet your daughter, Lena," I said.

"I can arrange that," he said.

"I'm just a little nervous, because I don't know sign language."

"You'll be fine," he said. "Lena's a loving little girl and she's smart. She'll be able to understand you. Besides, I'll teach you all you need to know. Sign language isn't that difficult once you get the hang of it."

"Does Lena smile a lot, like her dad?" I asked.

"Yeah," he said as his face lit up. "She's my little princess."

I touched the dimple in his cheek. "She's a lucky girl."

❖❖❖❖❖

I knocked on Isaac's door. We were taking Lena to The Baltimore Aquarium. He opened the door and I saw her peep from behind his legs. She smiled and signed a message to me.

"She says you're pretty," Isaac said.

"You're pretty," I told her as I walked inside the house. "Are you ready to see the fish?" Isaac interpreted for me. She nodded *yes*. I bent down on my knee and held her tight. "We're gonna have fun, Lena," I said.

She didn't look at me to read my lips when she kissed my cheek. At that moment, I felt like I was in another world. A sweet place filled with newness and possibilities. A world free of lies and sadness. A world I hoped to call my own.

Secrets

Lucas had me dancing on his damn dining room table. Pashen was gone most of the time, doing her own dirt. When she was home, she was usually too faded to care about what was happening to me. Tonight was another reminder that life was a bitch when you didn't travel down the straight and narrow road.

He had *Between The Sheets* by The Isley Brothers playing. I wore a black leather teddy with thigh high boots to match—an outfit he'd picked out.

"That's right, work that ass," he said sipping on his scotch.

I stared straight through him, pretending to enjoy myself. I hoped that when the song ended, he'd let me get off of the table. The doorbell rang. I stopped moving and quickly got down. I walked towards the staircase.

"Where you goin'?" he asked frowning at me. "You ain't finished."

"Lucas, someone's at the door," I said. "I'm not decent."

He snapped his finger at me like I was some dog. "Come back here. It's probably just Lamont, dropping off receipts. He's not gonna see you from the foyer." He went to answer the door. I sighed and sat down at the dining room table. I was too scared to talk back to him and too mad to cry. A few seconds later when I saw Lucas walk into the dining room with Isaac, I thought I was gonna shit on myself.

"Hailee, you have company," Lucas said, taunting me with his deceitful grin.

"Hello, Hailee," Isaac said, briefly making eye contact with me. He was uncomfortable seeing me as a tramp. I was ashamed to be one. I crossed my arms over my chest, trying to shelter my body.

"Professor," I said looking down at the carpet.

"You left your leather jacket in the studio," Isaac said. "I figured you might need it, and I'm going out of town tomorrow."

I felt the jacket graze my shoulder. I looked up, hoping Isaac would see the sorrow in my eyes and understand. He wasn't holding the jacket, though. It was Lucas. I snatched the jacket away from him and focused on Isaac. I could tell he didn't know what to make of this scene. Lucas broke our silence.

"Hailee looks good in leather. Don't you agree, Professor?"

Isaac didn't answer, and I didn't want him to endure Lucas any longer. "Thanks for bringing the jacket by, Professor," I said. "Have a safe trip."

"I will," he said as he turned to leave.

"Let me walk you out, man," Lucas said.

Isaac looked at Lucas, and for the first time, I saw anger in his face. "No thanks," Isaac said. "I know the way out."

Isaac left. Lucas winked at me. I wanted to scratch his eyes out.

"You see that nigga grittin' on me, in my house? Your little boyfriend was real bold to come here."

"He's not my boyfriend," I said.

"He better not be," he said. He walked over and gave me a kiss. "Thanks for my table dance."

I looked at him out of the corner of my eye as his lips rested on my cheek. "I hate you."

He laughed. "You think you brand new just because you got that nigga open?" he said. "Hailee, you ain't shit. All you will ever be is a stripper hoe that owes me money. You got that?"

I didn't respond as I climbed the stairs. I didn't care what he thought of me. He was a dog. All dogs have their day. It was just a matter of time.

❖❖❖❖❖

When Isaac got back in town he paged me. He said he'd be

volunteering at *The Baltimore Museum of Art* today, and wanted to know if I would meet him there.

At first I told him *no*, then at the last minute I decided to go see him. When I arrived, he was in the African Art section, setting up a new exhibit. Security was all around due to the value of the art pieces, so I knew I wouldn't be able to talk to him as freely as I wanted. I walked over and stood beside him. He placed a ceremonial mask on a stand.

"That's a pretty piece," I said.

He looked me up and down and smiled. "Yes it is." He stopped smiling when he saw concern on my face. "I'm sorry for intruding on you the other night," he said.

"Isaac, never come to that house again," I said. "If you need to contact me, you know how to reach me."

"Am I overstepping my bounds, trying to get to know you?"

"No, but I told you things are complicated. What you saw the other night meant nothing to me. It was something I felt I had to do to keep him from harassing me."

Isaac shook his head. "Hailee just leave him," he said. "I have an extra room. You can stay with me."

"I can't Isaac. Besides, I'm not trying to create a situation that may be confusing for Lena," I said.

He looked down. "Maybe you're right."

I touched his shoulder. "Isaac, I am trying to get my shit together. I need you to give me time to do that. You have to trust me."

He held my hand. "I trust you," he said. "I don't trust him."

❖❖❖❖❖

Isaac and I were at Woodmoor Gardens, a cemetery in Baltimore County. This was not just a final resting place, it was a haven of beauty. Isaac loved taking me there. He said it was the only place where I smiled. Woodmoor Gardens was my getaway from Lucas.

I could get married here, I thought as I picked up the rose from the fountain platform. I waited for Isaac to change the lens on his camera. He designated today as, *Hailee Day*. I got my hair done. He took me on a shopping spree and I found this nice dress I wore from Lord and Taylor. I never felt classy when I bought clothes with Lucas's money. Never felt my femininity. Always felt like a gangsta bitch.

I whistled at Isaac. "Hurry up camera man," I said. "My time is valuable. I'll have to raise my fee if you keep me waiting much longer."

He bowed. "I'm so sorry Miss Shaw," Isaac said. "I'm trying to make sure my camera is properly equipped to capture all of your magnificence."

"No excuses. Chop, chop. I have to prepare for a runway show in London."

"Oh really?" he asked smiling.

"Yes," I said as I flicked my hair the way Cher used to do. "Designers are all over me, begging me to model their latest creations. So, get your shots while you can. You won't be able to afford me next year!"

We laughed. Isaac shook his head as he walked closer to me with the camera.

"All right glamour girl," he said. "I'm ready now."

"How do you want me?" I asked.

"In my arms forever, but that's besides the point."

I stopped smiling. "You caught me off guard."

"I know." He bent over and gave me a gentle kiss. "Don't mind me. I'm in love."

I grabbed his hand. "Why do you love me, Isaac?" I asked.

"Why would any man not love you? Just look at you," he said. "You are truly model material. Tyra and Naomi have nothing on you."

I sighed. "Yes they do. A fat bank account," I said.

Isaac sat down beside me. "You equate money with happiness?" he asked.

"Money would definitely be a means to a happy ending for me right now. I'd be singin' *Oh Happy Day* if I had the green to get Lucas off my ass."

Bringing the devil up spoiled Isaac's Kodak moment. He looked at his hands. "Isaac, I didn't mean to bring him up," I said. I embraced him. "I'm sorry."

He caressed my face. "I'm sorry you're unhappy," he said.

"When I'm with you I'm happy. It's just hard to suppress negative thoughts and step out of a life that I'll have to step back into a couple of hours from now."

"Don't worry about a couple of hours from now. Enjoy this moment in creation."

I nodded. "I'll do that," I said. "So, are you ready?"

"Ready when you are," he said. "I got an idea. Take your sandals off and step up onto the platform. Okay, turn to the side. That's it. Now take the hem of your dress and pull it up to your thigh."

"Like my legs, huh?" I said as I raised the dress.

"No doubt," he said. "Lean your head back. Rest your left hand on your hair and close your eyes. Good, hold that." The camera clicked. He took a few more shots. "Well, that's a wrap unless you have any other ideas."

"Let's do a few more shots," I said. "Put the camera on the tripod. I want you in these with me."

"Your wish is my command." I jumped into the fountain. "What are you doing?" Isaac asked as he tightened the camera on the tripod.

"Giving you the perfect picture," I said. "Water captures the true essence of a woman. Didn't you know that?"

I let the water from the fountain wet my hair. Isaac looked like a statue, he was so still. The statue came to life as I saw its eyes move to the roundness of my breasts, burgeoning under wet silk fabric from my white halter gown. Then the eyes moved to the curve of my hips. I knew he liked what he saw. I stepped down from the fountain and he pulled me into his arms. I looked down at his Levi's as I felt him against my pelvis.

"I sense you like the wardrobe?" I asked.

"You sense correctly," he moaned. "So, either make love to me or let me take these photos."

I touched his lip. "Can't we do both?" I asked.

"Are you serious?" he said.

"Yes. I mean, a prize winning photo shoot wouldn't be

complete without a celebration, right?" I said.

Isaac smiled. "You're absolutely right, beautiful one. I'm gonna set the timer. You got a pose in mind?"

"Yep."

"Here we go."

He hurried over and sat with me on the fountain edge. I unbuttoned a few buttons on his linen shirt to expose his smooth chest. I laid down across his lap. He put his arms under my body and held me like I was the most precious gift on the earth.

"Get ready," he said. "You got about ten seconds."

I leaned my head back. I felt the soft touch of his lips at the middle of my neck. We stayed still. The camera clicked. We kissed and he lifted me up.

"Where do we go from here?" he asked.

I touched his face. "To Heaven."

Isaac and I swayed to a Roberta Flack ballad playing in our room at the Doubletree Hotel, near BWI Airport. A sliver of moonlight came through the window to illuminate the shadows. When the song ended, Isaac stopped kissing me. There was desire in his eyes. We undressed.

"Umph, umph Picasso," I said. "You're a stunning work of art."

He laughed. "How do you know, Paloma?" he said. "You haven't felt me yet."

I grabbed his hand and slowly dragged it down my abdomen, through the warmth of my secret garden, stopping at the waterfall. "I'm feelin' you baby," I whispered seductively. "Definitely feelin' you."

He pulled me close to him. "You're right," he said as he enjoyed my essence seeping over his fingertips.

"Now, Picasso before you start painting you'll need protection," I said.

"Got it right here," he said retrieving his jeans off of the floor. He removed the condom from his pants pocket. Condom in place, Isaac kissed me. Our breathing got intense. Isaac pulled away.

"I need to love you now," he said.

"I need you to love me like there's no tomorrow," I said.

I got down on the bed, instinctively moving onto my stomach. Isaac laid down beside me. I felt his warm lips rest against my ear.

"Hailee, I want to see your pretty face." He gently turned me onto my back. "I want to taste you," he said. "Will you let me taste you?"

I paused before I replied. I smiled at him because I was grateful. Nobody ever cared for me like Isaac.

"Yes, I want you to," I said. I let my finger trace the fraternity brand on his muscular chest. I opened wide for him. He went to work.

I felt like a delicate flower shedding its petal, waiting to receive the warmth of the sun again. Isaac didn't keep me waiting. Thunderstruck by his skilled tongue, I held onto him for dear life. Then the rain came, and melted the sun all over my body. He was gentle when he entered me, and we both cried out in ecstasy.

"Baby you feel too good," he moaned. "Am I dreaming?"

"I know I am," I whispered in his ear. I was delusional. He played a serenade in me that made me scream his name. He smiled and kept playing.

"I'm so glad I found you," he said. "I'm hoping that you'll be all mine one day."

I kissed his lips, admiring his light brown eyes. "I am yours, Isaac. I'll prove it to you."

"I'll hold you to that," he said.

"Just hold me," I said.

I closed my eyes. Isaac in me was so different. I wanted him inside of me. I wasn't afraid of the passion I felt. Our bodies moved as one. Intertwined, we began to paint our own mural. Satisfaction continued to build, and I couldn't control myself. Isaac ran his fingers through my hair as I whimpered. When my crying got louder, his hand touched my face. He stopped painting.

"Hailee, open your eyes." Tears flowed down my face. I didn't want to open my eyes, because I didn't want to wake from this precious dream. "Baby, look at me, please."

I finally looked at him. He caressed me in his arms. "What's wrong?" I didn't say anything.

"Am I hurting you?" he asked.

I locked my arms around him. "No, Isaac. You're loving me. That's why I'm crying."

Hell Broke Loose

I got home and to my surprise, Lucas was awake—kicked back in the family room recliner, watching *Sports Center* on TV. I figured he'd been up waiting for me, since he stopped caring about the late hours Pashen kept. I knew she wasn't home, because the house didn't smell like chronic, and Lucas had his hand inside his pajama pants. He obviously hadn't been tended to this evening, based on the tart expression I saw on his face as he got up from the chair.

"How was school today?" he asked.

"Fine," I mumbled as I walked to the kitchen. As I grabbed a bag of chips from the pantry, I felt his breath on my back.

"Why are you so dressed up?" he asked.

"Photo shoot," I said turning to look at him. "School project."

He licked his lips. "Can I have a few pictures?"

I glanced down at the ceramic tile floor. "No. The film is property of the artist."

"Lucky man," he said. I looked away and headed for the stairwell. "I didn't know you were taking a hotel management class this semester?" I froze. He smiled and walked towards me, sensing my nervousness.

"Yeah," he said with a devilish grin. "My boy Bremman just got back from St. Thomas. He said he saw someone that looked like you at the Doubletree Hotel earlier this evening. Same dress and everything."

He raked his long fingers through my hair. His touch wasn't rough, but it wasn't gentle. I closed my eyes, preparing for the worst. When the blow didn't come, I slowly removed his hand from my hair and took two steps back. He took two steps towards me.

"Lucas, I take a lot of classes you don't know about," I said.

"Is that right?" he said.

"Yes," I said as I turned away from him. "I gotta use the bathroom." That was my excuse to get out of his reach.

"Hailee?"

"Yes?" I said stopping on the steps.

He winked. "Sleep well."

I was awakened by the sensation of something hard pressed against my temple. I slowly opened my eyes. It was Lucas's gun. His hand around my neck let me know I wasn't dreaming.

"You givin' away my coochie!" Lucas screamed.

"No!" I shivered.

"You fuckin' that soft nigga from the art studio, ain't you?"

"No Lucas!"

"Yes you are, you ungrateful bitch. I lace you with platinum and diamonds. You are a twenty year old college student with a new Benz, and a closet full of clothes that I paid for! This is the thanks I get? You love to lock them legs when I want some, but it's open sesame with that punk, right?" I groaned in pain.

"Well since you like to feel the heat, why don't you try this stick on for size?" he said. He ripped my panties off and inserted the tip of the nine millimeter. "Like that?"

I closed my eyes. *God please, let me die. Make him shoot,* I prayed to myself. His Nextel went off.

"Saved by the beep," he said looking down at the phone clipped to his pants. "I hope you enjoyed your little fling, because from this moment on there will be no more sharing, you hear?"

I nodded *yes.*

He kissed me. "Sweet dreams."

I was officially a year older, and still clueless as to how to solve my situation with Lucas. Isaac had invited me over for dinner. I wasn't up to going, but I didn't want to disappoint him. His mother babysat Lena, and I knew he'd made a special meal for my birthday.

"The shrimp Creole was delicious Isaac," I said as we relaxed on his sofa watching TV. "Thanks for celebrating my birthday with me."

"You're quite welcome, sweetheart," he said.

I nudged him. "It wouldn't have been much of a birthday without you fussing over me," I said. "You better get your slice of strawberry shortcake now, because I'ma try to eat the rest of it before the night is over!"

He laughed as he leaned over to kiss me. As his tongue entered my mouth, his hands went under my shirt. He cupped my breasts and used his body to lower me down on the sofa. I felt his desire intensify. I wanted to feel more, but I knew he would ask about the bruises if he made love to me tonight; the bruises Lucas left on my body after he beat me for refusing him on my birthday.

My mind told me to stop Isaac, but my heart tried to convince my ass to stop thinking so much. I didn't have to fight the desire long, because within a few seconds, the seduction stopped. Isaac's hands had made it back up to my head. When he swept my hair from around my temple, he discovered a Band-Aid. I suddenly felt a headache come on as I saw the concern in his eyes.

"Hailee what happened here," he asked pointing at the bandage.

I bit my lip. "I had a rough night," I said. "Kept having bad dreams. I woke up from one when I rolled out of the bed, hitting my head on the nightstand."

He looked into my eyes, trying to discern the truth. I looked away, knowing that my lies were lingering on me.

"Hailee, you would've told me if you had bumped your head from a bad dream," he said. "What really happened?"

"Nothing. Lucas and I got into it, that's all," I said.

Isaac sighed. "That's all? If you have a bandage on your forehead, then *got into it* means he got physical. What kind of hold does he have on you?"

I moved my bang to cover the bruise on my head. "I told you he was possessive."

"You said he was tripping, because you told him you wanted to leave him, but I didn't realize he was being abusive," he said. He ran his hand over his hair. "I mean, is the situation with Lucas more than just a former sugar daddy letting you stay the rest of the semester in his house, rent free?"

I raised my palm. "Look," I snapped. "The Lucas deal is complicated. He agreed to let me stay with him in order to pay off a school loan he took out for me. I guess he figured he'd get his money sooner if he was my landlord."

Isaac squeezed my arm. "Hailee, are you still sleeping with Lucas, now that we're together?" he asked.

I folded my arms and leaned farther back on the sofa. "You ask a lot of questions," I said.

He slowly put his hand on my thigh. "I'm hoping to get some answers. I'm falling for a woman I know very little about."

"Well, take my word when I tell you there are certain things about me that I'd like to forget. So, I find it best not to disclose those things to you."

"Why?" he asked.

I frowned. "Can we change the subject?" I said.

He abruptly got up, placing his hands behind his head as he stood by the fireplace. "You always do that. Dismiss my questions when I ask about your personal life. I love you, Hailee. You should be able to communicate openly with me. I feel like I can trust you with anything. It bothers me that you don't feel the same way."

I got up and stood in front of him. "Stop this soap opera scene, Isaac," I said with my hands on my hips. "I told you I lived with a man from the very beginning. You didn't seem bothered when you were taking off my clothes." I rolled my eyes at him. His silence let me know he was hurting, but I refused to give him sympathy.

"Shit happens, Isaac," I said. I wrapped my finger around a

denim belt loop on his jeans, pulling him close. "If you love me, you'll have to accept how things are right now."

He shook his head. "I don't know if I can do that," he said. "Without honesty, what do we have?"

I was pissed as I walked back to the sofa to get my Coach purse. He came over and grabbed my hand.

"Hailee, sit down," he pleaded.

I snatched my hand away. "You want honesty!" I yelled. "That's what you want, Isaac? Okay, here's the truth. My mother isn't dead. She works for a drug dealer. The same one I work for . . . Lucas." Isaac's eyes widened, and his mouth opened slightly as if he wanted to say something.

"My mother used to be a cop, but money in the fast lane was more lucrative," I said. "She decided to become a dope representative. Her drug sales were good for business, until she got hooked on the heroin she sold. She messed up on the job, costing him his best client. He threatened to kill her, so I volunteered to be his whore in order to save her life. I have to live with Lucas, and screw him on command until he feels his financial loss from my mother is recovered. Is that enough background information for you?"

A tear broke through as I tried to fight my emotions. Isaac tried to embrace me. I backed away from him.

"Hailee, I can help you," he said.

I sighed. " No you can't," I said. "I care for you Isaac, but things are gonna get a lot worse before they get better. I can't change the past, and I can't change what's gonna happen to me. It's all fate. If true confessions bother you, then it's best we not see each other anymore."

I walked over to the closet to get my jacket. Isaac stood behind me.

"Baby, don't go." He gently pulled me into his arms. I blinked from tears flowing between my lashes.

"I have to," I said. I removed his hands and put on my jacket. "You're better off without me." I tried to walk past him to get to the door, but he blocked my path.

"No, I'm incomplete without you," he said. "Let me give

you the money you owe that bastard, so you can get out of his life for good. I'll even borrow the money. Whatever you need, I'll find a way to get it for you."

"Thanks, but no thanks. I don't need to owe another man."

"I'm not Lucas." He tried to comfort me, but I pushed him away. He held on as I squirmed to get out of his grip. "Don't fight me, Hailee. I only want to love you."

"Dammit Isaac, let go!" I finally freed myself. We breathed heavily as we stared at each other. "Why would you want to continue loving someone like me?" I asked. I quickly brushed passed him and opened the door. I looked back at him. "Don't you know whores can't be trusted?"

Before he could reply, I walked out.

❖ ❖ ❖ ❖ ❖

I watched the ducks waddle as I ate my lunch by the lake. When I felt soothing hands massaging my back, I glanced behind me and saw Isaac. He sat down on the grass and peeked at the open book on my lap.

"What are you reading?" he asked.

I showed him the book, then put it back down and continued reading without speaking to him. "*Family* by J. California Cooper," he said. "I love her short stories. Her words have a way of lifting my spirits up."

I nodded in agreement. He kissed my cheek and glided his hand down my hair. "I'm sorry about the other night, Hailee." I shrugged my shoulders and looked off to the lake.

"I've been paging you," he said.

"I've been ignoring you," I said, unnerved.

Isaac moved closer to me and wrapped his arm around my waist. "Don't you normally have a class at this time?" I asked with an attitude.

"Normally, but I let the students turn in their term papers and leave," he said. "I thought I'd give them a break to enjoy the nice weather. That way, I could have more time to find you."

I sighed. "I want to be by myself, Isaac. I thought I expressed that last night."

"You did, but I had to see you again," he said. "I gave Lena my word that I would make sure you got this." He pulled a box out of his briefcase and handed it to me. It was wrapped in rainbow paper.

"What's this?" I asked.

"A birthday gift from her," he said. "Open it."

I opened the box and removed a shiny kaleidoscope. I looked in and turned the bottom, admiring all the pretty images. I gave into a smile as I looked back at him.

"It's beautiful Isaac."

"I think so too," he said. "I believe my daughter is a true artist in the making."

"Lena made this all by herself?" I asked.

"I gave a few pointers, and helped her with the mounting," he said. "She did all of the drawings, though."

"Please tell her that I love it, and thanks for thinking of me."

"Well, she was hoping that you'd come to see her. So you could tell her thanks yourself."

My face turned sullen as I got up from the ground. "That's not possible," I said. I brushed grass off the back of my denim dress. Isaac stood up to face me.

"Why not Hailee? I still want to be with you," he said. "I was a fool last night, and I'll apologize a million times if you'll forgive me."

"There's nothing to forgive, and my decision about us is still the same," I said. "We can't see each other anymore."

I walked away. Isaac quickly caught up with me.

"Hailee, don't walk away. I wanna talk," he said.

I kept going. "There's nothing else for us to talk about," I said.

❖❖❖❖❖

Lucas asked me to join him in the shower. I didn't resist because I was tired of his threats every time I refused. The water ran hot against our bodies. Lucas moaned and held me close. I was still as he kissed my neck. I thought about Isaac. Thought about how messed up it was for me to be doing this with another man. I tilted my head back and let the water run down my face. Lucas took my movement as a sign of pleasure. We both stopped moving when we heard Pashen calling me.

"Hailee?" she said. Her voice got closer.

"I thought you said Pashen wasn't coming back home until this evening?" I whispered to Lucas. He didn't say anything. He just smiled. I tried to get out of the shower to get to Pashen before she got to me, but it was too late.

"Hailee, you in here?" Pashen said as she opened the door. Her face reddened immediately. "What the hell is goin' on!" she yelled. Lucas laughed as I tried to speak.

"Ma . . . I"

"Ma, my ass!" she screamed, pushing me back against the tile wall. Pashen was in the shower getting soaked with me. Lucas stepped out and leaned against the wall, enjoying the action.

"I'ma beat you good girl!" she shouted. I couldn't speak if I wanted to. Pashen threw punch after punch on me. "You slut! Was it good, huh?"

"Stop it Pashen!" I cried in agony. I crouched down on the tub floor, covering my head with my hands. Pashen kept hitting me. I felt the water stop and raised my head. Lucas pulled Pashen out of the shower. She was hysterical, wailing and flinging her arms.

"Pashen, that's enough!" he hollered.

"Let me go you bastard!" Pashen cried. She leaned against the counter. "Lucas, how could you?"

He shrugged as he rubbed his hairy chest. "You ain't takin' care of business no more, so I had to invest in some new pussy," he said.

"This is my daughter!" she shrieked.

He smirked. "Your point?"

I slowly got up as I wiped blood from my busted lip. "Pashen, please." I reached out to touch her. "Let me explain."

"Don't you say shit to me, you back stabbin' bitch!" she spat. "I should've aborted your ass when I had the chance."

"You should have, then I wouldn't be living like this!" I

screamed. "You have no idea what I've been going through." I got out of the tub and grabbed a towel from the rack.

"I know you fuckin' my man!" she shouted as she came towards me with her fist. Lucas stepped in between us.

"Pashen, calm down," he said grabbing onto her arm. She pulled away from him.

"You get off of me!" she yelled as she backed away. "Thanks for ruining my life!"

"Thanks for making it easy for me, bitch," he scoffed.

Pashen shook her head. I cried as I looked at the hurt on her face. There was nothing I could say to make her understand.

"Fuck the both of y'all!" Pashen yelled as she ran out of the house.

Lucas put his arm around me, but I pushed his naked body away. "We're over Lucas!" I yelled. I ran to the bedroom and slammed the door. He opened it and got up in my face.

"That's the first and last time you slam some door in my face!" he hollered. "We ain't over until my money is right. So, you might as well get comfortable taking off your clothes. I got a long laundry list of obligations, including your tuition. Did you forget?"

I ignored him as I went into my closet. I got some clothes and started to dress. "Where you goin'?" he asked.

"To find my mother!" I snapped. I put on my jeans and grabbed my Reeboks. I'd have to finish dressing downstairs. Lucas had a hard on, lusting after me in the mirror. I was tempted to get that knife from Pashen's nightstand and chop his shit off. He was to blame for Pashen hating me. I wanted to find her before she hurt herself over this loser. I left the bedroom and ran down the steps.

Angel Dust

In the midst of high pitched wails from rush hour commuters, and threatening shouts from police bullhorns, I saw her. I'd waited on a hard, wooden bench at the Lexington Market subway station for what seemed like an eternity. Subject to witnessing the aftermath of a troubled woman drawing the line. Faithful patrons of public transportation were trapped inside a halted train. Some remained frozen in their seats; others banged on closed doors. Obviously, they were traumatized by the scene of Pashen stepping into the middle of darkness, her body helpless from the penetration of speeding steel. Her weary soul was about to give up hope. Then she remembered His name, and in an instant, she was set free.

When law officials finally managed to clear the stampede of curious onlookers from the subway platform, a higher authority placed a beautiful rose in front of me. I stood and smiled at Pashen. Even under a stream of tears, her face glowed. She looked at me intently, as if she recognized me. Then she turned away, to stare at the silhouette etched along the tunnel tracks. I walked over to her and adjusted the ivory lace shawl that had fallen off her shoulder. She shivered at my touch.

"Sweetheart, that woman doesn't need you crying over her," I said softly. Pashen slowly looked at me, covering her mouth as she cried.

"I'm Anela," I said offering her my handkerchief. "Did you know the woman?"

She nodded *yes* as she took the handkerchief out of my hand.

"Oh, you may think you knew her, but trust me when I say, you didn't," I said.

"But . . . but I," Pashen said, confused. I placed her hand in mine and pulled her away from that dark hole. Slowly, we walked over to the bench and sat down.

Pashen released her hand from mine with her eyes directed at me, searching for answers to the confusion in the tunnel. "What am I doing here?" she asked wiping her tears. "I'm supposed to be dead."

"Chile, I'm supposed to be alive, but that sweet Negro I married sure had it in for me," I huffed. "Life will sometimes flip the script on you. The good ones gotta go, and the bad ones . . . I really don't know what happens to them. That's not my neck of the woods."

She frowned. "What?"

Pashen looked at me like I was crazy, and I had to chuckle. She had no idea what I had gone through, and now was not the time to let bitterness creep in from my past. I had to convince her that an ethereal life was worth all the tears and pain she felt.

"Don't mind me, Pashen," I said smiling. "I'm trying to warm you up to me, that's all."

"Who are you?" she asked.

"An angel. God heard you call out to Him. He sent me here to help you."

"An angel! Shit, I mean, shoot." She slid a few inches away from me, shaking her head. "Are you for real?"

"Depends on what you believe is real," I said glancing back at the train platform. "I am here to get you ready, though."

"Get ready for what?" Pashen said looking down at her garments. "Why am I dressed this way?"

"You don't like that dress? Girl, I shopped all day to find you something pretty. It sorta has that Norma Kamali feel to it. I'm jealous, 'cause I can't get my big buns in a straight gown like that," I said patting my hips.

Pashen looked unsettled. "It's nice, but. . . ."

I interrupted. "Scoot over, I'm not gonna hurt you," I said. She moved closer. Her reservation about my presence, and the chaos in the station was taking its toll on her small frame.

"Anela, I jumped in front of a train a few minutes ago, and now I'm sitting here with you," she whimpered. "I need to know what's gonna happen to me." She looked around the terminal. "It's so loud with all these people screaming. And the police officers: Tony, Kathy, and Jeff . . . Jeff was my partner."

She wrung her hands. The handkerchief dropped to the floor when she reached up to rub the inside of her left arm. Pashen swayed nervously to the sounds of sirens and code reds being amplified over the terminal's loud speaker. Then she got up and ran over to Jeff, who was on his knees, shaking uncontrollably. He was an emotional wreck. His comrades couldn't console him. He cried out for Pashen. She kneeled down and embraced him.

"I'm so sorry, baby," she said. Her voice was choked with tears. "I didn't mean to hurt you, Jeff."

Pashen's fingertips feverishly tried to wipe tears from Jeff's face, but his body was paralyzed with sadness. The two of them grieving together were not making my job any easier.

"Boss, you gotta help me get her through this," I pleaded as I looked up to Heaven. A wisp of warm air feathered my praying hands, reassuring me that I wasn't alone.

I walked over to Pashen and wrapped loving arms around her. "Sweetheart, Jeff can't hear or see you, right now," I said. "Let him go, Pashen. Let him go."

I had difficulty peeling her arms away from him. She finally gave in to the tender squeeze of my hands at her waist, lifting her off her knees. She put her head on my shoulder as we walked near the bench.

"I got everybody upset. My baby girl, Hailee. We had a fight over a damn dealer. I didn't get a chance to tell her I was sorry. I should've never let her move back into Lucas's house. He was a sick bastard and I knew it was only a matter of time before he'd be all over her. I was a terrible mother. All she ever tried to do was love me, and look at what I did!" she cried pointing to the melee behind her.

As Pashen wept, I smoothed down strands from her long

mane, then I closed my eyes in prayer. It was time for healing to begin.

The sirens were now silent. Frantic footsteps and the sour smell of a dank subway tunnel were blocked out by crisp, cream colored linen curtains. They resembled wide ribbons, like the ones my mother used to place around my girlish plaits for church on Sunday. Pashen was awestruck as she gazed at the baby blue sky. She stepped closer to me and held onto my arm, uncertain about the gold flecks of light raining down. We had a graceful and private sanctuary. A light breeze fringed the pleated curtains, causing a rippling effect. A cascade of calm ocean waves hummed in the background. The shadows of death had been transformed into a peaceful oasis. I closed my eyes and inhaled deeply, enjoying the intoxicating scent of jasmine in the air.

"Anela, what is this?" Pashen asked, tugging the ecru sleeve of my washed silk gown to get my attention. I opened my eyes and smiled.

"This is Heaven," I said.

Pashen's mouth opened slightly as she observed the change of scenery. "Heaven?" she said. "I . . . made it into Heaven?"

"You came a mighty long way to get here, but yes, you made it," I said.

She looked down at the hard cement floor. "I don't believe it," she said shaking her head.

I lifted her chin. "Believe, chile. God is real, and no matter what you see going on around you, He ain't never gonna change."

She grabbed my hand. "I'm afraid, Anela."

I took both her hands and raised them mid-air, making sure her palms touched mine. "Pashen, I want you to close your eyes." Her lips quivered as her wet eyelashes lowered. "Now, I want you to slowly open your eyes and tell me what you see," I said.

She was jolted by the image. I smiled because a miracle had mirrored the reflection of an exquisite angel. A woman with flawless tan skin and flowing tresses free of dyes and relaxers. A lovely spirit, shining brightly because her innocence had finally been loosed from the scab we call, *life*.

"Pashen, what do you see?" I asked clasping her hands tighter.

"Me!" she exclaimed. Her eyes were vibrant. Their hazel shade splashed with a hint of blue from the sky.

"Well, I see a beautiful lady who I think is ready to meet her first love," I said releasing her hands.

"My first love?" Pashen said in amazement. "Jeff's gonna be with me?"

"I'm not talking about Jeff, Lucas, or anybody else," I said. I exhaled as I wiped away the tear that had feathered my cheek.

Pashen touched my shoulder. "You okay, Anela?"

"I'm doing fine, sweetie. These are tears of joy, don't worry. I'm happy because you're gonna be with the One who will never leave you for another. The One who will never beat you, or call you outside your name. True love is right behind these curtains. Once you step on the other side, there are no more tears, no more drugs and no more loneliness. All you will ever need is just a few steps away."

I hugged Pashen, then stepped back to admire her in that size six satin halter gown. The same design I wore on my first flight home. Her smile lessened when she looked over at the curtains momentarily.

"What's wrong, chile?" I asked.

Pashen bit her bottom lip as she looked at me. "Hailee. Will she be all right?" she asked. "Lucas doesn't have a conscience, he'll. . . ."

"Shh. . . ," I said touching my index finger to her lips. "You gave that girl the right name. She's a tough cookie. Continue to say your prayers, and leave the rest to the Boss."

"The Boss?"

"Yes, and you're gonna meet Him right now." I looked down at her three inch satin sandals. "Take off your shoes."

"Huh? But Anela, I kinda like these," Pashen whined as she looked down at the sandals. I winked at her when she suddenly glanced back at me. The hard and dirty cement floor was now fine, toffee tone sand.

"See, that's why you don't need those heels," I said laughing. "I'll save them for you, though."

"Wait a minute," she said removing her shoes. "You're not coming with me?"

"No, I still have work to do."

"Can I help you?" Pashen pleaded.

"Afraid not, sweetie," I said touching her cheek. I looked up to the sky. "You're new, so Boss is gonna need you up there with Him to help manage the Call Center."

Pashen rubbed the inside of her arm as she looked at the linen fabric drifting in her direction. I gingerly massaged the arm that caused her discomfort.

"That arm gonna stop bothering you soon," I said. "Back home, the sugar is a hundred percent pure."

Her eyes watered again and she hugged me.

"Stop crying, chile." I rubbed her back. "Going home is something to celebrate, believe me," I said.

Pashen nodded as if she understood. She touched my hand. "Anela, I think I'm ready." She closed her eyes for a second, then looked straight into my eyes. "I'm ready," she said in a louder, more confident voice.

I beamed with pride. She was indeed ready for angel wings. "Pashen, draw the curtain back," I said.

Pashen parted the linen to reveal a tranquil body of crystal clear ocean water. Sunrays were baptized in simmering waves. Heaven patiently awaited her.

"You see that wonderful beach out there?" I asked

"Yes, it's beautiful," Pashen said. She took a deep breath as she marveled at the tropical surroundings.

"I want you to take one step at a time towards the water," I said.

"Anela, I can't swim," she said looking back at me.

I smiled. "Everything will be fine, sweetheart. You'll see." Pashen slowly walked towards the water as dense sand caressed her feet. She paused to glimpse back in my direction.

"See ya when I get back," I said.

She waved and turned away, moving closer to the sand's tide mark. Pashen's footprints were delicate and closely spaced. She walked with her head held high, her satin gown elegantly trailing each step. I looked to the east and noticed a larger set of footprints moving effortlessly across the sand. The footsteps were getting closer and closer to Pashen. At the median of dry land and water, they united. An infusion of intense sunlight caused me to turn my head. When I looked again, Pashen was gone. The larger footsteps were the only ones formed in wet sand. I took off my shoes and followed the imprints to the water. The tide washed a single red rose up to my feet and I realized, love had found its way.

How Am I Supposed To Live Without You

I never found Pashen. The police did. Two hours after my mother caught her man and her child in the shower together, she committed suicide. She jumped in front of a subway train. When the authorities arrived at Lucas's house to give the news, I cried and cried. My heart was heavy, because Pashen never knew the truth. She never knew I loved her more than my life. Loved her so much that I resorted to sleeping with the man she loved. I could blame myself for what happened. Perhaps Lucas wouldn't have killed her, but I didn't want to gamble with Pashen's life. I did what I had to do. Having regrets wouldn't bring my mother back.

❖❖❖❖❖

I didn't attend Pashen's funeral. Why would I eulogize my mother in the company of people that meant her harm? Lucas took care of the arrangements, which was the least he could do. Tiffani called and told me the service was nice. The Baltimore City Police Department did a special tribute. Tiffani accepted Pashen's flag on my behalf.

At the burial, I waited until people went their separate ways. When the funeral caravan departed, I entered the cemetery. The caretakers removed the chairs and the casket was released into the ground. I got out of the car, holding the oil painting I'd done of my mother. The one where she was dressed in her white gown, being held by The Savior. Slowly, I walked up to the opening in the earth. One of the caretakers approached me.

"Miss? I'm sorry, but it's really not safe for you to be around this area right now," he said.

I looked up from where my mother's silver casket rested. "Nothing is gonna happen to me," I said staring at him. "This is my mother, and I need to say goodbye." He nodded and backed away. I brought the canvass up to my face, kissing the image of her. I bent down and reached as far as I could before I released the painting. It traveled down fast to the casket, but it remained intact. I rose and wiped my tears. "Death only makes our love stronger, Pashen. Enjoy the good life. You deserve it."

When I left the cemetery, I went over to Isaac's place. He held me as I cried myself to sleep.

❖❖❖❖❖

Lucas walked into the kitchen with a petite, older black woman. She was very pretty. Her fine hair had silver streaks and was pulled back in a neat bun.

"Hailee, this is Anela Grace," he said. "She will be helping us out around the house."

I stopped eating my ice cream and got up to shake her hand. "It's nice to meet you, Anela," I said. "Please have a seat."

She sat down at the dinette table as Lucas pulled a beer out of the refrigerator. "Would you like something to drink, Anela?" I asked, annoyed at him for being rude.

"No thanks. That strawberry ice cream sure looks tempting, though," she said.

"Oh, let me get you some," I said.

She looked at Lucas. "Is it all right, Mr. Blacke?" she asked. "I am on the job."

He shrugged. "It's fine with me," he said. "Hailee, show her around the house when you all are done." He walked out.

Anela whispered. "He doesn't talk much, huh?"

"He talks plenty," I said. "It's just he usually doesn't have anything interesting to say." I smiled. "I'm glad you're here. I'll have somebody to talk to besides Lucas."

"If you don't mind me asking, have you and Mr. Blacke been an item for a while?" she asked.

I took the ice cream box out of the freezer. "He told you we were an item?" I said.

She folded her hands. "Yes, he said you were his fiancé."

I laughed. "In his dreams," I said. "Let me say this . . . I'm with him, but I'm not with him. I'll leave it at that."

Anela looked down at her lap. "I didn't mean to pry," she said.

"That's okay," I said. "No harm done," I said. I scooped the ice cream into a bowl. "So, do you live in Baltimore?"

"Well, I'm from up North, but I moved here about fifteen years ago when my husband died," she said.

I handed her the bowl. "Do you have any children?" I asked.

"Thank you, sweetie," she said taking the ice cream. "No children. How about you?"

I shook my head as I sat back down. "No, I'm too young and too stressed for kids right now. I'd like to have a child one day, though. A little girl."

She smiled. "I bet a little girl would be perfect for you."

I sighed. "Yeah. I'd have someone to love me for the right reasons," I said. "I'd try to give her a better life than what I've had. My baby right now is school. That's all I'm focused on. Hopefully, I'll graduate in May."

Anela touched my hand. "You will, and you'll have a good life," she said. "We all hit some crooked train tracks from time to time that set us back. Things straighten out eventually, though."

I frowned as I looked out the kitchen window.

❖ ❖ ❖ ❖ ❖

Anela had only been working for Lucas two months, but we'd already gotten close. When I came home from school, she'd have a nice meal cooked. Lucas was rarely home during the day, so we could talk. I helped her with chores around the house. After we finished housework, I'd drive her home. We had tea and she would show me her old scrapbooks. One night, time escaped us. We decided to pamper ourselves, and watch a movie. Anela said I wasn't taking care of my hair properly. She washed it for me and greased my scalp. Her soothing hands seemed to erase all my problems.

Anela brushed my hair as we watched *Down In The Delta*. I sighed. "Anela, my mother committed suicide." I didn't say anything else as I looked up at her. I didn't need to. She understood. She continued brushing my hair. "I owe Lucas a lot of money," I said. "That's why I'm living with him." I began to cry. "I'm trapped."

She bent down and hugged me. "Ease your mind sweetheart," she said. "Everything is gonna be fine."

"When I think back to how my mother and I fought right before she died, I get sick," I said. "I could feel the hurt in her eyes. She died hating me."

"That's not true," she said. "I'm sure she was a beautiful woman, just like you. When the Lord took her to be with Him, he wiped the slate clean. Hailee, you're not trapped. Trust me. Things work out for the good of them that love the Lord. Continue to pray for change, and it'll come."

Free

A surge of Isaac's strong pelvis made me forget the venom that Lucas released inside me when he invaded my soft folds the night before. Each place on my body singed from Lucas's hot tongue was soothed by my secret lover's balm of sweet kisses. I had to remember the relief Isaac's smooth lips gave to keep me sane during the nights we couldn't be together. I watched the sweat roll down his forehead as I slid down his long shaft. His eyes connected with mine. We rode out an insatiable high that somehow, despite our collective efforts, managed to come crashing down.

He moved on top of me, cupping my breasts as he licked the middle of my cleavage line. I wrapped my arms around his wet back. The vulnerability I felt made me wonder if Pashen had felt something similar when the heroin abandoned her veins. A blissful moment with Isaac was what I treasured, because it was a fleeting niche, trapped inside a horrific cell. A cell cluttered with dirt, deception, and Lucas. A place I sadly called, *home*.

Isaac exhaled as he slowly lifted his body. I placed my hands on his firm ass, pushing him back into me. "Don't pull out, Isaac," I moaned. "Not yet." My expression was serious when I touched his face.

He kissed my lips. "You okay?" he asked, concerned.

"Fine, baby," I said. He gradually lifted from me to discard the condom, then laid back down. He closed his eyes and snuggled on my breast. I grinned as I smoothed down the unruly curls from Isaac's afro that tickled my skin. I'd arrived at his studio to cornrow his hair. A sexual escapade interrupted the hair braiding.

Our retreat was a plush, wine colored micro fiber futon. The futon that got more wear from our sex funky bodies than customers who waited for art pieces. Candlelight shimmered on the walls as we rested. A bottle of Merlot waited on the hardwood floor nearby. I looked around at the wondrous works of art hanging in the studio. Then I focused on Isaac, who sleepily looked up at me.

"Tired?" I asked as I brushed my finger across his thick eyebrow.

"Just trying to catch my breath, as usual," he said laughing.

"I'm not that bad," I said as I licked his earlobe.

"You're incredible. You know that, right?"

"Only when you tell me," I said staring at his gorgeous face.

"I'm sure someone told you how incredible you were before we met," Isaac said propping himself up on the pillow.

"You're convinced of this, huh?" I said as I rose to my elbow. He nodded. "Well, I'm certain a special lady told you the same thing, many times before we met."

Isaac blushed as I rubbed my hand down his muscular arm. Everything about Isaac was trustworthy. He had an angelic heart. I thanked God for bringing him into my life, even under risky circumstances. I ignored tomorrow and enjoyed each second I had to feel real love.

Isaac kissed my cheek. "You look like you're deep in thought."

"Sorta," I said biting my lip as I traced the outline of his goatee.

"What's on your mind?" he asked.

"Tell me about Lynnette. What was her personality like?"

Isaac looked puzzled. I looked down, thinking I'd made him uncomfortable.

"Isaac, if it's bad timing, we don't have. . . . "

He reached over to lift my chin. "No, it's okay," he said. "I don't have a problem talking about her. I'm just surprised you wanna talk about this, right now."

I shrugged. "You once told me that I reminded you of her. I'm curious about the woman I resemble."

Isaac smiled as he stroked the hairy shadow on his chin. I laid my head on his shoulder. "I met her in college, at The University of Virginia," he said. "She didn't like me at first. I was a fledgling architect major, soft spoken and seriously in need of a barber for my crooked high top fade. Lynn was a party girl. Energetic and feistier than you." He pinched my side. I squealed as I pushed his hand away. "She tried to give me a hard time, but eventually the pink roses I left outside her apartment door every morning won her over."

"Aw, how romantic," I said smiling at him. I took Isaac's hand. "I know you're glad you have Lena."

"Definitely," he said staring at his daughter's portrait over the fireplace mantle. "Lynn gave me the greatest gift. Even illness couldn't stop her from being the perfect mother. She loved that little girl so much." Isaac looked away, then removed his hand from mine to wipe his face. He sniffled. "Sorry. I got something in my eye."

I placed my hand on the side of his face, gently turning him towards me. "It's okay to miss her, Isaac," I said.

He wrapped his arms around my waist. "Hailee, sometimes I hear her voice in my dreams. The familiar touch of her hand on my chest wakes me up in a cold sweat," he said looking down at the floor. "I always remember her last words in the dreams when I open my eyes."

I remained silent as tears flowed down Isaac's face. His fingers swept my cheek.

"Love her," he said. "Those were her words."

"Love Lena?" I asked.

"My love for Lena is like breathing; it 's given. I believe the words were meant for *you*," Isaac said as his lips parted mine for an enduring kiss.

❖ ❖ ❖ ❖ ❖

The time had come for me to stand up to Lucas. I wanted to move on with my life. I found him sitting in his library reading *The Wall Street Journal*. I walked up to him.

"Lucas, we need to talk."

"Yeah?" he said.

"I want to take care of my debt," I said.

"You want to what?"

"I wanna pay what I owe you. I would like to set up a payment arrangement."

He closed the newspaper and looked at me. "We already have an arrangement," he said.

I sighed. "I'm talking about a monetary arrangement," I said. "I wanna stop screwin'."

"Is that right?"

"Damn right. I plan on leaving soon."

He frowned. "Oh you plan on leaving, huh?" he said.

"That's the plan," I said placing my hands on my hips. "So, how much do I owe you?"

"Including the car, clothes, and jewelry?"

"All that shit stays with you when I leave," I said. "How much? Make sure you subtract the free sex."

He smirked. "That still leaves about forty G's," he said.

"What!" I hollered. "I know my mother didn't stick that much shit in her arms."

"Humph. You must be on crack, then," he said. "That's on the low end. You owe me fourteen grand in college money alone. You know Hailee, it hurts me to hear you talk this way. You just gonna brush me aside like I'm some sucka? Haven't I been good to you?"

"Yeah, let me count the ways," I said. "How do you say zero in your native tongue down under?"

He got up from his chair and walked closer to me. "Funny girl again," he said. "Well, I'm glad you got jokes, 'cause you gonna laugh your ass off when you hear this." He made a fist and pretended to hit a door. "Knock, knock."

I stared at him, disgusted. He slapped me, leaving the left side of my face burning. Tears welled in my eyes.

"Knock, knock, bitch," he grimaced.

"Who's there?" I whimpered.

"Three."

"Three who?"

"Three pigs: one from Homicide, one from Forensics, and one from the Coroner's office who will scoop your dead ass up if you keep talkin' shit!" he said. "Your little artist friend is a bad influence. He got you back talkin' me. Don't think you special just 'cause you got that nigga pussy whupped. You tryin' to be his woman or somethin'? Make a happy home with him and his deaf daughter?"

I looked up, surprised that he knew about Lena. "Leave Isaac out of this!" I screamed. "This is between you and me!"

"I agree, so remind that faggot or he gon' be dealt with!" he shouted.

"Lucas, can we settle this or what?"

He folded his arms. "I don't know, can we? I ain't Baltimore Gas and Electric. Budget billing don't work here. Chump change from Wal-Mart or some fast food joint ain't gonna cut it, either." He pointed in my face. "Don't even think about taking your clothes off on Baltimore Street anymore," he said. "Give me all my money, or your ass continues to be kept. That is, unless you want to attend a couple more burials. Too bad little Lena can't hear. Then again, maybe it's good. She won't know what hit her, or her daddy when my Holocaust hits."

"You cruel bastard!" I yelled. "You wanna kill somebody, you kill me. Do it! I don't care anymore!"

"Be careful what you ask," he said.

"You make me sick," I said.

He grabbed me by the waist and pulled me into his chest. His serious expression turned into a smile. I knew why. I could feel the bulge in his pants.

"I love it when you get angry, Hailee. Makes me hot."

I kicked him below. Twice. He collapsed to his knees in pain, screaming every curse word in the book at me. I darted for the foyer to get the hell out of his house. When I opened the door, I heard him yell, "You can't hide from me!"

I knew he was right . . . But I was gonna try.

❖❖❖❖❖

I picked up my cell phone and dialed Tiffani's number as I

sped my car down the highway.

"Hello?" she said.

"Tiff, it's me," I said, exasperated.

"What's wrong with you?"

I pushed the A/C button to cool my frazzled nerves. "I left Lucas. I told the devil I was not gonna be with him anymore."

There was a pause. "What did he say?" she asked.

"He told me I wasn't leaving until he said so," I said. "We got into it, and he hit me. I broke out after I kicked him in the nuts."

"Shit, where are you now? You comin' over here?"

"Naw," I said. "Your apartment would be the first place he would check. I am headed your way, though. I'm going to Montgomery County to meet Isaac at this hotel. He's waiting for me."

"Girl, you better be careful," she said. "You know how Lucas gets when he's pissed. Don't get me wrong, I'm happy you left him. I just want you to run smart. His crew is gonna be deep, looking for you."

"I know," I said. "I'm sure Lucas will be paging me soon on my two-way. I'll deal with that when the time comes. I just want to see Isaac right now to make sure he's all right. That bastard threatened to hurt Isaac and Lena."

"What!" she yelled.

"Yeah. Lena's out of town with her grandmother, so she's safe. I may have to convince Isaac to hop on a plane, though."

"What about you?" she asked.

I exhaled as I ran my hand over my hair. "What about me?" I said. "I left Lucas, but I'm not stupid. I got finals in two days. I didn't live in sin for three years to not finish my degree. I wanted Lucas to know where I stood. If he wants to shoot me in my cap and gown, that's his prerogative. I'm getting my degree, even if it's the last thing I do."

❖❖❖❖❖

Isaac and I stayed at the Residence Inn in Bethesda. Lucas paged me, nonstop. I knew I wouldn't be safe for long. Last night while Isaac slept, I left the hotel. I didn't want him in danger. The last message on my cell phone from Lucas read: *I'm giving you 48 hours to face me. Don't show, and I'll kill your boyfriend.*

I paged Lucas back, saying I would be there in the morning.

Isaac called me on the cell phone. I answered it. "I miss you," I said in a hushed voice.

"Hailee, where are you?" he asked. "I'm worried."

"I know, Isaac. I can't tell you where I am," I said. "I'm fine, though. You don't have to worry."

"Please tell me where you are," he said. "Baby, I'll do anything for you, even if it means my life."

"Isaac, I love you so much. You're the only good thing in my life. I want us to be together, but not at the risk of losing you because of a thug. Lucas is dangerous. He will hurt you if you interfere."

"I don't care," he said.

"Yes you do," I said. "You adore Lena. I can't let you sacrifice your life to save mine. She needs you more than I do."

"Hailee I'm going crazy not knowing where you are. I'm not afraid of Lucas. I won't let him hurt you anymore. I own a gun."

I held my head. "No, Isaac, stop it!" I cried. "Lucas isn't worth jail time, and neither am I. If you love me like you say you do, then stay away for now. Don't try to find me, and stay clear of Lucas's house. You promise?"

He sighed. "I can't promise you," he said. "I never break a promise, and I would break this one. I want you to be with me."

"Isaac, think about Lena," I said. "For no other reason, keep a cool head for her. I'm a big girl, and I know how to play that bastard's game. I have to go back temporarily. I have a feeling he's gonna be moving back to New York soon. The Feds have been sweatin' him strong lately."

"You know he's gonna want to take you with him," he said.

"No, he's probably gonna beat my ass, then jet," I said.

"Don't talk like that, sweetheart," he said.

"That's reality," I said. "I'm becoming too much of a liability for him. Lucas wanted to hurt me more than my mother. He got a rise knowing I tripped every time he threatened to take Pashen's life. When she took her own life, I think the thrill left him. Without Pashen as collateral, him screwing me is just another screw."

"He needs to pay for what he's done to you," Isaac said.

"He will, but that's not for you or me to handle. I have faith that he will be dead and back to where he belongs in due time." I exhaled. "Isaac?"

"Yeah?" he said.

"Thanks for loving me," I said.

"I still love you."

"I know, but you have to let that love go for now."

"I can't."

"Yes you can," I said. "Do it for me. What's that saying, *If you love something, set it free?*"

"Yes," he said.

"Let me find freedom, my way. I'll keep in touch with you."

"I want you to be safe."

"I will," I said. "I prayed to God last night. I asked for forgiveness of my sins. I asked Him to forgive the sins of my mother. Then I asked Him to remember all of Lucas's sins, and destroy his ass. I slept well last night. You know, God answers prayers."

❖ ❖ ❖ ❖ ❖

I drove back to Lucas's house. My cell phone rang as I merged onto the Northwest Expressway.

"Girl, where you at?" Tiffani asked.

"I just got on I-695," I said. "I'm headed back to the house, why?"

"Jeff told me he's been paging you all morning."

"I got his pages, but I'm not trying to talk to him right now. When did you talk to Jeff?"

"He called me after he couldn't reach you," she said. "Speed your ass the rest of the way home. There's been an emergency!"

I put my phone on speaker and laid it on the passenger's seat. "What?"

Tiffani laughed. "Today musta been The Second Coming, chile, 'cause Lucifer is dead!"

I almost ran off the road. "Huh!" I said steadying my car.

"Lucas was in a car accident," she said. "Jeff heard it on the police scanner."

I was in shock. "Oh my God," I said with my mouth open.

"Thank you God, would be more like it!" she shouted.

"Tiffani, are you sure it was him?" I asked.

"Almost a hundred percent," she said. "Jeff said the car is the same, and his description matches. His car went over the guardrail and down a hill while he was going through Patapsco State Park. Apparently, the car collided head on with a tree. He was killed instantly."

I pushed the lever to roll down my car window, because I began to hyperventilate. "Tiff, I'm free?" I asked.

"Hell yeah!" she cheered. "And we gonna have a Mardi Gras tonight, but this is what you need to do now."

"What?" I asked.

"Get as much shit from that house as you can stash, then break out," she said. "Drive to D.C. And meet me at my place. We'll decide what to do from there. I can store some stuff at my homeboy's crib until things blow over."

I exited off the highway onto Reisterstown Road. "I don't want none of that stuff Lucas owned," I said.

"Bump that!" she yelled. "Girl, green wasn't next of kin to that fool. Get your ass in his crib and search his drawers for money. That nigga owe you 100 acres and 10 mules. Give yourself ten minutes from the moment you get there. Don't drag your butt. Jeff's on the case. He said he can stall the search for a minute, but they gonna be snoopin' around the house soon. Hailee, hurry up. Stick to the small stuff. Just jewelry and cash. No statues or portraits, Mona Lisa."

I giggled. "Tiff, he got some top dollar artwork in there. I helped him pick out the stuff," I said as I turned onto Greenspring Valley Road.

"Leave it," she said. "You can buy more of that ugly, abstract shit later."

I shook my head. "I'm here," I said as drove up the driveway.

"Good. Keep your cell phone glued to your hip in case I need to call you."

"Okay, Tiffani."

"Take care of your business," she said. "Peace."

I stashed as much cash as I could. Tiffani was right. I didn't have a lot of time. I screamed and dropped some cash on Lucas's bed when I heard Anela say my name.

"I'm sorry Hailee," she said smoothing down her work uniform. "I didn't mean to scare you."

I walked up and gave her a hug and kiss. "That's okay, Anela," I said. "I didn't think anyone was home." I noticed her looking at my stuffed backpack.

"You seem in a hurry," she said. "Going on a trip?"

I scratched my head. "Yeah. I'm going to Virginia for the weekend to visit Luray Caverns and do some shopping at Potomac Mills," I said.

She nodded. "Sounds good. Must be an expensive trip," she said fanning the money that was on the bed.

I looked down at the floor. Anela lifted my chin and smiled. "I'll let you finish your packing," she said. "I gotta do some packing, too, with Mr. Blacke dead now. Time to move on and find another job."

My heart pounded with anxiety. "You knew about the accident?" I asked.

"Yes indeed," she said. "I got a good friend that keeps up with all the news. When I turned on the TV and saw the car, I knew it was Mr. Blacke." She put her hand on her chest. "It's a shame a man had to die with so much anger in his heart. Rest his soul."

Anela and I looked at each other for a moment. Then I started stuffing more money in the back pack. She touched my shoulder. "Hailee, sweetheart," she said smiling. "You can relax now. Old things are passed away." She put a loose strand of my hair behind my ear. "From now on, it's going to be all right. You may need more traveling money, though." She walked over to the picture above the bed and removed it to reveal Lucas's safe. She proceeded to turn the combination.

"Lucas gave you the numbers?" I asked.

Anela laughed. "No. One day he complained about how I didn't make his bed right, so I paid attention to him turning the numbers while he chastised me. I figured I'd take me a little Christmas bonus when the time was right." The safe opened. She pulled out a box. "A bonus is overdue," she said. When she lifted the cover, diamond light was all I saw. Two bracelets, a necklace, and more cash. I stood still as I looked at all that loot.

"Take this stuff," she said. "It would be auctioned, anyway."

I shook my head. "I don't know Anela," I said.

She winked. "Go ahead and take everything," she said. "He bought the jewelry for your mother a while back." She pulled out the stacks of money and gave them to me. "His serious money is scattered at a couple of banks abroad. I overheard him talking on the phone one day. This should hold you for a while."

"What about you?" I asked.

She hugged me. "I already got my reward," she said. "I saved the rest for you."

I bit my lip. "Anela, I lied earlier. I'm not going on a trip. I was just trying to get a few things, so I wouldn't have to see this place again, you know. Start over."

"I understand, baby," she said. "I'll miss you."

I held her hand. "I'll miss you," I said. "Maybe we can stay in touch."

"You concentrate on you for now," she said. "I'm in the process of moving on to another place. Once I get settled, I'll contact you." She walked to Lucas's closet and came back out with a large Louis Vutton duffel bag. "Transfer everything in here. Don't worry about the money. It's not traceable."

I frowned. "How do you know?"

She patted me on the back. "Trust me, I know," she said.

"You best be goin' now, chile."

Roses rested on my feet as Isaac rocked me close on the dance floor. We were alone, sheltered by a canopy of cobalt colored balloons and silver lights, configured in a luminous arch. I rested my head on his chest as we glided to *Never Felt This Way* by Brian McKnight.

I casually mentioned to Isaac two weeks ago that I regretted not going to my prom when I was sixteen. That year was everything, but sweet to me. Pashen had suffered a miscarriage and a broken heart from Jeff. We had been stressing over bills, and didn't have a lot of money to spend for one prom night. If there was a reason to believe that dreams come true, tonight was the night. Isaac rented the observatory of The World Trade Center in Baltimore and gave me a prom. He'd succeeded at making me feel like a queen.

The floor was a pool of pink flower petals. Each bare wall in the reception hall was covered with an enlarged picture of me, from birth through adolescence. Isaac wanted to have a few more older shots, but I wanted to showcase the early times. Times when I breathed easily, and I never looked over my shoulder in fear.

"Having fun?" he asked.

"Man, Isaac. I haven't had this much fun in years," I said. "I can't believe you did all of this for me."

"This is just the beginning," Isaac said. He squeezed the satin fabric that clung to my hips. "You're wearing the hell out of that red dress. The spilt running up your thigh is making me weak."

"I'm your Billie Holiday, baby," I said patting the white orchid that highlighted my shiny coffered hairstyle.

"You're my everything," Isaac said as he leaned over to kiss my neck.

"Hmm . . . That felt nice," I moaned as I closed my eyes.

"Do you like love songs?" he asked.

I kissed him. "Yes, I do," I said.

"Say that again?" he said holding his ear closer to me.

"Yes . . . I do, Isaac," I whispered in his ear.

He held up his hand. "Wait a minute," he said. "Let me get on one knee first."

Isaac kneeled and pulled a sparkling, pear shaped diamond from his tuxedo pocket. "Hailee Renee Shaw, will you marry me?" he asked placing it on my finger. I covered my mouth as Isaac kissed my trembling left hand.

"I'll spend a lifetime loving you, if you'll let me," he said. Tears of joy streamed from the corners of my eyes. I was speechless.

"You like the ring?" he asked. I nodded *yes*. "Good. When the jeweler showed it to me I thought to myself, *This is just like my Hailee. A flawless raindrop that has showered my soul.*" He placed my hand on the jacket lapel that protected his heart. "*A soul that's been trying to heal from losing love in the past.* Hailee, I didn't think I would have another chance to feel this way, but *you* are the one keeping me alive. I adore you."

Overwhelmed by Isaac's words, I joined him on bended knee. We cuddled inside of a monument that camouflaged the cries of angels, who perished in its sister buildings in New York City. I looked up to God in praise. I finally had my life back. A life filled with butterflies, smiles and cocoa kisses that I recalled from childhood. Pashen was gone, but He gave me a new heart. Despite a world drenched in blood from global warfare, local genocide, and my previous terror with Lucas—there were still good people on earth. Isaac was one of them. I lovingly told him that I would be his wife.

❖❖❖❖❖

Eight months later, I tried to call Anela to invite her to my Graduation/Engagement Party celebration that would be held the week of Christmas, but she was never home. After several attempts, I decided to drive by her house. There was a "For Sale" sign on her front lawn.

One of her neighbors saw me outside and walked over. "Can I help you, Miss?" the elderly gentleman asked.

"Hi Sir," I said blowing on my hands to keep warm. "I came by to see Anela. Did she move?"

He shook his head. "You don't know, do you?"

I frowned as I adjusted my chenille scarf. "Know what?"

He removed the fedora from his head. "Nela passed last week. She got pneumonia real bad. Died from fever."

I broke down in tears. The neighbor touched my shoulder to comfort me. He told me when the funeral would be held. I had to be there.

Depressed Diva

2003

Rescue Me

Man, I need another job, I thought as I crossed my arms and stared at my secretary's pale ass. She raved about her ugly daughter's dance recital. I smiled at Kate, trying to seem interested, but I didn't give a damn about pudgy Kaylee wobbling in a tu tu. I'll tell you why. Kate is a classic case of a person that wants to be heard, but brushes you off when you have something to say. I'm subjected to her stories about her redneck family's activities, yet when I give accounts of my family business, all I get is a fake, "That's nice." I pray I won't have to endure Kate, or the other backstabbers in this office much longer. Once my demo is finished, I'll get a record deal. I want my singing to propel me out of the insurance business for good. I work for Banner Insurance Company as a claim adjuster. Kate finally stopped boring me when the phone interrupted her mouth going a mile a minute.

"Banner Insurance Company, Onyx Devoe speaking."

"Yes, Ms. Devoe. This is Jon Navarti."

What does he want? I thought. Jon used to be a claim rep in this office, but he became an insurance agent a couple of years ago.

I logged back onto my computer. "Hello Jon. How are you?" I asked.

"Well, I'd be much better if I knew you were doing your job properly," he said.

"Excuse me?" I said.

"My policyholder Wayne Griffin has not been contacted about his claim. I'm wondering why."

"Jon, when was the loss reported?"

"Yesterday afternoon, around four o'clock."

I glanced at the clock on my desk. "It's quarter to nine the next morning. New claim files haven't been released yet."

"I can't fault you for not having the claim file, but since I have called, that is of no consequence now," he said. "This is a high profile policyholder, and a multi-line client. I will give you his contact information. I want him called within the next ten minutes. He had a fire loss, and he is expecting someone to assess the damage today."

"Jon, is Mr. Griffin's home uninhabitable?" I asked.

He sighed. "No."

"Then he will be contacted when the claim file is re-ceived. I may not even be the adjuster assigned to the case."

"Are you refusing to provide excellent customer service to a client whose jewelry floater alone yields a premium of $3,000 annually?" he said, irritated.

I squeezed the neck of my stress reliever troll, pretending to wring Jon's neck. "No. If assigned to the case, I will provide quality service," I said. "I do my best for every policyholder I work with, whether they pay premiums of $300 a year or $3,000. Presently, I'm working on a total fire loss for a young woman who lost her home due to her ex-boyfriend being an asshole and arsonist. I think that takes precedence over how much jewelry your client has insured."

"I'm getting nowhere with you. Let me talk to your super-visor!" he shouted.

"Fine Jon Navarti," I said in an octave that could be heard by others around me. "Before I transfer you, let me leave you with this: *My grandmother used to tell me never forget where you came from.* You've been an agent for two years, and already you act like your shit don't stink. Jon, you may have conveniently chosen to forget your claim rep days, but I remember your tenure in this office vividly. Let's go down memory lane, shall we? I used the company car after you on two occasions and found empty beer cans on the back seat. You begged me not to tell the supervisor. I didn't. I caught you kissing Lisa, your own co-worker, at Brookeville Park during the lunch hour. Did I tell the supervisor, or your wife, who also works in this office? No, I didn't. Yet you wanna complain to my supervisor, because I refuse to let your status as an agent intimidate me? Well, I'm not in the mood this morning to deal with your condescending demeanor. Let me transfer you, so I can free up my line to call your agency field executive. I think I'll give him some insightful information. Hold on."

I pressed the transfer button and dialed my boss's extension. "Banner Insurance, this is Dylan Bates," he said.

"Hi Dylan, it's Onyx," I said, annoyed. "I have Jon Navarti on the line. He would like to speak with you."

"Onyx, is everything all right?" he asked. "You sound perturbed."

"Everything is everything. I'll talk to you about it after you finish speaking to him."

"Send him through."

I transferred the call. Kate looked as if she wanted to talk about my conversation with Jon, but she saw my scowl and decided to keep her mouth shut. I got up to go to the bathroom. When I returned, there was a Post It note on my desk from Dylan, asking me to come in his office. I walked over there.

"Hey Dylan, I saw your note," I said in his doorway. He motioned for me to sit down.

"Onyx, when you transferred Jon he wasn't on the line, so I called him back," he said. "All he said was that he had a professional basketball player insured, and he would like to be contacted by the adjuster if problems arise concerning the claim. Apparently, this customer is a nuisance."

I folded my arms. "Was that all he said?" I asked.

"Yes, why?" Dylan asked. "Is there something I should know?"

I shook my head and stood up. "No. I think the problem I had earlier resolved itself."

Briefcase in hand, I slowly trekked up the long driveway to

my policyholder's house. I had been assigned to Wayne Griffin's claim. I'd also decided that I didn't care for him, since he insisted I not drive my company car up his driveway. Who did he think he was, the President? The sooner I got this claim resolved, the better.

I tried not to seem out of breath when I got to the doorstep. I opened my briefcase for a bottle of Sweet Breath. I put a few drops on my tongue. Eating home fries and onions this morning was not a good idea. Breath now satisfactory, I pressed the intercom button. The door opened and I got a crick in my neck as I looked up at the *Leaning Tower of Pisa*. This man was extremely tall.

"Ms. Devoe?" he said.

My face remained neutral, but my insides were heated. He was a cutie. "Hello Mr. Griffin," I said, extending my hand for him to shake. "How are you today?"

He smiled. "Just fine. Please come in."

Rick Fox, look out. You got some competition, I thought as I walked inside. He led me through the Italian marble foyer into the kitchen.

"May I offer you something to drink?" he asked.

I shook my head. "No thank you," I said. "I had something just before I came here."

He laughed. "Must have been strong from all those breath drops I saw you douse at my door."

I smiled, trying to play off my embarrassment. "You saw me?" I asked.

"Yeah, I have video surveillance. Please have a seat." We sat at the kitchen counter. "Forgive me if you thought I was being rude about you parking on the street. I just had the asphalt driveway paved. The contractor advised not to have any cars on the surface for another week. My cars are parked on the street as well."

"I appreciate the explanation," I said.

He looked around in his kitchen. "As you can see, my floor and stove are jacked up," he said.

"I noticed. What happened?"

"I gave my cook the week off to attend her granddaughter's wedding in Detroit. I tried to fry some chicken, then remembered I couldn't cook. Flour and grease started going all over the place. Grease hit the flame, and the whole pan caught fire. In the process of trying to put the fire out, I dropped the pan on the floor."

"An honest mistake," I said. "You may have had the burner turned up too high."

"I don't know, but I quickly found out that water will make friends with a grease fire," he said. "Shit, who knew?"

I laughed. "Use a fire extinguisher next time," I said. "Don't you recall from your science days in junior high that water and oil don't mix?"

"No, I was a 'just get by' type of guy in school," he said. "I did the bare minimum. Except in math. I did pretty well because I didn't want nobody fuckin' with my money when I turned pro. Excuse my French."

"No problem," I said. I got up to look at the damage more closely. "Mr. Griffin, it's not too bad. The hardwood floor, your range assembly and stove will have to be replaced. Perhaps a fresh coat of paint also."

He surveyed the walls. "It may not need paint," he said. "Those guys you sent to clean the smoke residue did a good job."

I pushed up the sleeves to my polo top. "I'm glad Service King was able to help you out," I said. "They do good restoration work."

I leaned down to open my briefcase as Wayne stared at my every move. I pulled out my Polaroid camera and diagram pad, placing them on the counter.

"You all don't use digital cameras?" he asked.

"No, Banner is a great insurance company, but we're a little slow when it comes to utilizing the latest technology," I said.

He smiled. "But you're the biggest insurance company in the country?"

I shrugged. "And?" I said. We both laughed. "Anyway, let

me take a few photos and measurements. I can have your estimate ready by this afternoon."

He got a bottle of water from the refrigerator. "I appreciate your efforts," he said. "I wanna get my place back in order
before I head down to Orlando for training."

I stood up from the counter stool and searched my briefcase for my measuring tape. "Yes, I heard you were a professional basketball player for the Washington Warriors," I said
pulling the tape out of my bag.

He took a sip of water and placed the bottle on the counter.
"Oh yeah? What else did you hear?" he asked.

"Nothing," I said putting the measuring tape at the floor's
edge.

"Here, let me help you with that," he said. He got up and
held the tape steady.

I smiled at him. "Thanks Mr. Griffin."

"Do you like basketball?" he asked.

"It's all right," I said as I wrote down a measurement. "I'm
not into team sports that much. I like tennis. I'm actually taking lessons right now. I'm a big fan of the Williams sisters."

"I like them, too," he said. "Good luck with your lessons.
Maybe I'll see you on TV playing in the US Open in the next
couple of years."

He helped me measure another section of the kitchen. "I
don't think so, Mr. Griffin. I'm too lazy to practice that hard."

He held up his hand. "Please, call me Wayne," he said.
"You say Mr. Griffin like I'm an old man."

I took the tape from him. "I'm trying to be professional," I
said.

"You're doing a great job, but I don't need you to be formal
with me," he said with a wink. He took a sip of his water. "I
thought you were a white woman when we spoke on the phone,
but when you said your name, I knew you had to be a sista."

"The name Onyx would be contradictory to a Caucasian,
wouldn't you think?" I asked.

He licked his lips. "Yes, but it's very fitting for an ebony
queen like you."

I blushed when he kissed the back of my hand. He made me nervous. I bent down to put the measuring tape in my briefcase. "I need a few photos, and then I'll be out of your way," I said standing up.

He slanted his head as he looked at me. "Can I ask you something? Actually, can I ask you two things?" he said.

I gripped the camera in my hand as I looked at him. "Yes, Wayne?"

"May I call you Onyx?" he asked.

I nodded "Yes, you may," I said.

"Do I make you uncomfortable?"

"No," I said as I snapped a photo of the stove. "You're just very tall, that's all."

He felt my sleeve. "And you're very fine, which leads me to another question."

His touch made me jittery. "What is that?" I asked, almost dropping my camera on the floor.

"Do you have a husband or boyfriend?" he asked.

I laughed as I took a picture of the floor damage. "No, and I'm not looking for either."

He raised a brow. "Oh? You're not looking for a girlfriend, are you?"

I rolled my eyes. "Very funny."

He smiled. "Hey, these are the times we live in."

I put the camera on the granite countertop. "I'm not a lesbian," I said.

"I didn't think so," he said. "Well, would you mind going out with a single, basketball player who is very much interested in getting to know you?"

I sat on the stool to view the photos I'd taken. "Thanks for the offer, but I can't."

He walked behind me and leaned close to my ear. "Why not?" he asked, his voice a sexy baritone.

I stood up in an effort to stay composed around this fine man. "You are a policyholder. Our interaction must strictly be about business."

He picked up my camera and aimed it at me, like he was

going to take a picture. "Says you, or the company you work for?"

I snatched the camera from his hand. "Says both," I said. "It would be a conflict of interest."

He moved closer and kissed my cheek. "It wouldn't be a conflict of my interest," he said.

I stepped to the side, giving him a nervous laugh. "Uh, Wayne," I said as I moved away. "I need to do a diagram of the area, then we will be done."

He frowned. "I'm sorry to hear that. I was hoping we were just getting started."

I took a deep breath. "Wayne, this meeting is starting to stress me out."

He smiled. "Are you not attracted to me?" he asked.

I looked away from him. "That is not the point," I said.

He rubbed his hand down my shoulder. "You didn't answer my question," he said.

I put my hands on my hips. "Do you have children?" I asked.

He nodded. "Yes. Fathers don't need love?" he asked.

I ignored his question. "By the same woman?"

He smirked. "No."

I sucked my teeth. "Typical," I mumbled.

He looked at his watch. "Last time I checked, the name Wayne showed on my birth certificate, not Jesus."

I glanced at his crotch. "Last time I checked, condoms were readily available in every drug store, gas station, and grocery chain."

His jaw tightened. "So, I guess that's why you're single. You're looking for a perfect man."

"As I said before, I'm not looking," I said. "However, if I was, I'd want a man who knows what he wants."

"Well, I told you. I'm a man that wants to spend time with you," he said grabbing my hand.

I let my hand go. "Yes, but what about the lady you told that to yesterday?" I asked.

He smiled. "Oh, my mother Lucy? She can't wait to see

me. I'm flying down to Houston next week to be with her."

I shook my head and picked up my note pad. I did a quick diagram of the kitchen while Wayne leaned against the sink, staring at me. Once I finished my sketch, I promptly put the rest of my stuff inside my briefcase and picked it up.

Wayne grabbed my elbow. "Onyx, put your briefcase down for a second. I would like to talk to you some more."

I sighed. "No, Wayne. I really have to go."

He looked down. "I understand." He extended his hand. "Thanks for your help."

My, "You're welcome", was cut short because he kissed me. I was surprised, but I liked the feeling of his lips. I let my briefcase drop to the floor and kissed him back. We paused for a moment. I looked down at the floor. He read what I was thinking.

"Onyx," he said gently lifting my chin. "Trust me. There's no conflict of interest, and there isn't a video camera right here."

❖ ❖ ❖ ❖ ❖

I wanted to kick myself in the ass for kissing Wayne. I couldn't believe he got to me like that, charming motherfucker. I sighed as I leaned back in my chair and looked at the clock. Wayne was expecting a call at 12:30 p.m. To discuss the claim settlement. It was lunch time, and Kate was out of the office. I figured now was a good time to call him since my eavesdropping secretary was gone.

Onyx, get a grip, I thought as I dialed his phone number.

"Hello?" he said.

"Mr. Griffin, I have your check and your estimate ready," I said.

He laughed. "It's back to Mr. Griffin, huh?"

I cleared my throat. "Yes. Would you mind if I mailed it?"

There was a pause. "Can I come by and get it?" he asked.

I snatched an envelope out of my organizer to prepare his paperwork for pick up. "Certainly, I'll have it waiting in the lobby for you," I said.

"Will I see you in the lobby?" he asked.

I held my head. "No."

"Then, I'd prefer to have it hand delivered by my Banner adjuster," he insisted.

I sighed. "Fine. I can drop it by your house within the hour," I said.

❖ ❖ ❖ ❖ ❖

Wayne stood at the door as I walked up the driveway. He had a bouquet of beautiful red roses in his hands. "For you," he said giving them to me.

"The flowers are nice. You didn't have to," I said inhaling the sweet fragrance.

He smiled. "I wanted to."

I handed him an envelope. "Here's your check. Please look the estimate over carefully. If there's anything you feel I've missed, let me know."

He gave me a sly grin. "Is your home phone number on the estimate?" he asked.

I pursed my lips. "Let's not get into that, okay," I said as I turned to walk down the driveway.

He touched my back. "Onyx, stay for a few minutes," he pleaded. "I'm not gonna attack you, come on. We're both adults. If you don't want anything to happen, nothing will happen."

I sighed. "All right, for a few minutes," I said as I walked to the door and entered.

He closed the door. "I have lunch ready, " he said rubbing his hands together. "Sandwich platters, fresh from Sutton Gourmet."

I ran my fingers across my short feathered hair. "I'm not hungry right now."

He smiled. "Maybe later, then."

I bobbed my head to some music that I heard playing in another room. "I like that piano solo. Sounds like a Joe Sample groove. Is that his CD?"

He shook his head. "It's not a CD," he said. "I have a baby grand that is programmed to play."

"Really? I'd like to have a white baby grand one of these

days," I said.

"You play?" he asked.

"Yes," I said adjusting my purse on my shoulder.

He pointed to a room down the hall. "Come check it out."

I held up my hand. "Wayne, listen. You're cool, but I don't want to lose my job. I've been working for this insurance company for five years."

"I don't see how that would happen," he said. He leaned against the wall and folded his arms. I almost fainted from the muscles I saw formed under his maroon silk shirt. "I'm a very private person. We're not out in a public area where perhaps a co-worker or your boss would run into us. Besides, as far as I'm concerned, our business matter is finished." He opened the envelope and briefly glanced at the paperwork. "You've given me my estimate. I'm pleased with the figure on the check, and I'm pleased with the way you handled my loss. The claim is closed."

I folded my arms. "A claim is never closed for good. I would like to see that baby grand piano, though," I said looking down the hall. He took my hand and smiled. "Let's go."

❖ ❖ ❖ ❖ ❖

Wayne's conservatory was impressive, filled with pictures of all the great jazz artists like Louis Armstrong, Charlie Parker, and Nancy Wilson. I sat comfortably next to him as he played the piano.

"You play very well," I said.

He leaned against me. "On a good day," he said. "I'm trying to impress you."

"So far, so good."

"Does that include my kissing technique as well?"

I stopped smiling and looked away from him for a second. "What happened earlier was a mistake."

He smiled. "No it wasn't."

I cocked my head to the side, trying not to smile. "How do you know?"

"Because I can look into those pretty brown eyes and tell you'd like to kiss me again," he said as he coolly swiped the piano keys.

I got up and walked over to the window. "You certainly are cocky, and presumptuous," I said.

He stopped playing. "And you like to avoid direct eye contact. Onyx sit back down beside me, and stop tripping," he said.

I exhaled and sat next to him on the piano bench.

His finger touched one of my spiked curls. "I like your haircut," he said smiling. "Reminds me of the style Toni Braxton had when she first came out." He smirked when I brushed his hand away. "So, is Banner a career for you, or are you in insurance temporarily?"

"The latter. My first love is singing. I'd like to sing professionally one day. I'm working on my demo now." He purposely touched my leg with his thigh. I scooted a few inches away from him.

"An aspiring singer, huh?" he said. "See, I knew you were a woman after my own heart. I sing also."

I reared back, looking at him. "Is that so?" I said.

"Yes, ballers have other talents besides basketball," he said.

I folded my hands in my lap. "Do you like your job?"

He shrugged. "I like the money the sport brings to me. I don't like most of the people associated with that money, including my ex-lovers."

I looked down. "I see."

He touched my cheekbone with his finger. "I'm trying to find a good woman. Find someone who can be a friend when my shit ain't necessarily going right. I want unconditional love."

I removed his hand from my face. "Well, I'm sure your search would be easier than mine. There are a lot of women that will give you the world if the price is right."

"Are you that type of woman?" he asked.

"No, I'm not. I'd rather be happy," I said.

He held his chin in thought. "What if we started going out?" he asked. "What if I paid off all of your bills, financed your demo, and put enough money into your bank account to enable you to quit pushing paperwork? Would you be a happy woman?"

"I'd be a dependent woman," I said.

"I'm sure you have a degree to fall back on, so answer my question," he said.

I shook my head. "I don't know. I guess I'd have to be in that situation to know if I'd be content with living that lifestyle."

He looked to the ceiling. "Onyx, please."

I held out my hands. "What?"

He smirked. "Never mind. Let me hear you sing."

"Why?"

"You're not shy are you?" he asked.

I stuck out my chest. "Of course not," I said. "I matriculated through the music department at Morgan State University."

He nodded as if he was impressed. "Then I know your shit is correct."

I smiled. "Yes, it is."

"All right, let's do this," he said positioning his fingers on the keys. "Name the tune."

"Do you know *Get Here* by Brenda Russell?" I asked.

"You're in luck. I know that well," he said.

"Play that then."

"Cool, Ms. Devoe."

I cleared my throat and he played. He admired my voice. I admired his smile. We got up from the bench and hugged.

"Onyx, I want us to be friends," he said rubbing my back.

"Give me some time to think about it," I said.

He slowly bent his head down to give me a kiss on the lips. "Time's up," he said.

❖❖❖❖❖

"You did what!" my co-worker Sanai screamed over the phone.

"I screwed him on the piano keys," I said. "Girl, don't be mad at me. It just sorta happened."

"Yeah, the wind sorta blew down your draws," she said laughing. "I'm not mad at you, I'm just shocked. How does a Banner employee go from adjusting a policyholder's claim, to adjusting her sexual position on his piano?"

I bit my nail. "You're not gonna say anything, are you?"

"Now you know me better than that. This conversation goes no further."

"Sanai, I know I was wrong to get involved with a customer, believe me. I just couldn't resist him for some reason. He has a way about him. When he pressed up against me, I lost control. Nothing mattered at that moment."

She laughed. "You shooting for that celebrity stardom anyway you can get it, huh?"

"It was definitely a scene made for the big screen," I said.

"Well, I hope you weren't so mesmerized that you forgot to use protection," she said.

I sucked my teeth. "Yes, we used protection."

"Music to my ears. So, Ms. Devoe, now what? What do you want from this guy?"

"I'm not sure. He said he wants to start seeing me," I said.

"He's already done that. So, is he talking anything that sounds remotely like an exclusive situation?" she asked.

"Your guess is as good as mine," I said cradling the phone. I took off my clothes in my bathroom as I got ready to take a long shower.

"You might want to take a step back from this guy. He could be a big time baller with a big time rap sheet, including doin' tricks," she said.

I shook my head. "I appreciate that Sanai, but I don't think it's gonna make that much of a difference. I've already sexed him, so there's no need to act precocious now. Unless you told me that he was a mass murderer or a fairy, I really don't think there's much else that would stop me from fucking him at least one more time."

She howled. "Onyx, you are a trip."

"I'm also feeling satisfied right about now, so if Wayne is down, I'm down. I'll put his drama on the back burner for the moment," I said as I gyrated in front of the mirror.

"He's that good of a piano player?" she asked.

"Superb," I said.

I'm Afraid

Wayne left several messages on my answering machine after our little rendezvous in his piano parlor. I hadn't spoken to him, because I wasn't trying to get all caught up in a baller dude. I mean, who was I kidding? Did I really expect him to commit to me, when I allowed him to sex me like some tramp? I enjoyed his company, but I was prepared to let him be cavalier with the next female. I had to regroup. Focus my energy back on my demo.

❖ ❖ ❖ ❖ ❖

Today, I was at Spectrum Recording Studios in Rockville, working on the second track for the demo. It was late October, and my producer Ace said we were behind schedule. He had some trade shows and listening sessions with new artists coming up, so he wanted to get through the second song before he got too busy. More studio time meant more money. The credit union at work wouldn't lend me anymore due to two outstanding loans. I had to max out one of my credit cards. Yet another injection of stress for a diva with no recording contract to date. I sang in my booth, trying for the fifth time to give Ace the "crunked" energy he had requested.

"*Day by day, my love's gettin' stronger. You got the look, you got that vibe, I can't hold out much longer. You don't know me, but you know how to turn me on. You don't love me, but I need you in every way. Black magic you give, got me in a daze. It's crazy, but I pray you'll be mine. Day by day. . . . *"

Ace interrupted. "Hold up, Onyx. I'm still not feelin' it, baby."

I opened my eyes and looked up at the sound booth.

His face was close to the glass as he shouted at me through the microphone. "What, you on your period or something! There is no vibe from you today," he said.

I sighed as I put my hands on my hips, pissed. "Ace, I don't know what else to do. I'm givin' you all I got!"

"No you ain't Anita Baker, so unless you ready to retire, I had better see some improvement!" he snapped. "There's plenty of honeys ready to break this door down, so I can hear them sing. I don't have time for mediocre shit. Let's do it again." He lunged back into his seat.

I looked down as the music started. After about ten seconds into the introduction, the music cut off once more. "Now what!" I screamed.

When I looked in the sound booth there was no one there, except a person I didn't expect to see, Wayne. He walked out of the glass door and came down to where I was standing.

"Wayne, what are you doing here?" I asked. "I thought you had a game."

"I did," he said wrapping his arms around my waist. "Now I'm back. Which reminds me, I need to get you a new phone. Obviously your present one is broken, because you have not returned any of my calls."

I shook my head. "I can't believe you remembered that I'd be in the studio today."

"I remember things that are important to me," he said as he kissed my cheek. "Too bad I can't say the same for you."

I rolled my neck, trying to release some of the tension. "What are you talking about, Wayne?"

He massaged my shoulders. "You've been dissin' me, but we'll talk about that later. I want you to relax." I gave into his soothing touch and dropped my head.

"Nice track," he said. "Those drum beats are slammin'. Is the song about me?"

"Don't flatter yourself," I said nudging him with my elbow. "I wrote it before we met."

"I think I know why Ace was so upset," he said. "You can't

just sing the lyrics. You have to feel them from your center."
He gently pressed his finger on my stomach and turned me
around to face him. "Come on, breathe." I followed the
rhythm of his inhalations and exhalations.

He smiled. "That's right," he said. "Now close your eyes
and relax your neck. Good. Think about the way you felt when
you wrote the song. Bring the attitude out. That's what your
producer wants." He slowly caressed my face. "Onyx, look at
me. The demo is gonna go fine, and you're gonna be fine." He
gave me a kiss. "I'm proud of you."

I blushed. "Thanks Wayne."

He looked up at the booth. "I told the fellas you needed a
break. They'll be back soon. You think you're ready to give it
another shot?"

I nodded *yes*.

"Cool," he said giving me a pat on the butt. "Do your
thing. You want platinum, right?"

I put my hands on my hips. "Yeah," I said.

"Well, this is where it begins," he said as he walked back
towards the glass door.

Ace and his assistants came back into the sound both. I took
a deep breath. Wayne was with Ace at the sound board, smiling
at me. I smiled back at him as I waited for the track to begin.

❖ ❖ ❖ ❖ ❖

After my studio session, Wayne and I went to Zanzibar for
dinner. The waiter brought our drink orders to the table. "So,
what's the reason for giving me the cold shoulder these past few
days?" he asked.

I shrugged. "I don't know," I said. "I guess I didn't want to
kid myself into thinking we had something going just because
we got busy."

"Didn't I tell you what my intentions were before you left
that night?"

"Yeah, but lots of people talk a good game."

He took a sip of his wine. "Well, lucky for you, you don't
have to deal with lots of people. All you have to do is deal with
me."

I looked down, fidgeting with the napkin in my lap. "That's what I'm afraid of," I said. "Dealing with you."

He frowned. "I did something to make you afraid of me?" he asked.

"No, but. . . . "

Wayne reached out for my hand. "Never be afraid of passion, Onyx. I mean, I ain't prepared to walk down the aisle, but I'm not walking away either." He smiled. "Give us a chance. Give love a chance."

"You're not in love with me," I said pulling my hand back.

His warm hand grasped hold of my wrist. "I'm in love with the possibility of loving you," he said. "Besides, you don't love me, either. You're being stubborn. Brushing me off to ease your conscience about us getting intimate the second day of knowing each other. I don't want you to have any regrets about what happened. We became one, and you can't take that back. No matter how hard you try. So, let's just move on from here, together."

❖❖❖❖❖

A month after our first meeting, Wayne and I moved in together. He paid off all my credit card accounts, took me to the Bahamas for a weekend getaway, and flew his mother Lucy up from Houston to meet me. Needless to say, she and I did not hit it off too well.

Wayne left me to entertain her the whole weekend, while he played ball. She told me that Wayne was still rebounding from his heartbreak from a girlfriend in college. She said he'd been jumping into fires with females ever since. To top it off, she had the nerve to ask me if I was gonna trap her son into paternity payments like his former girlfriends did. After a few minutes of trying to be diplomatic, and a few glasses of Chardonnay, I told her it wasn't her damn business what went on between me and her baby boy. She paged Wayne all upset, talking about she was ready to leave. I was glad she had an attitude. That way her jaws could stop moving, and I could go upstairs to rest. I had been feeling worn down for the past two weeks.

Before I went to sleep, I offered Miss Lucy an apology. She blew me off. I offered her some tea, but she declined. She said she didn't want anything from me, and didn't understand what Wayne saw in me. She rolled her eyes, I rolled mine and took my sleepy ass up the steps.

I was awakened from my nap when I felt a kiss on my forehead. "Onyx baby, you all right?" Wayne asked.

I sighed as I slowly pulled myself up. "Is your mother still here?"

"No," he said softly. "I took her to dinner in Pentagon City so we could talk. Then she wanted me to check her into the Hilton. She's flying out of Dulles Airport tomorrow morning."

"Well, I'm sure she criticized me the entire time you all were out," I said.

His finger tapped my nose. "She doesn't know you well enough to criticize you." He sat on the bed beside me. "I know how my mother can be. Mothers try to protect their sons, even at the expense of someone else's feelings. I'm sorry if she made you uneasy."

I shook my head. "I'm sorry too," I said touching his chest. "I wasn't feeling well, and I guess I let my feelings get the best of me. I'd like for your mother and I to get along. Especially if our relationship continues to grow."

He kissed my fingers. "Focus on us right now. In the meantime, I'll work on my mama." He rubbed his hand over my belly. "She's gonna have to learn to like you. For our daughter's sake."

I gasped as I jumped up. "Our what?" I said folding my arms over my stomach.

He laughed. "You know you're pregnant, Onyx."

I looked away. "No, I don't know that," I mumbled.

Wayne stood up and embraced me. "Well, I know. I've been around women enough to know the signs."

I closed my eyes as I held my head. "Damn, I hope not," I said. "I have stuff I need to do before I go there. Not to mention the fact that we are not headed for matrimony any time soon."

He shrugged. "Unmarried people bear children all the time."

"Yeah, but I don't want to be in that clique." I sighed. "You would be happy if I was pregnant?"

"I'm happy that I didn't create life with another girl. You're all woman, sweetheart."

I slanted my eyes at him. "Real deep, Wayne," I said.

He bent down and kissed my stomach. "This is reality now. Let's deal with it."

❖❖❖❖❖

Sanai and I were in Laurel headed for Olive Garden for lunch. She turned the car radio off and looked at me.

"Onyx, don't get all quiet on me, now. A baby is a blessing," she said.

I picked a piece of lint off my skirt. "I know," I said. I shook my head. "I'm just shocked. I mean, I'm thirty-one years old, and for six years my GYN doctor has been telling me that I probably wouldn't have kids because of endometriosis. That's why I didn't protest when Wayne wanted to ease up off the condoms. I figured freestylin' a couple of times wouldn't hurt." I leaned my head back on the headrest and sighed. "So much for that."

Sanai patted my shoulder. "Well, doctors don't know everything," she said. "Obviously this was supposed to happen."

"I wonder what's gonna happen next," I said. "Wayne told me last night the Warriors are trading him mid-season to Houston. My demo is not finished. Wayne's financing it, but Ace has been snubbing me. Talking about he needs to focus on his signed artists right now. Wayne wants me to move with him to Texas. So, basically if I quit working at Banner, I'll be at his mercy."

Sanai smirked. "Not necessarily," she said. "We got claim offices in Texas. Just put in for a transfer."

I chuckled. "To be honest Sanai, the way I feel right now, I'm not thinking about handling claims," I said.

She laughed. "I ain't mad at you girl! Listen, you're gonna be fine," she said. "Keep your head up and don't worry about tomorrow."

On a rainy Thursday morning, I told Banner I was out. By Saturday, I was on a plane with Wayne, headed for Houston. I leased my condo to a co-worker, and said goodbye to friends. Leaving was difficult, but it was reassuring knowing that true friendships follow you anywhere. I didn't shed a tear when I resigned from Banner. My qualm was starting over. A new man, a new environment, and a baby on the way, terrified me. Wayne and I didn't even know each other that well, but I had suddenly left my life behind to be a part of his.

As he slept soundly on the plane with his arm wrapped around me, I thought about my singing. I closed my eyes in prayer, asking God for discernment. I knew good and well this prayer was belated. Better late than never. Would I still become a singer, or would I just be content being in Wayne's shadow? Since I asked myself the question, I guess I had to be bold enough to find out. I exhaled as I opened my eyes. One thing was for sure. I wasn't gonna do jack shit until my morning sickness subsided. I said a soft, "thank you" when the flight attendant brought me another ginger ale. No ice.

❖❖❖❖❖

Living in Houston has been an overrated experience. The city was nice, but I'd enjoy it better if Wayne stayed home more often. I wasn't able to make many friends, because I'd been so sick from the pregnancy. All I seemed to do was eat, puke, pee, and sleep. I felt blessed to have been able to conceive a child. I just thought I'd be *happy go lucky* like those pregnant women on the show, "A Baby Story". I thought about Wayne and me going on that show to celebrate our child's birth. We'd probably have a good chance of getting on, since Wayne was a professional athlete. As I pondered more on the thought, my blissful vision became distorted. I began to think about people looking at our segment, shaking their heads disdainfully. Saying, "*Look at that wench. She thinks just because she got knocked up by a baller dude, she gonna live happily ever after. He got all that money, and he hasn't even given her a ring yet.*"

Yeah, there'd be people hatin' on me. Calling me a wanna be. Well, maybe I was one. I wanted to be loved by the man who took me away from my family. I wanted to be a successful singer, and mother. I had to stay positive and work on my demo. I would try to stay healthy as my due date approached, and pray that Wayne marries me.

Mamma Drama

I banged on the piano keys, frustrated as I tried to create a new song for the demo. I heard the doorbell and got up. When I looked through the peep hole, I saw a brown skin woman with immaculate hair. I opened the door. We stared at each other for a second. Then she smiled and extended her hand to me.

"Good afternoon, I'm LaKeisha Sanders. Wayne's son's mother."

I shook her hand. "Nice to meet you LaKeisha. I'm Onyx Devoe, Wayne's fiancé." She chuckled. I gave her a slight frown, confused by her humor.

"I'm sorry, Onyx. When you said fiancé, I had to laugh at Wayne's butt. He's had quite a few of those, including me."

I didn't think she was intentionally being condescending, but I was still annoyed. The last thing I needed was the baby mama blues today. I had to get this song finished.

"Wayne's not here," I said with my hands on my hips.

She shook her head. This was an uncomfortable moment for me. I knew I would have to deal with Wayne's past. I just wasn't prepared to do so this soon. I could tell she sensed my insecurity.

"I have some information to give Wayne concerning his son," she said as she peered into the foyer. "Do you expect him back soon?"

"He had practice and then a meeting," I said. "I don't expect him for another hour or so. I can take the information for him, if you like."

She flung her hair. "That's fine," she said, aggravated. "Shall I stand out here while you get a pen and paper?"

I looked down as I rubbed my shoulder. It was tacky of me not to invite her in. *Damn Onyx, you're a better woman than that*, I thought. "I'm sorry, LaKeisha," I said. "Please come in."

She stepped into the foyer and observed the fresh floral arrangement in the corner. "Your flowers are beautiful," she said.

"Thanks," I said.

She admired herself in the mirror. "I can't believe Wayne. He's balkin' over what he gives me monthly, livin' in this palace," she hissed. "I should ask for more."

I glanced at the marble floor for a second, then back at her. She was in her own zone as she raked her fingers through her hair. I slid my hand down my nappy nape, suddenly regretting that I'd canceled my hair appointment this morning. This girl was decked in a cream linen pantsuit with leather sling backs, the perfect color match, while I stood in a red house dress that screamed maternity clearance rack. I hated to admit that sista had it goin' on, especially after all the stuff Wayne said about her. But, his story was his story. And right now that didn't count for shit. I was going to say something, but she beat me to it.

"Onyx, can I sit for a minute?" she asked. "I have been on my feet all day, styling hair."

"Sure," I said. She followed me into the family room. We sat down on the couch. LaKeisha looked at the piano.

"You play?" she asked.

I rubbed my belly. "Yes. I'm a singer and songwriter," I said. "I hope to have an album out shortly."

She smacked her lips. "Don't we all. Where you from?" she asked.

I leaned back on the leather cushion, offended by her sarcasm. "I'm from Silver Spring, Maryland. It's near D.C."

She surveyed her French manicure. "That explains the lack of southern hospitality. Can I have something to drink please?"

she said looking up at me.

I didn't flinch. *Nobody asked you to make your ass at home heifer*, I thought. It was rude not to offer her something, so I apologized.

"Forgive my manners, LaKeisha," I said. "I have a lot on my mind today."

She crossed her legs. "I understand. Wayne will do that to you," she said as she picked up the *Black Enterprise* magazine from the coffee table.

I sighed as I wobbled to my feet. "What would you like?" I asked.

"Water's fine," she said reading the pages.

"I'll be right back," I huffed. I came back with the water and sat down. She put the magazine down and folded her hands over her knee.

"So, you got anything to ask me?" she said. "I'm sure Wayne talked a bunch of bull." She took a sip of the water.

I shrugged. "No, nothing in particular," I said. "The last time I tried to get to know one of Wayne's ex-girlfriends, I got slapped. Then, Wayne and I got thrown out of the club after I promptly beat her ass."

She frowned. "What girl you talkin' about? Simchi?"

"Simcha," I said.

She adjusted her position on the couch. "Her name should be Simple," she snapped. "That crossed eyed bitch tries to fight everybody over Wayne's ass. I'm not her, give me a little more credit." We laughed. "Wayne wasn't in the right frame of mind when he fucked her half Korean ass. Talkin' 'bout she a model. I ain't seen her in Essence or Elle, have you?"

I just shook my head.

She drank some water. "She needs to be doin' ads for Pearle Vision," she said putting the glass on the table. "Wayne trips on me, but I know he regrets fathering that hoe's baby. I heard she done slept with half of Houston. I hope the little girl has more sense than the both of them. What's her name?"

"Kwan," I said.

"Huh?" she said.

"Kwan," I repeated.

She flicked her palm in the air. "Whatever. Well, here are my two little ones." She beamed with pride as she opened her Gucci bag and removed two pictures from her wallet. She handed the photos to me. "And they have names you can pronounce. This is Wayne's son Chandler. He's five, and Brooke is three."

The children were beautiful. Wayne's son had deep dimples like him. I felt melancholy when I looked at the photo, wondering why Wayne didn't have any photos of his kids around the house. Wondering why he tried to hide innocence created from his sins. Would he be ashamed of our love child too?

"You can keep that picture for Wayne," she said. "He hasn't seen Chandler in almost a year. He's grown a lot since then. Now that Wayne's back in Houston, he has no excuse not to spend time with his son. That's why I'm here. I want to give him all my information so he can contact me."

"Okay, I'll give you our new number as well," I said. I grabbed some paper off of the piano. I handed her a piece, and we wrote down our information.

"You thought I was gonna start some mess when you saw me at the door?" she said. "Be honest."

I sighed. "I really didn't know what to think." We exchanged papers.

"Well, rest your mind, 'cause I'm not some fool trying to give grief to a sista," she said. "My gripe is with Wayne. I'll let that fool Simcha handle the drama. Wayne and I were together when I realized he had some unfinished business with her. She showed up at our apartment with a newborn in her arms, cryin' and carryin' on. I was four months pregnant at the time. I cussed Wayne out for not telling me about her. She came to my job, tryin' to act out. I took a quick break from curling my client's hair to beat her down. I know Simcoo-coo was grateful, 'cause I knocked her eyes straight for a day. Don't think twice about that girl." She finished up her water. "So, where did you meet Wayne?"

"At his house in Maryland," I said. "He's insured with the

company I used to work for. I handled a claim for him."

She took a compact mirror out of her purse to apply some more lipstick. "I met him through my cousin Patrick. He and Wayne are good friends. They used to play ball together in college. One night Patrick had a fight party, and Wayne was there. We stayed up all night talkin'. Stayed up drinkin'." She winked at me. "And you know the rest."

"Yeah," I said as I looked at my brittle nails.

She stood up and stretched. "Back to back babies turned Wayne into Roadrunner. I expected that, though. That's why I got the best attorney in Houston to set him straight. He may be a no show around my son, but that check faithfully shows up at my P.O. Box. You live and you learn from these ballers," she said. "You gotta take care of you, in case they start to show off. My little girl is by a basketball player too."

Now why didn't that surprise me? I opened my mouth slightly to act like it did. "Really?" I said.

She nodded. "Yes, Rynell Roman. He plays for Dallas. We hooked up at a fashion show and lived together for a year. He wanted a baby, so we decided to have one." She yawned. "We were supposed to get married, but it didn't work out. We're still friends, though. Unlike Wayne, he acts his age." She sighed and looked at my stomach.

"Congratulations are in order?" she asked.

"Yes," I said smiling and holding my belly.

She snickered. "Good luck, girlfriend. You take it easy." She touched my arm. "I don't wanna keep you any longer. Thanks for the water."

"No problem," I said as I got up. I noticed her looking at my hair.

"Listen, I don't know if you've already found a place, but I just opened my own hair salon downtown," she said. "It's real nice." She took a business card from her purse and handed it to me. "Why don't you swing by and let me tighten up that haircut?" She leaned over and gently patted the back of my hair. "You could use a perm in the back, unless you goin' for that natural look?"

I quickly covered the back of my hair with my hand, embarrassed. "Thanks for the offer, but I already have a salon," I said. "I had to cancel my appointment today, because I wasn't feeling well."

"Well, the offer still stands." We walked through the foyer. She held her hands up. "Free of charge, courtesy of Wayne and Rynell," she said as she opened the door and left.

Wayne strolled in the house at one thirty in the morning. I kept my head focused on the piano keys as he walked up to me. He planted a fake, *I'm guilty as shit*, kiss on my cheek. I stopped playing.

"I'm sorry I'm so late baby," he said sitting down beside me on the bench.

"Did the game go into quadruple overtime or something?" I asked as I folded my arms.

He laughed. "Something smells good," he whispered in my ear.

I moved away from him. "I made beef brisket for dinner, and it was delicious."

"Any leftover?" he asked taking off his watch and putting it on top of the piano.

I shook my head. "No," I snapped. "I gave the rest to Dibo. I think it's a shame that the damn dog appreciates me more than you."

He plopped his hands on his thighs. "What's wrong now? You don't feel good?" he asked.

"Hell no. I don't feel good about us at all, Wayne. This pregnancy has been so rough for me, and I'm lonely," I said, my voice cracking. "I need some TLC from my man. Is that too much to ask?"

He sighed as he looked down. "Baby, I have to work."

"What type of work keeps you out past midnight!" I banged on the keys and got up from the piano.

Wayne grabbed onto my arm. "Onyx, chill."

"Get off of me!" I yelled. "You don't understand what I'm going through! You don't even know me. Why did you bring me here?"

His jaw tightened. "I thought you wanted to be with me?"

I smoothed my nightshirt down over my belly. "Wayne, when are we getting married?"

He put his head in his hands. "Onyx, marriage scares the shit out of me."

"What?"

He looked up to the ceiling. "Do we have to talk about this now?"

I clenched my teeth. "Yes, I want to talk about it. I'm not asking you to marry me tomorrow. I just want to get things solidified in my life. You didn't seem uneasy about marriage when I told you I was pregnant. Remember?" I grabbed his hand. "You said I was the one," I said brushing a tear from my face. "You said you wanted a family."

Wayne held my hand firmly in his. "I meant all of those things," he said. "I knew you didn't want to be an unwed mother, so I let you know I was fine with the idea. I was afraid you'd abort the baby if I didn't do right by you."

I slapped him. "You're selfish, and you're a liar!" I cried. "You have yet to do right by me. A righteous man wouldn't have me crying like this. He'd spoil me. Take me to nice places, instead of having me cooped up in this house. He'd make me feel proud to be the mother of his unborn child."

He scowled as he rubbed his face. "You startin' to sound like Simcha and Keisha. Always looking for handouts."

"Fuck you!" I ran towards the steps.

"Onyx, wait," he said coming over to me. He rested his head on my shoulder as his hands wrapped around my stomach. "I didn't mean that. I'm just stressed right now, baby."

I released his hands from me. "Join the club. Leave me alone, Wayne. Why don't you go back to where you came from? I still smell her on you."

❖❖❖❖❖

The day after our fight, Wayne brought me breakfast in bed. After I finished eating he gave me the Platinum AMEX card. He said he had a romantic weekend planned for us, and told me to pick out some nice things for myself. While a shopping spree barely settled our score, it did brighten my mood. Wayne's cousin, Dayna, accompanied me to the mall. Dayna was the only person I hung out with. Wayne introduced us at a family cookout. We've been friends ever since. She and I are the same age, and were sorors—both members of Delta Sigma Theta.

"Damn," she said. "You got some nice stuff today. That halter pantsuit is definitely tight."

I held my wrist, admiring my new Movado watch. "I figured since Wayne is paying, might as well do it up lovely," I said. "You feel like looking at some shoes? Maybe I can buy you something for putting up with me all day."

"No, I'm straight girl," she said looking in the Bebe store display window. "As long as you feel up to it, you enjoy yourself." She shook her head. "What's gotten into Wayne?"

I sighed as I arched my back. "I don't know. I think he feels bad for being a cheating asshole."

We sat down on a bench at the Food Court. "Girl, don't trip," she said. "That's just a day in a baller's life. Shit, any man's life for that matter. There aren't too many men who haven't slipped up on some alien coochie at least once. The ones that deny cheating are the worst. So, after getting my feelings hurt a few times I decided to join the game." She winked at some guy who walked past. "I only pimp six figure men, though. Before they hit the pussy, I get the SSN and run a credit report. Then, I make them show me bank statements to see if they got decent savings. If everything checks out, I'm bout it, bout it."

I laughed. "Well, I'm not exactly in a position right now to creep," I said tapping my tummy.

"Chile, please," she said. "I got the most tail when I was pregnant."

I covered my mouth in surprise. "Your ex-husband knew?"

"Uh huh. He came home to find Mommy practicing labor positions. His ass thought he was slick creeping on me, so I flipped the script. I found better dick, and sent him to find another place to live," she said slapping me a high five. Dayna always knew how to make me laugh.

She pointed at me. "See Onyx, you too soft with Wayne. The only way to hurt a man is to hit 'em in the pockets. You better stop thinking about ribbons in the sky, and start planning your child's portfolio. Wayne is my cousin, but Babyface, he is not. Learn to take care of yourself first. Save the sob stories for your demo."

❖❖❖❖❖

Wayne and I were at a birthday party for one of his buddies from college. I really didn't want to go, but he convinced me. He said there wouldn't be a lot of folks over, so I could rest in one of the bedrooms.

I was achy, definitely not in a partying mood. I had indigestion and was tired from doing the baby's gift registry earlier that day. I took advantage of that spare bedroom, and got some sleep. After about an hour, I told Wayne to drive me home. I could tell the Heineken consumption had gone to an all time high, because the fellas kept waking me up with their yelling.

Wayne took me back to our place, then said he wanted to go back to his boy's house to watch the ball game. I was so tired, I didn't mind. When he wasn't back home by seven the next morning, I got worried. Wayne didn't return any of my calls, so I went straight over to his boy Barry's house.

Barry opened the door, looking very hung over. "Hey, Onyx," he said wiping his eyes.

I threw my car keys in my tote bag, annoyed. "Barry, is Wayne here?"

He looked at his feet and coughed. "No, he left out about an hour ago. He probably went to Denny's or something to get some breakfast."

"Well, I need to get my earrings," I said as I pushed him aside and walked in. Barry did a two step shuffle to get in front of me as I walked towards the bedroom.

"Why don't you let me get those for you," he said, anxious. He scratched his head.

I removed my sunglasses. "That's quite all right," I said walking right past him. "I know where they are. It'll be faster if I get them."

I walked into the room and smelled the aroma of sex and alcohol. I looked at Barry tapping his foot at the doorway. I guess he was sworn to secrecy, but I had other means of telling if Wayne was busted. I headed to the bathroom. Just what I'd thought . . . A used condom floating in the commode. Barry looked at me like he didn't have a clue. I went over to the nightstand for my earrings. I held my stomach in shock when I realized they were missing. I bet that unidentified skank stole them while Wayne freaked her ass.

I got home and Wayne was knocked out. My mood was foul due to his infidelity, so I decided to fuck with his head. I sat on the edge of the bed, and kissed his cheek, ever so softly.

"Wake up, darling," I said.

He smiled as he opened his eyes. I kept a happy face as I pulled my head away from him, trying not to get sick from the stench of stale cologne and liquor mixed together.

"Hey baby," he said. "Where you been?" He raised himself up on the headboard.

I smiled and held my two fingers up. "Oh, I was out shopping. I found a new desert recipe in a magazine that I wanna try for dinner. Here, taste these," I said as I moved my fingers toward his mouth. "See what glaze you like the best."

My index and middle fingers were raised, ready for the competition. He went for the index finger first. "No Wayne, try this one first." My middle finger was straight up in his face. He sucked my middle finger, then slowly pulled back on it. He sort of shrugged, as if he really didn't have an opinion one way or the other.

I raised a brow. "You don't like that?" I asked. "That one was my favorite."

"It doesn't taste bad," he said. "It's sorta bland."

I nodded. "All right, well try this one." I gave him my index finger. He got to half of the finger, then jerked his mouth away.

"Damn, what kind of glaze is that!" he shouted. "It's too salty. The other one was definitely better."

I know it was bitch, I thought. "I'm not sure what kind of glaze the last one is, Wayne. I was hoping you could tell me. I'm surprised you didn't find it appetizing. You seemed to indulge in plenty of it last night, from the looks of Barry's guest sheets."

His eyes got big. I poked him in the chest. "The first glaze was my pussy, but I guess you forgot what it tastes like, since you been eatin' skank pussy lately."

He held his arms up. "Onyx. . . . "

I put my index finger over his lips. "Don't try to find words to say on my account. Let me talk. My next OB appointment is in two weeks. If any of my tests come back positive, due to your creepin' bullshit, my ass will be in a lawyer's office without hesitation. And God forbid, if our baby has something other than half of your chromosomes," I said. "I swear I will kill you."

He kneeled on the bed and clasped his hands. "Onyx, I'm sorry," he pleaded. "Baby, I was drunk. I don't even remember last night. I would never intentionally do anything to hurt. . ."

I threw the pillow at him. "Shut up, Wayne. You just did." I yanked off my Nine West loafers and stomped over to the walk-in closet. "You got fifteen minutes to get showered and dressed," I yelled.

"Why?" he asked.

I took off my blouse, and peeked out of the closet. "We're going downtown to Tiffany's," I hissed.

He folded his arms. "I thought you just came back from shopping?" he said.

I nodded and shook my finger at him as I walked out. "You know what? I am sort of tired. You go without me." I pulled one of his old jerseys from the dresser and threw it on.

He got up and pulled me over to the bed. "I don't need anything." He licked his lips. "I'm tired too," he said cupping my breasts. I smacked his hands.

"You know they're sore," I pouted as I looked down at my chest.

He smiled and kissed my hand. "My bad. We could relax in the Jacuzzi."

I put my hands on my hips. "Wayne, I can't use the Jacuzzi while I'm pregnant. Yet another detail of my life you would know if you stayed your butt at home! You being tired is nothing new. Hoes and Vodka tend to wear you out. Now, I know I didn't stutter when I told you to get out of that bed!"

"All right," he huffed. He dragged himself to the closet. "What do you need at Tiffany's that's so important?"

I laid down on the bed. "Where are my diamond earrings, Wayne?" I said adjusting the pillows under my back.

He tapped his chin as he avoided direct eye contact. "I don't know. Didn't you have them last night?"

I rolled my eyes at him. "Yeah until I laid down at Barry's. I took them off. I guess Goldilocks thought they were her door prize for comin' first. So, your trip to Tiffany's is urgent." I held up my hand. "First, I want a replacement set of carat studs. This time make sure they are one carat each. Second, I'm your fiancé and the mother of your child, so my ring is due. Select the prettiest platinum solitaire you can find. No less than three carats. Ring size five and a half. And finally, Mama needs a new pair of shoes. Stop past Nordstrom's and get me these stilettos." I tossed the catalog to him. He stood there, mouth wide open. "Shoe size seven," I said. I puckered a fake kiss at him and closed my eyes.

Wayne mumbled under his breath as he left the bedroom.

"I love you too, sweetheart," I said.

Smooth sounds emanated from the piano downstairs and pleasantly woke me from my slumber. Hearing live music was always good for my soul. I sighed as I walked downstairs to greet Wayne. I wanted to make up and wipe the slate clean, once again.

Wayne smiled when he saw me enter the family room. "Madame," he said as he continued to play his tune.

Mutt, I thought, but bit my tongue. I sat down on the piano stool beside him.

"What are you playing?" I asked.

He winked. *Melodies of Love* by Joe Sample.

I smiled. "Sounds nice."

Wayne was a very good musician and singer. That's what attracted me to him. I often thought he was better in music than in basketball. He said basketball was more of a sure thing. I begged to differ. I thought Wayne was gonna turn into a basketball; he'd bounced from team to team so much. You weren't a sure thing if teams traded you at the drop of a dime. A thirty-two year old with constant knee problems caused his franchise stakes to go way down.

I stopped thinking about his NBA issues and focused on him playing the piano again. He always knew how to get back into my good graces. I promised him that if I ever made it big, we'd sing a duet on my first CD, if we were on good terms.

Wayne stopped playing and gave me a soft peck on the lips. "I got something for you," he said as he reached under the piano. He pulled up a cute Kangaroo stuffed animal.

"You bought a stuffed animal for me?" I asked. "I think I'm past the age. . . . "

He shook his head. "No. The kangaroo is for the baby," he said. "Your gift is in the pouch. Reach inside."

He handed the kangaroo to me. I reached inside and pulled out a small baby blue box adorned with a white ribbon. Authentic Tiffany's wrapping paper, no doubt. I opened the box to find a beautiful square cut solitaire. I smiled as Wayne placed the ring on my left finger. "Wayne, the ring is gorgeous, but it means nothing if I don't have success at loving you."

He touched my cheek. "Baby, you don't have to change a thing," he said. "Thanks for putting up with my crap."

"I'm trying to save you from yourself Wayne, but you keep letting me down. You know, love can only stretch but so far," I said.

"I know." Wayne moved out from the piano and took my hand as he got down on one knee. He kissed the back of my hand softly. "Forgive me?"

"You sound like a broken record," I said.

"Well?"

"Yes, Wayne. I do." I sounded like the same record . . . Broken.

Papa Was A Rolling Stone

It was ten o'clock when I got home from the hair salon. I was so tired. Why did it take an average of four hours to do a black woman's hair? And four hours was just for basic shit. If you added a perm, a haircut or color, you'd better be prepared to camp out with a blanket and pillow.

When I walked in, the house was dark except for a dim light coming from the dining room area. Wayne was home for a change. I found him with his head down on the dining room table. I went over and rubbed his back.

"Wayne? Wayne, baby?" He breathed hard as he slowly lifted his head.

"Why don't you go upstairs and rest?" I said.

"Hi baby," he said.

He gave me a hug and sat back down. I sat on his lap.

"Your hair looks nice," he said.

"Thanks," I said. "Hard day?"

"Yeah, I have a lot going on. I gotta make some changes," he said rustling some papers that were on the table.

"You feel like talking about it?" I asked. He looked serious as he kissed my cheek and held me tighter.

"Well, if you feel up to it, I guess now is as good a time as any," he said. "Onyx, the team decided not to renew my contract. I got the news today. I called my agent and told him to get busy on a trade deal, but he started hemming and hawing, talking about I needed to be patient. He said it would be difficult to get what I was asking, considering my age, my knees, and the lack of minutes played these last few years. I fired him and called my boy Harrison's agent, Dean, and signed with him. Just yesterday, he thought he had a deal worked out with Dallas, but management bailed at the last minute. They decided to take on a Rookie being traded from Cleveland."

"What about the other teams?" I asked. "There has to be someone else interested."

"Dean talked to Washington," he said. "They are under new ownership and interested in tightening up the roster, but not with veterans. They already have Harrison and Leon, and those brothas ain't goin' anywhere. Teams want young blood these days. Jersey offered a year, but that's a year of playing behind two other Power Forwards and a decent Center, which leaves me riding the bench all the time. Besides, they want me to play for the league minimum, which is an insult for a former Olympian and All-Star."

I rubbed his arm. "But Wayne, a year with a new team and a new agent could make all the difference," I said. "Things might work out in Jersey. They could renew the contract, or possibly work out a better deal for you elsewhere."

He sighed. "See Onyx, that's the thing. Possibilities are endless, but they can make or break you," he said. "There is no job security in this league. One day you think everything is fine, the next day you're being moved around from team to team like some chess piece. You're always at somebody's mercy, having to accept shit at a moment's notice. So, after talking it over with Dean some more, I decided to give myself a break from the NBA."

"What?" I got up from his lap and leaned against the table to face him.

"Yeah baby," he said, tapping his fist in his palm. "Dean got a decent deal for me to play in Italy. We gotta leave next week."

I touched my stomach, because the baby reacted when I jerked after Wayne said, *Italy*. I held my hand to my mouth. "Italy, Wayne?" I muffled. "Couldn't you have at least consulted with me before you made that type of commitment?"

"Onyx, you're a smart woman, but you don't know this profession. I got about three years left in me to play ball, that's it.

And with you talkin' about you need to be spoiled, and Simcha and Keisha glued to my ass for the next decade, what was I supposed to do?"

"You were supposed to consider my feelings before you made a decision that affects the both of us, Wayne!" I shouted. "I'm six months pregnant. All my doctors are here. Did my health ever come into your mind?"

Wayne stood up. "Women change doctors all the time. Onyx, stop acting like you're the only pregnant woman on the earth. They have doctors and everything else you'd need in Italy. Italy is a beautiful place." He took my hand. "I know it's a lot to take on right now, but I have to make this move. Financially, I'm hurting. I met with my accountant the other day and he set a budget. I wish I would have done that years ago, but I was hard headed when I was younger. I thought the money would last forever. I had to learn the hard way. Bad investments, gambling, and two kids have made me realize that those millions don't stretch as much as I thought."

"Wayne, you exaggerate," I said. "You only stress about money, because you try to keep up with the Joneses. Who gives a shit about what other players got, or what they're doing?" I looked around the room. "Half of the stuff in this house we didn't need, but you just had to have the latest whatever."

He frowned. "I don't see you complaining about being retired from Banner," he said. "You know why, because you like livin' nice, without some supervisor sweatin' your ass. That's why we gotta move to Italy. I wanna keep you satisfied, so are you going with me?"

I held my head. "Are you going to marry me in Italy?" He walked out of the room, not saying another word. I didn't say a damn thing either.

❖ ❖ ❖ ❖ ❖

Two days after his breaking news regarding the move to Italy, Wayne still wasn't back home. He claimed he had to go out of town on business, the usual lie. I didn't trip on him being away. I tried to adjust to the fact that I'd be moving out of the country. I decided to go out and get baby furniture and a few other items. I didn't want to worry about buying stuff for the nursery after we moved. An all day shopping spree was not what I expected, but the sight I saw as I approached the driveway caught me off guard even more. The front door was open and my landlord was on his cell phone standing against the railing. I parked the car and watched in disbelief as movers brought furniture out of the house. A "For Sale" sign was firmly planted in the lawn. I felt dizzy as I slowly got out of the car. I walked across the grass towards the landlord, fearing the worst. When I reached the steps, Mr. Nazarian quickly got off the phone and walked down.

"Ms. Devoe, are you all right?" he asked with a deep Armenian accent.

I didn't answer him. I looked away briefly, then went up the steps and inside the house.

"Ms. Devoe?" he repeated while following behind me.

"What's going on?" I asked. "Why are movers here? Wayne didn't mention moving any stuff this soon."

"Wayne called me early yesterday morning," he said. "He told me he was sending a courier over to give me a final check, because he was moving out of the country, and needed to break the lease ASAP. I had to be here to let the movers in. "

Tears formed in my eyes. I wiped my face and sighed before speaking. "Do you know where Wayne is by chance?" I asked.

"No, I'm sorry," he said. "He just said he was out of town. I was under the impression that you were with him. He said there would be no one home to meet the movers."

I bit my lip. "I see. Well, Mr. Nazarian, Wayne moving his shit out behind my back lets me know for sure that I've never been with him." I looked over at the movers wheeling the piano across the marble tile in the foyer. "Excuse me," I said as I walked over to them. "The piano stays here. It belongs to me."

The mover spoke. "But we were instructed to. . . . "

"I don't care what you were instructed to do," I said to him. "The piano is mine. If your client has any problems with that he can contact me."

He threw up his hands. "Okay, lady," he said leaving the piano in the foyer. He walked away.

"Uh Sir," I said to the mover

"Yeah?" he said.

"Have you moved all the items from upstairs?"

"All the furniture is gone. There are some women's clothing and accessories left. A man with an Expedition came over to get Mr. Griffin's clothes."

Patrick, I thought. "Okay. Thanks for the info," I said.

"No problem," he said.

"Mr. Nazarian?" I said.

"Yes, Ms. Devoe?" he said coming closer.

"I have a favor to ask."

He nodded. "Certainly. How can I help you?" he asked.

"I was wondering if I could at least have a couple of days to get my things out and find another place to live."

"Why don't you take the rest of the weekend. I don't have any prospects coming over until Monday afternoon."

"I really appreciate it, Mr. Nazarian."

"All right, have a good evening." He left out, the movers left out, and Wayne left me hanging.

❖❖❖❖❖

Dayna offered to take me to the airport. I was leaving Houston for good.

"You sure you don't want to stay at my place until your tenant moves out of the condo?" she asked.

"No," I said. "There's nothing here in Houston for me, not anymore. I'll miss you and Dibo, but it's best that I go back home. Try to be the best mother I can be, and re-build the life I had before I loved Wayne."

She hugged me. "Well, I want you to know I'm here if you need me. Don't worry about Dibo's big ass. My brother and I already got plans for him. We gonna make him for hire. Hook him up to a vegetable cart or something."

I nudged her. "You better not!" I screamed.

She laughed. "Just jokes. You know Onyx, I probably shouldn't feel this way, but I'm embarrassed by how Wayne acted. I knew he was capable of doing some jacked up shit, but this?"

I sighed. "I thought the same thing," I said. "But you know what? I can't think about him right now. He sure didn't think of me when he fled to Italy. I'm just ready to go. You feel like taking me to the airport?"

She glanced at her watch. "You got about a two hour wait," she said.

I picked up my purse. "That's fine," I said. "I'm used to waiting."

Lost Melody

I was at the piano writing on the fourth track of my demo when the phone rang.

"Hello?" I said.

No one said anything.

"Hello?" I moved my finger close to the Off button to hang up, then I realized who was on the line.

"You coward," I said aloud into the phone. "You're thousands of miles away and you still aren't man enough to speak to me."

Wayne was silent. Tension and tears started to build within me. "What did I do to deserve you leaving me, huh?" I cried. "Tell me. I gave up everything to be with you, and I'm about to have your child. Wasn't I at least worthy of a goodbye note?" His silence remained.

I sighed as I wiped tears off my face. "I guess not. Well, I'm tired of questioning whether or not you ever loved me, because it doesn't matter anymore. I don't want a man who doesn't want me. However, your baby girl is in my womb, and she's gonna want her daddy." I took a deep breath. "Wayne, please promise me that you'll be in her life," I pleaded. "No matter what went down with us, she's still your family."

"Did you get the checks I sent?" he asked in a hushed tone.

"Our daughter is worth more than a check," I said. "Are you going to be there for her?" A dial tone was his reply.

❖ ❖ ❖ ❖ ❖

Something wasn't right. I hadn't felt the baby move all day. The baby was very active the night before. I decided to call my midwife, Therese. She told me to come in right away.

When I got to the office, Therese put me on the fetal monitor. Nothing was heard. She did an ultrasound. There was no movement. I saw the concern on her face.

"Therese, you're scaring me. What's going on?" I asked.

A doctor came into the room. Therese grabbed my hand and said, "We're taking you to the hospital."

❖❖❖❖❖

A few minutes after I arrived at the hospital, Therese sat by my bedside with tears in her eyes.

"Onyx," she said touching my face. "The baby is dead."

"No!" I screamed. Wails of sorrow exploded as medical personnel stood in silence.

"No God, please . . . Don't hurt me like this," I cried. "It can't be true. Check again. She's just sleeping. She's not dead, I know she's not dead. Therese, I'm begging you. Please check again."

Therese held me. "You would re-check if it were your baby, right?" I asked.

Tears ran down her face as fast as they ran down mine. "I would," she said.

"Please do this for me," I whimpered. "Check again."

❖❖❖❖❖

A final check was done. Therese's answer was still the same. She induced labor:

10:00 p.m.—Contractions were stronger. I breathed through them.

12:00 a.m.—Contractions were unbearable. I cried through them.

1:30 a.m.—Back labor began and I prayed for God to give me strength. I asked Him to make the pain go away, after this day. I was in the bed, lying in a fetal position, rocking and moaning as the pressure of the baby increased on my pelvis. Her death, heavy on my mind. Therese pleaded with me to accept some pain medication.

"Onyx, sweetie. You don't have to suffer," she said. "You've been through enough. Let the doctor give you an epidural."

"No, I want to feel everything that's happening to me, because as God as my witness, I'll never let another man hurt me like this again."

At 5:00 a.m., I pushed three times to deliver my baby. I reached for her immediately as I heard Therese tell the other nurse, "Record the time of death."

"I wanna hold her," I moaned.

"Of course," Therese said. She cleaned the baby and gently placed her into my arms.

I smiled at her beautiful caramel face, long eyelashes like her father. She looked perfect, like she was just resting.

"Sweet, sweet baby. Melody Arie, Mommy loves you so much." I kissed her as I hopelessly looked for any signs of life. My angel remained still. A few moments later, my denial ceased. Melody was dead. She had been strangled by her umbilical cord.

I continued to hold my baby as Therese removed the afterbirth from me. I heard the nurse tell Therese that the Chaplain was right outside. I panicked. "Please don't let them take the baby from me!" I yelled.

"I won't let anybody take her," Therese said.

"I know we need to pray, but I wanna sing to her first," I said.

"Take all the time you need," Therese said as she finished my exam.

"Can I be alone for a few minutes?" I asked.

"I'll be right outside," she said.

The room was quiet. I sang Melody a lullaby.

Starting Over

Six weeks had gone by since I'd lost Melody. I dealt with her death the best I could. I was back to work at Banner. I was also back in the studio working on my demo. The past would never be forgotten, but I knew I'd die if I kept holding onto yesterday.

It was the end of May, and City Council Elections were being held. I stood at the polls, waiting for an open booth. The woman in front of me was summoned to the registration desk. She was handed her information pamphlet, but hesitated to walk to the booth. I overheard the volunteer at the desk say to her, "What do you mean you can't read?"

I felt the volunteer could have been more discreet with her words, especially since the woman put down the paper and headed towards the exit sign, obviously embarrassed.

I quickly got out of line and followed her. "Miss? Excuse me, Miss?" I said.

"Yeah," she said as she turned to me.

"Hi, I'm Onyx," I said extending my hand. She shook it reluctantly. "I don't mean to hold you up, but I noticed you didn't get to the booth. This is important. All of our votes are needed."

"Yeah, well I ain't got time for people who ain't got time for me," she hissed.

I touched her arm. "I know what you mean. These voting machines can be confusing. If you wanna stick around, we can go over the pamphlet. I'm sure the volunteers won't mind, as long as you don't tell me who you're voting for."

She looked down at her feet. "You'd do that for me?" she whispered. "I mean, I'm a little slow."

I smiled. "I have plenty of time," I said. "I'd love to help." Her face seemed to glow when she smiled.

"Thanks Onyx," she said. "My name is Anela Grace."

After Anela and I voted, I asked if I could help her learn to read. She agreed, and we soon became friends.

I started to feel like my old self again. Work was boring as usual, but I was proud of the fact that my demo was almost finished. Anela made tremendous progress in her reading. She was a widow and retired from working the assembly line at the Wonderbread factory in D.C. We'd get together three times a week to study and review her worksheets. My mother was a school teacher for over thirty years, so she helped me gather materials for Anela to use.

Tonight Anela cooked some of her homemade spaghetti, which was my favorite. We finished studying and sat down at the table to eat.

"Are you feeling okay, Anela?" I asked.

"I'm doin' all right, but I've been feelin' worn down the past few days," she said, rubbing her neck. "My legs are swollen too."

I placed the napkin in my lap. "Do you think your blood pressure is up?"

"No, 'cause I had the pharmacy clerk at the grocery store take my pressure. She said it was fine. I called the doctor, though. I see him next week. For now, I'm just gonna cut down on the salt."

I poured some ice water in her glass. "Keep me posted," I said.

"I will," she said. "Now let's say grace so we can eat." I took Anela's hand as we prayed.

"Glomerulosclerosis?" I said, holding her hand. "What's that Anela?"

She sighed. "Some kind of kidney disease," she said. "It

makes you swell up and it causes you to be tired all the time."

"Is it serious? They can treat it, right?"

"Yeah, but it depends on how bad off the person is. The doctor needs to run more tests on me to see how to go about treatment. If my kidneys are damaged real bad, then taking medicine might not be enough."

"There's a possibility you might need a transplant?" I asked.

"Maybe," she said.

I walked over and embraced Anela because she looked scared. "It's gonna be okay, Anela. Keep praying."

Anela was worried, but I tried to assure her that everything would be fine. Kidney transplants were pretty common these days. Time was miraculously on our side. As a potential donor, I was tested immediately. My kidney was a perfect match.

❖❖❖❖❖

Anela and I recovered from the surgery. Anela's body seemed to tolerate the kidney, and I was glad I had a part in saving my friend's life. I put the magazine I was reading on my stomach and closed my eyes. When I opened my eyes again, Anela was at my bedside, smiling in her wheelchair.

"Anela, you're like a little church mouse. I didn't even hear you come in. Shouldn't you be in bed?"

"I was, but I got bored. I came to check on you," she said.

I sat up in the hospital bed. "I'm doing great," I said. "I'm a little groggy from the medication, but I'm getting my second wind."

"Good," she said.

"Are you still eating dinner with me?" I asked. "I got some homemade crab cakes being delivered."

She rubbed her tummy. "You know I'm for that, but maybe I should check with the doctor. Make sure I can eat them."

I nodded. "You're right. Well, if you can't have them, I'll enjoy them for you."

We both laughed, then Anela's complexion turned pale. She reached out and grabbed my hand. I got out of the bed. "Anela?" I said. "Do you want me to get the nurse?"

She shook her head. "No, get back in bed," she said. "Rest yourself." I got back under the covers.

She grinned. "I have a surprise for you," she said.

"Really?" I said.

"Yeah." She handed me a small rectangular package, wrapped in gold.

"Anela, why did you give me a gift? I don't have anything for you."

"You already gave me the best gift of all. Not just the kidney," she said pointing to her side. "You saw something in me that no one else could see. You believed in me."

A tear rolled down her cheek. "Onyx, I can never repay you for all you have done, but you will be blessed. I promise you, on my life."

I squeezed her hand and reached over to wipe her cheek. "Anela, I'm already blessed," I said. "Just meeting you was a blessing, because I was grief stricken over Melody at the time. I needed you in my life."

She smiled. "I didn't mean to get mushy on you. Open your gift." I tore off the wrapping paper. It was a book of poems by Maya Angelou.

"This is nice Anela," I said. "Maya Angelou is one of my favorite authors."

"That's not all of my surprise," she said taking the book away from me. "I wanna read something to you. I've been practicing for a while." She flipped through the pages. "This poem is called *Phenomenal Woman*. This is how I feel about you." She began reading. She took her time . . . And I cried the whole way through.

❖❖❖❖❖

Three weeks post surgery, Anela was doing fine. I'd returned to my job handling claims. I was in the basement of an upscale house in Potomac. Undoubtedly, the residents of this abode had serious money. Luckily, the water damage from the sump pump leak wasn't severe. I wanted to get the claim resolved quickly because high valued homes sometimes meant high maintenance policyholders. I was not in the mood for

Rockefeller drama.

Based on my assessment of the damage, the Berber carpet and padding would have to be replaced. I'd also take care of the small inventory of contents damage. After taking a few more photos, I decided to cruise over to the piano on the other side of the room. It had been calling me the entire time I wrote my damage estimate. I figured I'd give it a quick inspection to make sure it hadn't been affected by the water. I did a few taps on the keys. Then, I did the scales. Before long, my ass sat on the bench and played full force.

"You play very well," a voice said from behind me.

I quickly got up from the piano. A woman who I believed to be the owner of the home was a few feet away.

"I'm sorry Mrs. Katz," I said, embarrassed. "I'm Onyx Devoe." We shook hands.

"Nice to meet you," she said. "I'm sorry I wasn't home earlier. I had a meeting in D.C."

"No problem," I said. "I was testing the piano to see if it had any damage from the water leak."

"Well, does it?" she asked with a smile.

I shook my head. "No, I don't think so." I spanned the keys with my fingertips. "It plays beautifully. However, if you want a professional to come out and inspect it, Banner will pay the expense."

"Based on the way you play, I'll consider your assessment professional enough," she said. She motioned towards the piano. "Why don't you sit back down? Finish what you started. You're not doing Phyllis any justice by ending *Meet Me On The Moon*, midway."

My eyes got big. "Wow, you knew I was playing Phyllis Hyman?"

She folded her arms. "Why wouldn't I? She's one of my favorite artists. Did you assume I wouldn't be familiar with the tune because I don't look like you?"

I looked down. "I guess I did make that assumption. I apologize."

She laughed. "Don't apologize, just finish playing."

I sat down. "I sing also," I said looking over my shoulder at her. "I could start the song over with the lyrics if you like?"

"By all means," she said as she sat in the leather recliner and watched me in action.

❖❖❖❖❖

Mrs. Katz and I sat in her sunroom drinking lemonade. "Onyx, I think Phyllis would have been proud," she said. "You have a wonderful voice."

"Thanks," I said. "There will never be another Phyllis, though. She was the best."

"True, but you certainly have her caliber of talent," she said.

"You think so?"

"I know it. I can tell a trained voice when I hear one."

"I went to Morgan," I said. "Majored in Music."

"Dr. Carter, huh?"

"Yes," I said, surprised that she knew my professor.

"He's well renowned," she said. "Besides, he's a good friend of mine."

"It's a small world."

"Yes, it is," she said. She took a sip of her drink. "It's also a world where time is of the essence. So, tell me. Why are you sitting in my house explaining insurance coverage when you should be performing at Constitution Hall?"

I wrung my hands. "My dream is to become a professional singer, but life for me has been a little rough lately," I said. "I've had some roadblocks to get over. I don't know, sometimes I think the idea of becoming some well known singer is far fetched. I mean, singers are a dime a dozen."

She placed her beverage on the end table. "Well, with that attitude, you will be just another struggling singer, settling in a dead end job. No offense Onyx, but I have an idea of what adjusters make. My brother works in insurance. The stress must exceed the pay. My philosophy is that it is better to put all of your energy into something you really want, instead of allowing a mundane job to consume you. You can always get a job, but you won't always have the opportunity to do what your heart longs to do. Trust me, there are a lot of fabulous singers waiting to get their big break. So, I suggest you not let your gift go to waste."

I sighed. "I hear you Mrs. Katz, but it's not easy making it in the business. You have to have connections," I said taking a sip of my lemonade.

She raised a brow. "How do you know I don't have connections?"

I almost choked on my drink when she said that. I put the glass down. "You do?" I asked.

"Perhaps," she said laughing at me.

I smiled. "Are you in the business?"

"No, but I know music. I'm a professor at Howard University. My husband is in the business. He is a successful entertainment lawyer. His firm is in New York City." Dead silence on my part.

She reached over and touched my hand. "What's wrong, Onyx?" she asked. "Cat got your tongue?"

I shook my head. "No, I'm just trying to take all of this in." I bit my lip. "Do you think your husband could get me an interview with a record executive?"

She shrugged. "That depends on how serious you are about coming into the industry. My husband's time is very valuable. He meets artists every day. He only has time for people who believe they can be superstars. Are you willing to let go of that nine to five and work your ass off to make it big?"

I grabbed her hand. Tears welled up in my eyes as I thought of the possibility. "Yes, Mrs. Katz. I am."

"Do you have a demo?" she asked.

I nodded. "It's not finished, but I have five tracks completed," I said. "I wrote them all."

She smiled as she got up from the wicker chair. "All right," she said. "Let me see what I can do. Excuse me while I make a phone call."

❖❖❖❖❖

Mrs. Katz spoke to her husband. I sang for him over the phone, which landed me a formal audition with Clive Davis at

J Records. He loved my voice. Two weeks later, I had a record deal.

Several months had passed and I had been so busy traveling across the country to promote my debut album. Anela and I tried to get together, but our schedules conflicted. She did a lot of volunteer work at the library, and I was tied up with interviews and appearances. Christmastime was near, so I hoped I'd get a chance to see her when I came home. Last night, my mom called with bad news. She saw Anela's obituary in the newspaper. She had died of a bacterial infection, according to the notice. I was an emotional wreck when I heard the news, because Anela and I had been close. I stopped blaming myself for not spending more time with her. I would make peace with her at the funeral.

Working Girl

2004

The Interview

Russell was going full steam ahead, riding past the crack of dawn. "Who's pussy is this baby?" he grunted.

"Yours Russ," I said holding on with minimal enthusiasm.

"Who's!"

"I said yours, you deaf?"

He opened his eyes to see my ticked off expression. I'd already come twice, and I did not have time for a third. Russ fucked well, but after two bouts it was time to stop. I had to get ready for a job interview this morning. He frowned slightly, then ignored me. His eyes closed and he started to jam a little harder. Like he was gonna make a point of finishing his business, no matter what.

"Baby!" he screeched during his ejaculation.

"That's right. Get it all out," I said as I patted his back and looked up to the ceiling. My milk chocolate body was strong for 115 pounds, but I wasn't Superwoman. He needed to raise up off me. Russell had the physique of a Sumo wrestler on steroids. Muscular, but flabby around the mid-section.

He lifted from me and got out of the bed, removing the condom from his limp dick. He raised it in the air and admired the milliliters. "Damn Paris," he said. "This here could make a whole football team." He waved the semen filled condom in front of my face. "Why do you insist on me flushing my future down the toilet?"

I rolled to my side as I looked at him. "You answered your own question," I said as I yawned and stretched my legs. "*Your* future. My future doesn't include a child."

He grabbed tissues from the nightstand and wrapped the condom up. "But you got a son?" he said tossing his trash in the waste basket.

I folded my arms. "Exactly. Now I want a husband. You for the taking?" He was silent.

"I thought so," I said as I tried to get out of bed.

Russell hopped back into bed and pulled me close to his body. He slowly let his fingers stroke my nipples. It felt good, but I had to go. His dick was engorged again. I felt him try to enter me. I bucked him away.

"Russ, there will be no growth in me until you get the marriage certificate, and a nine to five."

He started to pout. "You had Maurice's seed."

I sucked my teeth. "That was seven years ago. I was eighteen and naïve, Russell," I said as I ran my fingers through my afro. "Why did you have to bring him up? He was a girlfriend beater, mad at the world for no good reason." My body stiffened as I recalled the physical abuse from my ex-lover.

"I'm sorry," Russell said. He put his hand on my waist and leaned his face close to mine. I kissed his full lips, mesmerized by his walnut colored eyes.

"I want a family with you, Paris," he said touching my face. "You know I'm yours forever. Why do you need a piece of paper to believe that?"

I tapped his chin with my finger. "No paper, no family Russ. We both know you don't have your dick trained like you should." Russell liked to play poker with the ladies.

His deep brown face actually turned red from blushing. "I'm not that bad," he said as he glanced away with a smile. I jabbed his stomach with my elbow. "Freaking one more than me is bad enough."

"Marriage would tame me," he said, winded from my blow to his side.

"Marriage would make you worse," I huffed. "We were friends before we hit it, remember? I know your ass."

He clasped his hands. "I'll give up slidin' if you'll keep lovin' me," he pleaded.

I laughed. "Don't sweat it, Russ," I said. "I already love you. Will my love last? I don't know." I hugged him. "Let's just enjoy shacking up for now."

He kissed me. I let him rub against my body, but grabbed his dick when he tried to play poker. "Respect me, Russell," I snapped.

He winced. "All right, Paris! Damn!" I stuck my tongue out at him and got out of bed.

"Baby, you got plenty of time to get ready." He folded his hands behind his head and relaxed on the bed. "Lemme tear dat pussy up one more time," he said in his switched on Jamaican accent.

I sighed as I headed to the bathroom. "Nice vernacular, Russ," I said.

"Nice what?" he shouted. "Paris, I need to use a dictionary to talk to you these days. You're becoming a goodie two shoes, and I don't like it."

I peeked out the doorway at him. "Ask me if I care."

He scowled as he got up. "That's cold," he said.

"That's the truth," I said. He walked into the bathroom. I was at the mirror, applying oil to my natural hair. Russell wrapped his arms around me, resting his chin on my shoulder. "Why did you cut your twists out?" he asked. "They were beautiful."

"Not professional enough," I said massaging my scalp.

He frowned. "Says who? Those phony people you tryin' to work for?" he asked.

"No, says me," I said pointing to my chest. "I'm about to enter the work world. I want to be taken seriously, so that means having serious hair."

"No, that means selling out."

I broke free from his embrace and went over to the shower to turn the water on. "Do you have a $40,000 a year gig lined up?" I asked looking over my shoulder at him.

He looked down at his crusty feet. "No," he mumbled.

"Then, shut up," I said as I stepped into the shower.

❖❖❖❖❖

I crossed my ankles under the conference table as I tried to calm my nerves during the intern interview at Stockard & Gray, an investment firm in D.C. I wanted this job so bad I could taste it. I knew I was qualified, but who wasn't these days? The economy was in a slump and the competition for jobs was rampant.

I had to get this position. My son depended on me. Interviews tended to make me anxious, but the brotha conducting the interview put my mind at ease. Garvey Daniels was light skin with wavy hair, clean shaven and definitely a Hugo Boss man, based on his tailored gray suit. He gave my résumé a final glance.

"Well Ms. Parker, your credentials look good," he said.

And you look good, I thought as I kept my interview face.

He leaned back in his chair and rubbed his chin. He put the résumé and pen on the table. "I must tell you our firm runs at a very fast pace," he said. "The demands are great, and a lot is expected from our interns. You'll be required to take the Series 6 and 7 examinations. Overtime, occasional Saturday shifts, and travel are also par for the course. Do you think you would be able to handle a taxing workload, and maintain your studies at Maryland?"

I folded my hands on top of the table. "Mr. Daniels, how do you know this job would be taxing for me?" I said. "You only know what you see on paper, but you've never seen me work. Any job can be taxing. Believe me, I wouldn't be wasting my time or yours if I didn't feel I could successfully fulfill the job requirements of this position. All I ask is for an opportunity to prove that I am qualified."

"Humph," he said as he raised his eyebrow, appearing to soak in my information. "I have one last question for you. Where do you see yourself in five years?"

"Being your boss," I smirked.

He smiled and even laughed a little at my answer. "Interesting," he said. "You seem very confident."

"Why shouldn't I be?" I maintained my serious look. "I've done very well in school for three and a half years, destined to graduate suma cum laude from The University of Maryland at

College Park. I am a single mother who solely looks after the well being of her son. I love, nurture, and tutor him, along with keeping myself focused. I have enough life experience and book sense to master this job." I eased a smile on my face. "So, am I the woman you're looking for?" I asked with a hint of flirtation in my voice.

Garvey swiveled in his executive chair. He didn't give a verbal response, but the sensuous curve of his full lips told me I was definitely being considered.

I slammed the front door to wake Russell's big butt up from the sofa. "Hey sugar," he jerked, pushing one of the sofa cushions onto the floor.

"Did you have a nice nap," I said throwing my keys onto the dining room table.

He straightened up the sofa and walked over to me. "How'd it go?"

I smiled. "I think it went well. The guy interviewing me was a young brotha. He seemed to be impressed."

He folded his arms. "Impressed with what?" he asked with a scowl.

I sighed. "My hang time when I jumped his bones. My résumé, Russell."

He cocked his head to the side. "Would he be your boss?"

I shrugged. "I don't know, why?"

"Because I know brothas, that's why," he huffed.

"Whatever," I said waving him off. I headed towards the bedroom to change my clothes. I heard Russell walking behind me. He tapped me on the shoulder.

"Don't I get a kiss, Paris? I haven't seen you all day."

I shook my head. "Hit that Listerine first Russ. From the looks of the film around your mouth, I know that breath is hummin'."

"You ain't right," he said as he stomped into the bathroom. I laughed. He came back into the bedroom a minute later. "Am I good to go now?" he asked.

"Yes, much better," I said giving him a kiss on the lips.

"Where's Maceo?"

"Oh, I let him go upstairs to play with his friend," he said looking up to the ceiling.

I put my hands on my hips. "Did you ask him if he had finished his homework?"

He gave me a goofy grin. "Uh, no."

"Then you can go get him so he can do his school work," I said, annoyed. "I know it's not done. I'm gonna take a nap."

"Baby, you're not gonna cook?" he asked.

"What's wrong with your hands?" I hissed. "You cook."

"Damn Paris," he whined. "I had a taste for some lasagna."

I threw up my hands. "I had a job interview and went to school today."

His jaw tightened. "I worked all day."

I pursed my lips. "Yeah, you worked all day at the club, flexing your arms at babes instead of guarding the door. Why do you expect me to fix all the meals?" I said. "It would be nice if you took the initiative to put dinner on the table."

"What's the use?" he said. "You criticize everything."

I shook my head. "It's the thought that counts, Russ."

"I work to put a roof over your head," he said with a sour glare. "That's enough. A man should have a decent supper from his woman after a long day." He grabbed a hold of his belt buckle to pull his jeans up over the exposed waistband of his boxers. "You know how many women would love to cook for me?"

I rolled my eyes. "Yeah, quite a few if you like dog food," I said. "If you're so fed up, go over to their houses and get your grub on."

He got indignant. "This is my apartment, you know?" he said.

"And this is my pussy," I said pointing South. "If you expect to get anymore in your lifetime, you will relax yourself and get out of my face."

Russell cursed under his breath as he walked out of the room. "I'm going to get a pizza."

"Thanks honey," I yelled lying down on the bed. "Don't

forget the extra cheese." I giggled as I closed my eyes, looking forward to a moment of peace.

❖❖❖❖❖

Russell walked in as I studied for my Accounting exam. He was usually all talk, but I knew from the expression on his face that something had to be wrong. He sat on the edge of the bed staring at me. I reached out for him, thinking about his grandmother who had cancer.

"Russ?" I said. "What happened? Is it Ma-tee?"

He leaned over, putting his head in his hands. "It's not Ma-tee," he whispered. "Joey let me go."

"What?" I said wrapping my arm around him.

"Can you believe that? After working for that fool for six years, he gonna fire me just like that," he said snapping his finger. I knew Russ hadn't done anything wrong, because he loved working at the club. He also trusted Joey too much, which is what I'd been telling him for years.

"What did Joey say?" I asked.

"He said he had too many bouncers on his summer payroll. He said money was tight from his renovations to the club, and he had to cut employees in order to keep up with his construction loan payments. I don't have seniority over two other guys, so I got cut." He cracked his knuckles. "Joey claimed it would only be temporary, and that he would call me to work a couple of private parties scheduled around Labor Day."

I shook my head as I stared at Russ. I wanted to tell him not to get his hopes up, because Joey was full of shit. I used to work for him as a bartender.

"What I don't get is that he kept Vinny, and that guy's only been working there six months," he said.

"Vinny is Joey's nephew," I said fingering the small curls my stylist left after my haircut. "Need I say more?"

"No," he said biting his bottom lip.

I squeezed his hand. "Russ, don't sweat it. There are other jobs out there. If Joey calls, he calls. If he doesn't, forget him." Russ nodded as he laid his head down in my lap. I kissed the top of his bald head. *Lord, please let this man find another job soon, or else we're gonna be up the creek*, I silently prayed as I held onto Russ.

Russ, Maceo, and I were at Camden Yards in Baltimore to see the Orioles play the Yankees. I surprised Russ with some tickets, because I knew he was down in the dumps from getting fired. I'd gotten the internship at Stockard & Gray, so I hoped I'd be able to carry us for a couple of months. I figured today we would focus on family time instead of stressing over bills and school.

The Orioles were losing, which was no surprise. Maceo and Russ loved the Yankees, anyway. It was the seventh inning and Derek Jeter was up at bat. I nudged Russell. "Hey, let me borrow the binoculars for a second," I said.

"Why?" he asked.

I smirked. "I wanna check out something."

He cut his eyes at me as he shoved the binoculars in my hand. "You wanna check out that pretty boy Jeter, don't you?"

I nodded. "That's right," I said as I put the binoculars to my eyes.

"You would leave me for a guy like him?" he asked crossing his arms.

I looked away from the field and pinched Russell's cheek. "Sweetheart, I'd never leave you for a guy like him. I would leave you for *him*, though."

I giggled. Maceo even laughed. Russ pouted. I hugged him. "I'm just playing Russ," I said. He hugged me back. *Shit, no I'm not*, I thought as I watched Jeter run to first base.

Russ up. "Russ, what is this?"

I woke up to find something glittering on my left hand. Something I knew we couldn't afford. I woke Russ up. "Russ, what is this?"

"What does it look like?" he said smiling.

"An engagement ring?" I asked holding my hand in the air as I leaned against the headboard.

"You got it," he said as he sat up in the bed.

I shook my head. "This isn't the one we had on layaway."

He kissed my cheek. "That little chip was played. Looked more like a friendship ring to me. That's why I did overtime at the car wash, so I could hook you up. That's a half carat you got there, baby!"

I sighed. "Russ, you didn't have to."

He pulled me into his arms. "You're welcome, Miss Manners."

"I am thankful Russell," I said kissing him.

"Does that mean you'll be Mrs. Jones?"

"Can we postpone the wedding until after I graduate?"

He nibbled on my earlobe. "That's cool," he said. "I wasn't trying to rush you. I just wanted to show you that I was down for the long haul. You and me, against the world. So, is it on?"

"It's on, baby. It's on," I said. I kissed his neck. Then, I sighed because I knew exactly what I was getting myself into.

Job Training

Garvey and I cursed at the computer as we tried to review the new training software. The intercom buzzed. "Excuse me for a second Paris," he said as he went to his desk.

"Sure," I said.

"Yes, Penny?" he said into the phone.

"Mr. Daniels, your wife is here to see you," she said. Garvey's sigh filled the room and I sensed tension.

"Garvey, do you need me to leave?" I asked. He slowly shook his head *no* as he pressed the button on his phone. "Penny, send her in."

I kept working, but froze when I heard a high pitched Southern drawl. "Honey, I've been waiting at Montgomery Grill for over an hour," his wife said. "Did you forget our lunch date?"

He rushed over to her. "I'm sorry dear," Garvey said kissing her cheek. "I've been busy in training."

She flung her hair as she rested a hand on her hip. "Well, you could've called me on the cell phone. Now I won't be able to make my Tae Bo class at the gym," she whined. "You know I hate to miss my workout."

My, my, I thought as I typed. Garvey got himself a Southern Belle. I was surprised. I figured he'd hook up with a Manhattan sista, the way he liked to brag about being from the Big Apple.

"Alicia, I promise I'll make it up to you," he pleaded as he held her in his arms. "You know Kim Waters is headlining at Blues Alley tonight. I'll reserve some tickets for the second set and leave work early. We can do some shopping before the show."

She shrilled like a school girl. "Garvey, you always know how to butter me up," she said.

I could not believe the two of them. I was about to barf from hearing all this generic syrup.

"Come meet my new intern, Paris Parker," he said escorting her over to the computer. I turned towards them. "Paris, this is my wife Alicia," he said.

"Hi Paris," she said with her hand strategically placed on top of mine, so I would notice the rock she wore during our handshake.

"It's nice to meet you, Alicia," I said in a flat tone.

"Likewise." She stared at my afro. "Interesting hair," she chimed.

"Yours too," I said. "Is that yak, or wet-n-wavy?"

Alicia got red in the face. I grinned. There was no way I was going to let her scrutinize my natural style when she had a weave going from here to Tennessee.

Garvey interrupted. "Alicia, let's go downstairs. I have to go to the bank."

"All right, honey," she snuffed as she batted her eyes at me and walked away.

Garvey said a quick goodbye as they walked out of his office. I turned back to the computer. No wonder he had constant migraines. I knew she gave him much drama.

❖❖❖❖❖

"I told Lucky I'm out!" Russ yelled storming into the kitchen after arriving home late for dinner.

"What?" I said as I washed out a casserole dish.

"I quit," he said.

I looked up to the ceiling. "I can't believe this."

"Well, believe it, 'cause that gig is played."

I dried off my hands with a dish towel and leaned against the sink. "Russell, you detailed cars for your cousin. He paid you well. You had it made!"

He frowned. "You think that's all I'm good for?"

"I didn't say that," I snapped. "But making $13 per hour beats sitting at home, being a proud idiot! We got bills, Russ!"

"It's the principal of the thing," he said waving his finger at me. "Niggas would come in there, lookin' at me like I was soft."

"You worked for a business, owned by your cousin. He probably would have let you become a partner. But no . . . you got to act tough and show niggas what time it is!" I hollered. "Well, dammit Russ, what time is it, huh?" I grabbed his wrist. "Oh, my bad. You don't have your watch on, because your battery went dead. Unfortunately, your watch will stay broken, since you're doing such a good job at fuckin' up our finances!"

He yanked away from me. "We'd have some damn money if you wasn't in school, tryin' to be bourgeois."

"If I was trying to act bourgeois, I'd be screwing some nice suit at work, not sticking it out with you!" I yelled. "See Russ, I'm more like Florida from *Good Times*. I stand by my man when shit gets thick. But that's TV." I stepped closer to him. "You working my nerves is straight up real. So, James get a job quickly, because Florida is real tired of being stuck up in your mess!"

Garvey leaned close to me as we navigated through a new program installed on my computer. "Paris, I really like your hair," he said. "It's stunning. Very progressive."

I gave him a phony grin. "That's me, progressive," I said typing on the keyboard. "Quite frankly, I'm surprised you like it."

He held out his hands as he sat down on the edge of my desk. "Why?" he asked.

I stopped typing and touched my hair as I turned in his direction. "You don't seem like the type of brotha that's into natural hairstyles."

He raised a brow. "Really? What type of brotha do you think I am?"

I grabbed my bottle of water on the desk and opened it. "One that likes a lot of cream in his coffee. I've seen your wife,"

I said cutting my eyes at him. I gulped some water before putting the cap back on.

He picked up Maceo's picture from my desk. "I can't help who I fall in love with."

"Yes you can," I said twisting my chair from side to side as I stared at him.

"Well, your son looks Latino," he said holding the picture in front of me.

"Filipino, actually," I said taking the picture from him. "His father is mixed."

He smirked as he moved his hand down the starched crease on his trousers. "So, aren't you being hypocritical? You must prefer cream as well."

I shrugged. "Yes, but my preferences have a tendency to change over time."

"Well, you misjudged me," he said. "I like all types of sistas."

"Yeah, but you married Vanity," I said. "I believe you would kick it with a woman like me, but I could never go home to Mama. She'd be devastated if her grandkids came out a shade darker than the grocery bag, not to mention having kinky hair like mine."

He reared back. "You don't even know my mother," he said in a defensive manner.

I folded my arms. "No disrespect, Garvey. Am I wrong, though?" He didn't respond.

❖❖❖❖❖

The tiny red light blinked on the answering machine, as usual. Nothing exciting, just the usual Looney Tunes. . . .

The first automated message said, "We've been trying to reach you. This is not a sales call. Please contact us at . . . Our hours are between 8 a.m. And 9 p.m. It is important. . . . "

"Yeah, yeah," I mumbled as I turned down the volume. Creditors loved to waste answering machine tape. "Again . . . Our number is. . . . "

How many damn times were they gonna give me a number that I wasn't gonna call? I hit the delete button.

I pressed the Forward button to move to the next call:

"Hello this is Sue calling for Paris. Please call me at 1-888. . . . " I don't know a Sue. None of my friends have 1-888 numbers either. I picked up the phone to call my mother and suddenly regretted it. There was a pause, then a fast pick up.

"Ms. Parker?" a woman said.

"This is she," I hissed.

"This is Ramona from Ameribank. Your account with Best Electronics is two months delinquent. I'll need you to make a payment for $122 over the phone," she said, trying to scare me with her condescending tone. I held the phone away from my ear and stretched my arms as she continued to fuss.

I interrupted. "How dare you scold me like I'm some child. I'll pay you when I get the money," I said as I walked over to the sofa.

"Ms. Parker, you must make a payment, or I'll be forced to report this to the Credit Bureau," she said.

"Do what you gotta do, girlfriend," I said sitting down.

She sighed in my ear. "Another month delinquent, and your account will be turned over to a collection agency," she said.

"I can send you five dollars," I said.

"Five dollars is unacceptable," she snapped.

"Then your company is stupid, because five dollars would have paid your tired salary for the hour," I said. "Suit yourself. I'll stick to zero." I kicked off my shoes and curled up on the sofa.

"This is a debt you created!" she shouted. "We offered you credit in good faith."

"Yes, and since you're taking my debt personally, like it's your damn money, let me offer you this . . . Kiss my delinquent ass!" I clicked her off and dropped the phone on the carpet. I made a mental note to call the telephone company in the morning to change my number.

❖ ❖ ❖ ❖ ❖

The firm was swamped with new accounts. You'd think after the September 11th tragedy, people would be slow to spend their money. However, we had business like there was no tomorrow. I even invested money in a college fund for Maceo and took out a life insurance policy in case something happened to me.

Garvey and I put in long hours at the office for weeks. I didn't mind, because the overtime really helped with the bills. What annoyed me was when Garvey tried to meddle in my personal business. He was Mr. Executive during normal business hours, but after hours he must've felt entitled to probe for information. I didn't sweat it; he'd done no harm so far. He was a great boss and I had learned a lot from him. I wanted to remain professional. However, we joked and laughed more and more as those late work nights progressed. He relaxed his corporate posture, and removed his suit jacket and tie when it was just the two of us. Every time he flashed that sexy smile at me I got heated, so I kept a case of bottled water under my desk to cool me off.

I sat at my desk, eating the Chinese food that I'd ordered. He sat on the edge of my desk, staring at me. I smacked my lips, hoping this bad etiquette would irritate him. No such luck.

"Is it good?" he asked.

"Um hum," I muffled.

He smiled. "It must be, because you haven't come up for air since you started eating."

I swallowed my last bite. "I'm sorry Garvey, I'm trying to rush, because I know we still have a stack of performance reports to review."

"Don't worry about the reports," he said folding his hands. "I'm used to pulling all niters. I can take them home, order a pizza, and have them reviewed in no time. When you're finished eating, we can set up the conference room, and get outta here."

"Thanks," I said discarding the food box in my trash can. "I'll be able to read to my son tonight before he goes to bed."

He touched my shoulder. "I must say, I commend your efforts. It has to be rough raising a child on your own, working here, and going to college. My hat goes off to you."

Garvey's hand stayed glued to my shoulder blade. I moved it as I got up and emptied the rest of my bottled water on a dead ivy plant. He was not gonna get me worked up tonight. I sat back down, rolling my chair closer to the computer, out of his reach.

"Well, tip your hat to the thousands of other women out there doing the same thing," I said. "What I do is not difficult. It's when I *don't* work that the going gets rough. I'm not trying to be in that predicament," I said taking a dry cloth to wipe the dust off my monitor.

"I see," he said as he glanced over at the framed photo of Russ and me. "May I?" He removed the picture from my desk before I could answer. "How does your boyfriend feel about all of these late hours?" He traced his finger around my body curves in the photo, and looked at me like he wanted to transfer his finger to my flesh.

I snatched the frame away from him and dusted it. "He's stays fed, so he's cool with it."

He rubbed his hands together. "Ah, so that is your significant other in the picture. A few days ago when I asked if you had a significant other, you told me *no*."

I placed the photo back on my desk. "A few days ago, I had my mind on business, as I do now." I gave him the *Don't Mess With Me* look that shook his mind back to corporate accounts.

"You ready to set. . . . ," we both said in unison.

"Yes," I said as I pushed my chair in. I had to use the restroom, but that would have to wait. Break time was over. Garvey's fine ass got to me, which meant I had to turn up my attitude a notch to combat his seductive persona.

❖❖❖❖❖

Russ came home grinning and laughing like he'd won the lotto. When he strutted over to me in the living room and planted a slobbery kiss on my cheek, I just stared at him. I wondered what B.S. He was about to throw down.

"I bought you some flowers baby," he said handing me the bouquet.

I sighed as I took the flowers and tossed them on the coffee table. "We can't eat flowers, Russell," I said. "You should have taken flowers from in front of the building if you wanted to give me flowers. Maceo does it all the time."

He frowned. "Oh, that's real nice. Teaching your son to be a thief."

"He's not a thief," I said. "He's just being a creative seven year old, trying to put a smile on his mother's face. At least his mischief is saving us money." I looked over at the bouquet. "How much did that cost?"

Russell threw up his hands. "Here we go," he said as he went to put his jacket in the closet. "I try to be nice to you, and I get the third degree! We can't have a peaceful evening, huh?"

"Hell no," I said standing up. "Not when we got bill collectors calling out the ying-yang."

"How many times you gonna remind me about our bill problems!" he shouted as he went to the refrigerator. I followed him.

"Russ, I will harass your ass every day until you find a job. I'm fed up, but the truth of the matter is that neither one of us is going anywhere. So, we gonna be some miserable motherfuckas up in here. I suggest you invest in some earplugs, because I will be hollering until you put your lazy ass to work!"

❖ ❖ ❖ ❖ ❖

Garvey and I got comfortable as we stood inside the file room, purging old documents. He told me stories about him growing up. How he wanted to be cool, but got teased, because he wore bifocals. He tried to wear the *School Boy* glasses that were popular back in the day, but they didn't make them in the prescription he had. He bought a non-prescription pair and got a concussion after walking into a pole. I laughed. We purged quite a bit of junk. When it came down to the last file we were face to face. The file dropped to the ground. I went into shock as Garvey wrapped his arms around me and gave me a warm, sensuous kiss on the lips. I felt a jolt that brought my vital signs into focus. Comfortable wasn't comfortable anymore. I let Garvey know.

I gently pushed him away. "Garvey, I implore you. Please

don't touch me."

He laughed. "Implore me? I'm not the ambassador."

I folded my arms. "I'm trying to expand my horizons, work with me," I said. "Look, I have a lot of respect for you. I'm not angry about you kissing me, because I kissed you back. However, I believe it would be in our best interest to remain professional."

He came close. "Paris, we've been feeling that vibe for a while. It was gonna happen sooner or later." He licked his lips as he touched the collar of my blouse. "What goes on in this office is between us. Affection after hours has no impact on job performance."

I frowned. "It has everything to do with job performance," I said as I moved to the side. "I'm clear on the difference between work and pleasure. Obviously, your loins have made you confused on the distinction."

"You speak for me now?" he asked.

I shrugged. "Whether I speak for you or not, you understand my point. We get into it, and I'm finished."

He slanted his eyes. "What do you mean?" he asked.

"I mean a guaranteed *blackballed* sign taped to my ass," I said as I looked out the doorway.

"It's not like that," he said standing close behind me.

I sighed as I turned to him. "What's it like then, Garvey? I'm engaged, and you're married."

"My wife thinks our marriage is in trouble."

"Are you getting a divorce?"

"Not unless she files for it," he said rubbing his temple.

I leaned against the file rack. "Why not?" I asked.

He buttoned his collar. "I have a reputation to maintain," he said.

"You mind elaborating?" I asked.

He paced the floor. "I'm a successful investment broker. I know my job, in and out, and I know what it takes to stay on top. A part of my success has been to remove the word *failure* from my vocabulary. I picked the schools I attended carefully. I picked my job and my wife the same way. Intuition when it comes to trading in the stock market. Trepidation when it comes to personal matters."

I shook my head. "You said a lot to say nothing," I said. "Why would you stay in a marriage if you're unhappy?"

He ran his fingers over his freshly trimmed curls. "I never said I was unhappy. I'm dissatisfied."

"Isn't being dissatisfied, failing yourself?" I asked.

"Not when you find ways to channel frustration away, so it doesn't have a deleterious effect on your life," he said. He winked at me.

I smiled. "Meaning what? Cheating with your intern?"

"Meaning, not letting good opportunities go to waste."

I looked at the ceiling. "Stick to stocks, Garvey. You definitely won't be getting the *Player Of The Year* award."

He shrugged. "I'm sorry that my perspective on life disturbs you."

"It doesn't disturb me," I said. "I just think you are among the echelon of brothas that like to bullshit folk. Living the *Leave It To Beaver* lifestyle in the public eye, but moonlighting in the sewer when wifey isn't watching."

He smirked. "I've never cheated on my wife."

I put my hands on my hips. "I didn't accuse you of doing so."

He held his chin as he rocked on his heels. "Are you happy at home?" he asked.

"Content," I said glancing at my watch.

He nodded. "Sounds like dissatisfaction to me."

"You have a right to your opinion," I said massaging my shoulder.

"Tell me about your fiancé."

"I don't get into details about my personal matters with co-workers."

"You seemed interested in my business outside the office," he said.

"I asked questions, you answered," I said. "Don't expect me to be as forthcoming with you when it comes to my life."

He exhaled. "Well, one thing's for sure," he said. "You and I probably have nothing to worry about. With all this damn dialogue, our libidos just said the hell with it, and left to find eroticism in Corporate Mergers down the hall." We both laughed as we walked out of the file room.

❖❖❖❖❖

Russ was slow to find another job, so I had to do something. I'd gone to a Mary Kay party that my girlfriend hosted and decided to sign up for a sales kit. She seemed to be doing well. She started out part-time and within six months she'd quit her retail job, because she was making more as a Mary Kay sales rep.

One day I sat on the sofa fuming from Russ's 007 phone calls. Then, I thought to myself, *Why should I run my blood pressure up over his hidden agendas. I gotta use my brain to get what I want.* Oh, I'm sorry, you're probably not familiar with the 007. See, that's when women called your house and hung up when you said hello. Sleazy women who liked to fuck your man. They didn't want to take the time to develop their own man into something decent. No, they wanted to steal your stuff. The brotha you'd spent years with trying to get right. The one you second guessed leaving, because you'd wasted so much time, you feared you wouldn't have the energy to go through those same laborious motions with someone else.

So, if you were a sista like me, you tolerated shit. You justified shit. You waited for a payback opportunity . . . Like today. I went to the coat closet and pulled out one of Russ's boots. The one he hid his hoochie phone numbers in.

"Oh yeah," I said fanning the pages of the little black book. "I'ma get paid." Russ officially had a first cousin he adored who sold Mary Kay. Shit, I had to get paid to pay the rent.

❖❖❖❖❖

Maceo watched television in my room while I went downstairs in the basement to fold the laundry. When I got back to the apartment, he had the TV blasting.

"I told that boy I didn't want him watching those rap videos," I said to myself as I walked into the bedroom. I dropped the laundry basket on the floor in shock. My son was sprawled out on the bed with a safety pin, punching holes in

Russ's condoms.

"Maceo Phillip Parker!" I screamed. I scared the crap out of him.

"Huh?" he said dropping the wrappers out of his hands.

I snatched the condom box from off of the bed. "What are you doing with this?"

He looked down at the floor. "Nothing," he whimpered.

I folded my arms. "Doesn't look like you're doing nothing." I grimaced. "Looks like you're up in grown folks business." I walked over and turned off the TV. "Now tell me."

He got up off of the bed to face his drill sergeant. "I put holes in Russ's rubbers," he whined.

"Condom is the correct name. Did you know that?"

"Yeah."

I sighed as I sat down on the bed. "Come sit down here beside me, Maceo," I said patting the bed. He slowly came over and sat next to me. I ruffled his curly locks with my fingers. I cracked a smile, because I knew he was gonna be a charmer, just like Maurice. He looked like his dad, but thank God he had my temperament.

"Remember when we watched *Law & Order* and I talked to you about AIDS?" I asked.

He nodded. "Uh huh," he whispered.

"We also talked about women having babies, right?" I said rubbing his back.

"Yes," he said peeping up at me.

I reached for one of the condom wrappers. "Well, that's why we have condoms in this house," I said holding it in front of his face. "So, Russ and Mommy won't have a baby."

He folded his arms and frowned, kicking the bottom of the mattress frame. "But I want a baby brother," he groaned. He stood up. "Kamau has one. He told me what to do to get one."

I raised a brow. "Did he tell his mom what he told you?"

Maceo shrugged his shoulders. "I dunno."

I sucked my teeth. "I bet he didn't, because she probably would've beaten his butt." I gave Maceo a slight scowl.

He screwed up his face and started to cry. "I'm sorry, Ma,"

he sniffled, wrapping his arms around me.

I gave him a gentle tap on his backside. "You should be," I said. "Don't you want me to finish school, so I can get a good job to buy you that X-Box stuff you're always asking for?" He nodded *yes* on my shoulder.

I rocked him and smiled. "Well, doing something like this might make Mommy go broke, if she has another baby to feed." He sat on my lap and I kissed his cheek. He was still my baby.

"I understand how you feel, Maceo," I said. "I was an only child. I would love to give you a baby brother, but I can't do that right now. I also want to give you a nice house, with a big yard, and. . . . "

"A Rottweiler, named Romeo?" he screeched in excitement.

I laughed. "I don't know about that," I said. "Listen, my point is . . . I got plans for us. I need to get some things straightened out in my life."

He rubbed his eyes. "You're still going to marry Russ, aren't you?" he asked.

"Russ and I are still talking about it, but you don't worry about that," I said. "You stop meddling in this room, you hear me?"

"Yes, Ma."

I tickled his ribs. "You wouldn't like it if I cut up your baseball cards, or punched holes in your Shaq jersey, now would you?"

He leaped off my lap. "No!"

"All right then," I said as I placed the condom box beside the nightstand. "Don't do this again. Why don't you go put your sneaks on? I'll take you to the park, so you can practice your catching."

"Okay!" He ran out of my room. *Kids do the damndest things*, I thought as I picked up the laundry basket.

❖❖❖❖❖

I invited Shannon and her cousin Bobbie to my Mary Kay party, and we had a good time. We ate some lunch, and then I did my thang. I'm a natural with presentations, so once Russ's bunnies broke out the checkbooks, I knew I had it made. I could tell Shannon was definitely down with buying stuff, as long as I kept the food coming. I knew Russ got back spasms, breakin' her fat butt in. I told her I was his cousin. Everybody was happy. Everybody but Russ. He got home and looked like he was going to pass out from the shock of seeing Shannon in our apartment. I sat back and smiled.

"Hey Russ, Russ!" Shannon shouted, ejecting herself from the now weakened folding chair. She ran over to Russ, planting a big kiss on his lips. He looked over at me, annoyed as hell. I shook my head and counted my money.

"Your cousin was so sweet to invite us over," she said. "I finally get to see you, honey." She tugged on his sweatshirt. He pulled away from her, still looking evil at me.

"Russ, Russ. Do you like this color on me?" she asked following him into the kitchen. Russ didn't say a word, so I asked him.

"Yes Russ, Russ," I said standing up and framing my hands around Shannon's face. "Don't these colors look fabulous on your lady?"

He rolled his eyes at me and turned towards Shannon. "Look Shannon, I hate to ruin the party, but you gotta go," he said. "I got called in to help out at *The Savoy* tonight. I wanna get some rest before I have to work." I turned my nose up when I heard him say, "work."

Shannon pouted. "Well, can't I get a kiss first?" she asked. He gave her a quick peck and headed straight to the bathroom.

"See ya later, cuz!" I yelled out to him.

"Later," he mumbled.

Shannon and Bobbie got their stuff together to leave. "Thanks for your patronage," I said as they walked out the door.

I walked to the bathroom. The shower was running. "Oh Russ, Russ?" I shouted from outside the door.

"I ain't got time to get into it with you right now, Paris!" he yelled.

I laughed. "You don't have to get nasty with me. I just wanted to say keep up the good work. You sexin' these hoes is good for business."

The Pressure

Garvey gave me a shit load of reports to analyze by the close of business tomorrow. I was swamped at work, and I was tired. I totally forgot Maceo's football tryouts, and he'd been riding me about it ever since. Bills were always overdue. Midterms were coming, and to top it off, Russ dangled on my last nerve.

As I dropped one of the quote sheets on my desk to rub my temple, I heard a sigh from my boss. He peered over my cubicle as his slender fingers tapped the metal divider trim.

"How's your review coming along?" he asked, agitated.

I sighed. "Fine Garvey, but I think I may need another day to finish. I asked Data Processing to run an analyzer on the Equity Fund for our retirement market and it hasn't been delivered yet. I need to go through that to make sure we have all the figures for the seminar at the Marketing Conference next month."

He shook his head. "Well, I was hoping you'd have all your documentation gathered by now. You've been working on the presentation for two weeks. What's the problem?"

"There is no problem, Garvey." I waved my hand. "Forget about the extension. I can handle it."

He nodded. "Fine. Finish what you can by ten tomorrow morning. I'll send everything down to Media Services for editing, and then we can move on. We have a new junior account manager coming in tomorrow. His name is Connor Drust. I want you to facilitate some of the fund training." He came around and leaned against my file cabinet. "You two will be working closely together on upcoming projects. As a licensed broker, I'm sure he'll be able to impart good knowledge on asset management. I hear he's a computer wiz also. Perhaps he can help you with some of the programs you and I haven't gone over yet."

I covered my face in frustration as he stood over me. I did not have time to train some employee. Garvey put a manila folder on my desk. "Would you take this downstairs?" he asked. "I need some transparencies made."

I snatched the folder off the desk and abruptly stood up. "Is there anything else you'd like to pile on me?" I snapped.

Garvey frowned. "Is there any place else you'd like to work?" he asked. "When I hired you, you assured me that you were equipped to take on the responsibility of a portfolio intern. Is that still so?"

"Yes Garvey," I said in a softer voice. Inside I was furious at Garvey for acting like I was one step away from unemployment. I had been working my tail off. I don't know whether he was getting laid at home, but it seemed as if my refusal of his sexual advances had him bent out of shape.

"All right," he said straightening his tie. "I'll be in my office if you need me." He turned and walked away. I started to walk down the aisle, making a brief stop at my secretary Penny's desk. She tried to act like she was busy on the computer.

"Is your ear okay, Penny?" I asked.

She appeared puzzled as she stopped typing to look up at me. "Pardon?" she said in a meek voice.

I cut my eyes at her. "I figured with your ear being glued to my cubicle, it must've stung like hell when you pulled it off an A and B conversation." Her mouth opened slightly as I strolled down the aisle.

I didn't get paid enough to handle all this stockbroker bull. I wish I would have done this internship my sophomore year. Then I would have known to change majors. Lately, Garvey had me playing receptionist, because Penny went out on medical leave to have some jive toe surgery. He thought I was a college gofer, but I was a grown ass woman. I wanted to manage fund accounts, not answer phones. Most of the calls I screened were his wife's. I knew I had a bitchy attitude, but she had me beat. I didn't know whether they were still having marital problems, but the both of them were trippin'.

This morning when Alicia called, Garvey gave me specific instructions to tell her he was in a meeting. She ordered me to interrupt him. I ignored her and she got furious. I sat at my desk, proofreading a letter when she walked into the office. She walked by my desk and asked me to get her a cup of coffee. I looked at her like she was crazy, which sent her butt switching down to Garvey's office. I guess he saw her coming, because he frowned at me when she passed. I rolled my eyes at him and went back to proofreading my letter. Stockard & Gray didn't pay me enough to baby-sit scorned wives.

❖❖❖❖❖

Tonight would be my last night for overtime. Either Garvey could accept that, or get rid of me. I missed Maceo. Russ didn't review his homework like I asked, and Maceo's interim report confirmed that I needed to spend more time with him.

As I walked into Garvey's office, he slammed the phone down. "Garvey, I need to talk to you," I said.

"What is it?" he huffed.

I folded my arms. "I won't be able to continue working extended hours. My son is having difficulty adjusting to my work schedule. I don't get enough time to spend with him in the evenings, and his grades aren't where they should be."

Garvey stood up from his desk and walked towards me. "Paris the job is what it is. Putting in long hours is the nature of the beast. Either you roll with the punches, or you don't." I shook my head as I handed him an envelope.

"What is this?" he asked.

"My resignation," I said. "Maceo is more important to me than crunching numbers. And I'm tired of you giving me your *Do or Die* mentality. I'm willing to work hard, you know that. But my son's failure in school is not going to be the cost of my success. I'll get a job elsewhere." I turned away from Garvey's blank expression and walked out towards my cubicle.

"Paris, may I see you back in my office?" he called out.

I sighed as I looked at the screen saver on my computer. "Please," I heard him say. I slowly walked back to his office. He was standing in the doorway.

"Have a seat Paris," he said closing the door.

"I prefer to stand," I said as I snubbed him and walked in.

He sighed as he leaned against the desk. "I apologize for my remarks. I should have been more understanding of your concerns about your son."

I nodded in agreement. "Yes, you should have."

He scratched his head. "I've been under a lot of pressure lately. The market's been crazy. Executive Office has been on me about revamping some of our hospitality portfolios, especially Marriott."

I raised my hands. "Don't you think I know that, Garvey? I'm right here working those reports and putting together your presentations, so you can shine for the big wigs." I looked at my hands. "I'm under a lot of pressure too, especially since you've been so grumpy."

He chuckled. "I know I've been a pain in the ass lately."

I smiled as I looked up at him. "I won't disagree. I thought about giving you some of my Midol. I tell Russell all the time that men get PMS worse than women."

He moved directly in front of me. "It's nice to see you smile again," he said as he gently stroked my cheek.

I blushed and enjoyed the warm sensation of his fingers. Then my eyes bugged, because I knew better. I turned my face away. "Garvey, I gotta go," I said stepping aside. I could tell he sensed my nervousness.

"Paris, listen. If you can just give me two overtime nights a week, at least until after I conduct the 401(k) seminar in L.A. Next month, I can cover the rest of the load."

I nodded. "That's sounds fair," I said.

"All right, then," he said as he looked me up and down. I gathered he was impressed from the smile that glistened on his face. "Periwinkle is a nice color on you."

"Good night, Garvey," I said as I fingered the pleated trim on my suit jacket.

"Good night, Paris. I'm glad we could work this out. You and I are a hell of a team," he said leaning against the door frame as I walked out. "I don't want to lose you."

I said a quick, "thank you", before I walked down the aisle. I heard an "Umph, umph" from a distance, and it wasn't coming from the ceiling speaker that played Musac. It was Garvey. I looked over my shoulder. He steadily watched me. Just what I needed, a cheating boyfriend, and a hands on boss.

❖ ❖ ❖ ❖ ❖

I came home to a dark apartment. Pepco cut the lights out right on time, as promised. Thank God Maceo was over at my mother's. I called her to see if she could keep him another day. It was ten o'clock at night. How was I supposed to study for my Econ test? My mind was made up. I'd sell the engagement ring Russ gave to me. He certainly wasn't handling things like he was ready to be a husband.

I walked towards the small candle that burned on top of the dining room table. I put my briefcase in the corner and sighed as I sat in the chair. "Lord, help me to hold out, because I can't take this stress much longer," I said aloud as I closed my eyes and massaged my temple. I heard a noise. I opened my eyes to see Russell slowly coming towards me. I closed my eyes and massaged my temple again.

He rubbed my shoulders. "Baby, the lights will be on tomorrow," he said. "I promise."

"If you don't get them turned back on, I will," I said. I pulled the engagement ring off and slammed it on the table. Russ grabbed the ring and tried to put it back on my finger, but I yanked my hand away. "Russ, I don't want it! I'm tired of living like this!"

"Paris, you have my word," he pleaded as he held the ring in his hand. "The money for Pepco's bill is on the dresser. I would've had the lights turned on today, but I didn't make it to Laurel in time. I stayed at Lucky's longer than I anticipated."

I turned to look at him. "Lucky?" I said.

He ran his hand over his head. "Yeah. I went by to see him. We talked things out. I asked for my job back. He gave it to me, and gave me an advance on my pay. Everything's gonna be all right now." He slid the ring back on my finger. I didn't move this time. Russell pulled me into his arms. "I wanna make peace, baby," he said kissing my forehead.

"I gotta study Russ."

"In a minute," he said smiling.

I stuffed my hands into the back pockets of his Sean John jeans. "Now, you know good and well you ain't *a minute* brotha," I said pinching his ass.

We laughed. He took my Terps sweatshirt off and unzipped my jeans. Russell pulled them down as I stepped out. He slowly kneeled in front of me, licking my navel on down to my lavender silk bikinis. I moaned and held his smooth head firmly in place as he teased my clit with his tongue. "Hello Kitty," he said as he pushed the fabric aside, slurping as my milk came down. He squeezed my ass just right and I collapsed onto the carpet, not giving a damn about lights, exams, or Garvey.

❖ ❖ ❖ ❖ ❖

It took a lot of guts for Russ to ask Lucky for his job back. Lucky was family, but he had a way of rubbing things in when he felt he was right. Nevertheless, he was our only hope right now. Russell needed a job. I was glad Lucky hooked him up.

My first class didn't start until two o'clock, so I decided to surprise Russ with a nice lunch that I'd gotten from our favorite deli. I got to the car wash in Hyattsville around twelve. I parked the car, and walked quickly to Lucky's office to escape the whistles and tasteless comments coming from three brothas buffing cars. The one talkin' the most shit knew I was Russell's woman. Asshole.

When I stepped into the office, Lucky was sitting behind his desk on the phone. He smiled when I mouthed *hello* and sat down. I looked around at some of the NASCAR posters he had on the wall. It appeared that Lucky was in deep conversation with a supplier, so I stood up to take a closer look at the pictures. I noticed one of a black car racer, Willy T. Ribbs. I had no idea brothas raced professionally. I'm sure they caught much grief from Duke, Billy Bob, and the rest of the crew. I looked at a few celebrity photos autographed to Lucky: Mike Tyson, Chris Webber, and Mo'nique. I guess they were his clients. Lucky was the best detailer in the D.C. Metro area. A millionaire at twenty-nine. I felt his eyes x-ray my ass through the wine colored suede skirt I wore. I turned back around. He had that same sinful smile on his face. A player just like his cousin. Ran in the family. I decided to look for Russ in the bay, but Lucky motioned for me to sit back down.

"All right man," he said. "I need that order by the end of the week. Okay. You down for some pool this weekend at the Magic Q? Bet. I'll talk to you later. Peace." He hung up. "What's up sweetheart?" He rose to come around to me.

I glanced at my ring. "No need to get up Lucky," I said.

He grinned, adjusting his pants as he sat back down. He ran his hand through his S-Curl, trying hard to look like Ginuwine. Bearing a close resemblance, I must admit.

"I see you're still prissy, as usual." He played with the toothpick in his mouth. "Still fine, though."

I sighed and crossed my legs. "How are Tia and the kids?" I asked.

"Everybody's well." He threw the toothpick in the trash.

"Good. Tell Tia I said hello."

He smirked. "I'll do that. So, what do I owe the pleasure of this visit?" he asked folding his hands on the desk.

I placed the brown lunch bag on his desk calendar. "I'm here to see Russ. I wanted to surprise him with a nice lunch, his first day back on the job."

"Well, you're telling me something I didn't know," he said frowning. "When did Russ start working for me again?"

I felt a knot swell in my throat as I opened my mouth to talk. "You didn't hire Russ back a few days ago?" I asked.

"No. He came to see me last Tuesday, and asked to borrow some money," he said. "He told me y'all had an emergency that came up. He never mentioned wanting to work here again."

Lucky picked up a loose paper clip, tossing it in the air. "Shit, I even asked him if he wanted to put in a few days a week, 'cause I wanted to know when he was gonna pay back my money."

I fiddled with the engagement ring on my finger. "What did he say?" I asked.

"He said he was gonna sell his Trooper," Lucky said. "Use some of that money to pay off bills, including my loan."

I looked down at my hands. I didn't know what to say. Finally, I grabbed the lunch bag and headed towards the door.

"Paris, hold up." Lucky came from around his desk and grabbed my arm. "I don't know what's up with my cousin. Obviously, you coming here means things are hectic."

I bit my lip as I looked at Lucky. The back of his hand gently wiped a tear from my face. "Paris, I'll call him. See what's going on. I'll gladly give him his job back. I never turn my back on family."

I took a few steps back from Lucky, because even though the October air outside was refreshingly cool, it was uncomfortably warm in his office. He moved back to his desk and turned a key to open the drawer. I saw him take out a wad of money from a gray metal box. He counted some money and handed it to me. I counted ten $100 bills and enjoyed the way the money felt in my hand. Crisp bills I knew I couldn't keep. I handed the cash back to Lucky. He wouldn't take it.

"Paris, take the money."

"No thank you," I said glancing out the window.

"You got a lot on your plate right now, with school and all. I'm mad that my cousin ain't keepin' stuff tight," he said.

"Everybody doesn't have the same ambition as you, Lucky."

"Yeah, but every man of sound mind and body can work."

"I don't dispute that," I said looking at the floor.

Lucky took my left hand and sucked on the finger that bore Russ's ring. "I know, because you're just like me. Aggressive. Driven. I love it."

I pulled my hand away. "I'm leaving," I said as I slammed the money down on the desk and opened the door.

"Wait a second, Paris," he pleaded.

I sighed as I closed the door. He picked up the money and held it in the air. "What is the difference in you taking this money now, and Russ taking it in increments, shining cars. Either way, it's still my money."

"Yes, but a brotha taking money from a brotha is different than a woman taking money from a man that would rip her clothes off, and sex her on his desk at the drop of a dime," I said pointing at him.

He smiled as he looked down at his pants. "You really think that low of me?" he asked.

I rolled my eyes. "I was gonna ask you the same question."

He fanned the money in front of me. "What about Maceo? If for no other reason, take the money for him."

"My son was the first thought that came to my mind when you handed me those bills. That's why they are no longer in my hands. I'm not desperate, and I'm not a skank. I'm a mother who's down on her luck right now. I'll find a way to get out of my predicament without owing interest to you. You are an excellent entrepreneur, but you are not my man." I said, my jaw clenched. "Russell is on my shit list, but as his woman, I'll give him one more chance to get right."

He put the money down. "I didn't mean to offend you."

"Don't worry about it," I said.

"Paris, Russ is family and all, but you could do much better."

I shook my head. "Like with who, you?"

He winked. "Something like that."

"I'm sure your wife would be thrilled."

Lucky rubbed his hand over his blue striped shirt. "Tia knows the deal," he said adjusting his gold cuff links. "Her only duties are to look good, fuck me, and take care of my kids."

I narrowed my eyes. "I'll pray for her."

He folded his hands right in front of his crotch. "She's fortunate to have me," he said.

"I wish she was here to tell us in person," I said, aggravated. "Money still doesn't make you all that, Lucky."

He licked his lips. "Sorry to hear that."

"I'm sorry more women haven't told you the same," I said as I opened the door. "Have a nice day."

I walked inside the apartment, vowing to stay calm. Russ was in the living room watching *The Young and the Restless. He* never missed an episode. No job having bastard.

"Hey baby," he said without taking his eyes off the TV.

"Hey." I sat down beside him.

He gave me a peck on the lips. "You all right?" he asked.

I raised a brow. "Fine. Are you?"

He scratched his stomach, unsure about how to take my question. "I'm good," he said with a reluctant stare.

"Yes, you sure are," I said shaking my head. I looked at the TV screen. "You know what I was thinking Russ?"

"What's that?" he said stuffing some cashews into his mouth.

"You love the soaps. Maybe you should try to get an agent. I think you'd be a great actor."

He smiled. "You think so?"

"I do," I said leaning back on the cushion.

"Well, you know I was an extra on *The Wire* last year," he said.

I nodded. "I remember. Why don't you do some research? Go to a couple of auditions?"

He snapped his finger. "I might do that. Thanks babe," he said patting my knee.

"You're welcome." I opened my book bag and pulled out a manila folder. I handed
it to him. "In the meantime, fill this out."

He opened the folder. "A McDonald's application!"

"Yes," I said.

"Girl, you must be crazy!" he shouted as he got up and headed for the kitchen. I was right behind him. He took a beer out of the refrigerator. "You think I would actually work in a fast food restaurant?"

I slammed the refrigerator door, almost catching his hand.

"Unless you have signed a contract to be in the next Spike Lee film, you will be meeting with Ronald tomorrow morning, 9:00 a.m."

"Listen Paris, I. . . . "

My palm went up in his face. "There will be no discussion, Russell. You had better be flipping fries, or working somewhere by the end of the day. You're not working for Lucky." His eyes bugged after he heard that. "The minimum wage thing will only be temporary," I said. "I'm sure you'll get your big break in Hollywood in no time. Lying and acting come so naturally for you." He looked away, veins bulging on his head.

I folded my arms. "Where's the Trooper?" I asked. He didn't answer. "Well, you can borrow the Sentra tomorrow for your interview. I don't have school. I'll take the train to work. Just drop me off at the Metro before you head out." I walked out of the kitchen. "And Russ?"

"What!"

I leaned back so he could see me. "Do me a favor. Bring Maceo a Happy Meal home, will you?"

❖❖❖❖❖

The Marketing Conference was underway. Garvey and I were across the country at a resort in Beverly Hills. I was excited to be in California, because I'd never been before. I was also proud to be a part of a marketing team known for its success in making money deals, and attracting wealthy clients. That's why I knew I had to be about business on this trip. The situation in the file room was something to be forgotten. I hoped Garvey felt that way. The hotel hosting the conference was real plush. We had the red carpet rolled out for us. I had a lot of issues to deal with back home, so it was nice to have a break from bill collector calls, and Russell. I did miss Maceo. I felt awful when I called and he cried, begging me to come home. He'd been sick, and I almost backed out of this trip. Russ assured me he had everything under control. When my mother told me she'd drop in every day to check on Maceo, I felt better. I still couldn't help thinking about him, though. This was the first time we'd been apart this long. I couldn't sleep. After a hot shower and a cup of tea didn't help, I decided to sit out on the patio, alongside the pool. It was one o'clock in the morning.

"Insomnia?" I heard a familiar voice say. I turned around. Garvey stood behind my lounge chair.

"Sort of," I said as I looked at the pool's waterfall.

He sat in the chair beside me. "What's the matter?" he asked.

I crossed my legs and straightened up in the chair. "Drama back home," I sighed. "My fiancé forgot to renew the registration on my car. Now I gotta deal with dead tags, and insurance issues. Maceo was sent home from school with 102 degree temperature, and I found out my rent is going up $50 a month."

"Murphy's Law," he said shaking his head.

I rubbed my arms. "Yeah, I wish I could veto that shit."

He smiled. "I'm sure everything will be fine," he said. "Can I treat you to a cappuccino? The café is still open downstairs."

I figured that was safe enough. "Okay," I said as I slipped my sandals on and stood up. Garvey and I walked to the lower level. There was a cabana and a fairly large indoor Jacuzzi. He and I drank coffee. I relaxed my mind a bit. Garvey suggested that I soak in the Jacuzzi to relieve my stress. I closed my eyes as I let the warm water reach my neck. I sensed Garvey watching and peeked at him.

He rubbed his hands together. "I give great neck massages," he said with a tempting grin.

"I'll pass," I said closing my eyes again.

Garvey coughed to get my attention. He kneeled behind me. "We're in a public area, Paris," he whispered in my ear. "Do you really think I would try anything dirty with you?"

I sighed as I looked into his alluring eyes, relieved that the Jacuzzi bubbles concealed my fingers working the middle spot beneath my hot pink swim bikinis. Garvey's warm breath in my ear made me tingle all over. I vowed not to yield to his advances, so as a consolation, I pleased myself under the water.

I licked my lips as I arched my head back at him. His face was only inches away from mine. "Garvey, remember what I said in the file room a few weeks ago?" I said. "A kiss is just a kiss. Those joined by the lips have the power to decide what comes next." I turned my body his direction. "I told you, I'm a woman of my word. This will not happen."

He had a somber expression as he stood up. I exhaled and lowered back into the bubbles. Just when I thought I was safe, I heard a whistle. I looked behind me to see Garvey's shirt on the ground. I looked up and saw his well toned, copper body stepping out of his linen pants, exposing black Speedo briefs. The hand that had been working my middle flew up over my eyes.

"Oh, my God, Garvey!" I shrieked, peeking at his protruding front. "Would you put some clothes on?"

He smiled as he stepped down into the water with me. He drew my body close to his. My lip quivered, preventing me from protesting his touch. He wasn't assaulting me, but he wasn't making it easy for me to resist him, either.

"You shouldn't have to please yourself, Paris," he said sucking on my neck. I sighed as a tear formed at the corner of my eye. I had never cheated on my man, and I didn't want to cheat myself out of being respected. I mustered the strength to push him away.

"Stop it, Garvey or this is gonna turn real ugly!" I hollered as I moved to the other side of the whirlpool.

He sighed as he sank down into the water, resting his arms on the concrete ledge. "Paris, we are attracted to one another." He shook his head. "What's wrong with that?"

"Everything," I said as I wiped my eyes. "It's easy for you to screw me, because you're where you wanna be in your career. I'm still climbing the ladder, and fucking you would definitely put me back at ground zero."

He closed his eyes for a moment. "Paris, you are a beautiful and intelligent woman. I'm captivated by you. I would not think any less of you as a person if we became intimate."

I grimaced at him. "You must also think I'm a fool, telling that lie." I stepped out of the water and wrapped the towel around my waist. "Thanks for the cappuccino," I said as I walked away.

Connor Drust, the new junior portfolio manager had my guard up. Some people had a certain aura that made me uneasy. I couldn't stand training him, because he thought he knew it all. After lunch, I came back to my desk to find Connor typing on my computer. This wasn't the first time, and I didn't like him in my work area while I was away. I decided to say something. "Connor, I would appreciate it if you would use the computer at the training desk."

"Why?" he asked.

I folded my arms. "Because this is my personal work area, and I'm accountable for the PC, laptop, and shareholder files I manage," I said. "I'd like to be around when someone is using my equipment."

He scowled. "Are you insinuating that I would tamper with, or steal your so called equipment?"

I sucked my teeth as I leaned against the desk. "It's my equipment while I work here. I'm insinuating that you are rude when you take it upon yourself to use my workspace without my permission."

He gave a fake laugh as he spun around in my chair. "Listen to you. You act like I'm some temp that just walked through the door." He puffed out his chest. "I am a stockbroker. You are summer help, dreaming of being in my shoes. I was on your computer, because Milt from International Accounts asked me to install some new software."

I frowned "How'd you gain access?" I asked. "The last time you used my system, Garvey gave you his password. He hasn't been here all week."

"Paranoid, are we Paris?" he asked. "I used Milt's password, although it really wasn't necessary. I strongly recommend that you don't use your son's name as a password. I'm sure HR instructed you on password guidelines during orientation."

"So Connor, what you're telling me is that you hacked into my computer?" I asked.

He got up from my chair and stood over me as I sat in the spare chair. "No. What I'm telling you is to squash your suspicions," he said. "You got a good job, thanks to Garvey being in your fan club."

I jumped up. "What did you say?" I said.

"You heard me," he spat.

"I earned this internship, Connor."

"Yeah right," he said lowering his voice. "Just like you earned that bonus for the Consolidated Expressway seminar you and I did last month. I did all the graphics and fund research, while you got up in a short skirt and talked stocks from a script Garvey helped you with."

I pointed at him. "You wait a damn minute. I did that presentation. No one helped me, not that I need to explain myself to you. You better watch how you speak to me."

He moved close to my face. "Or else, what?" he said. "You gonna beat me up?"

I felt the perspiration on my temple due to my anger. "Get out of my face, Connor."

"Gladly." He started to walk away, but paused and turned back. "Complain to Garvey, and I'll sue you for defamation."

"Envious over a little cash bonus?" I asked. "Unbelievable. Now I know why you're only a junior portfolio manager. Cry babies can't be trusted."

"We'll see who can't be trusted," he smirked as he left my cubicle.

❖❖❖❖❖

I got off the elevator to go to Data Processing when I ran into Andy. He was one of the custodians at the firm. We knew each other, because we used to work at *The Savoy* together. Andy was an exotic dancer who used to bring the house down on Ladies Night. *Long Ranger* was his stage name. The ladies loved him. Little did they know, Andy could work high heels better than any other. He loved to cross dress. Very convincing in drag. I enjoyed being around him at the club because he kept me laughing.

He was vacuuming the hallway when I walked over to him. "Hey pretty mama," he said turning off the vacuum cleaner.

I hugged him. "What's up Andy?" I asked.

He frowned. "Still working for this dump, and still pissed

off about it."

I laughed. "I hear that."

He pulled the vacuum cleaner cord out of the outlet. "I haven't seen you around lately," he said. "You doin' okay?"

I sighed as I rubbed my neck. "I'm making it. They got me working crazy hours. I barely see Russ and Maceo. I work so much it seems like I sleep here too."

He patted my shoulder. "Well, don't stress," he said. "You got other options. Your bartender's license still active?"

I nodded. "Yeah."

"Go back to the club if you have to." He removed his spray cleaner from his cart and winked at me. "You used to look cute in those fish net stockings." He looked around to make sure nobody saw us. "Not as cute as me though, when I did my thang!" he said, shaking his hips.

We both laughed. "Business still good for you at the club?" I asked.

"Always," he said. "That's the only thing that keeps me afloat. Torrance and I broke up, and do you know that bitch had the nerve to leave me high and dry? Ran up the phone bill, and all he left was a *kiss my ass* note for his share of the rent. Little balls bastard."

I shook my head. "I'm sorry to hear about the break up, Andy. You and Torrance were together for years."

He walked over to the elevators. "Four years to be exact," he said. "You think you know a person, and then they go crazy on you." He sprayed the steel doors then polished them with the cloth. "Anyway, I got over it. Now I'm in the stables like there's no tomorrow."

I walked over to him. "You be careful."

He bumped me with his hip. "Always. So, baby doll it's good to hear you're still with Russ. Y'all doing all right?"

I sighed as I looked down at my ring. "We're still together, but don't hold your breath on the wedding invitation."

Andy looked over at me as he polished the other set of elevator doors. "Still chasin' that stray kitten, is he?"

I looked up to the ceiling. "You know Russ. I'm trying to

keep sane, Andrew. If things get any more hectic around here, I may see you at the club. I got major issues going on."

"You feel like tellin' me, Paris?"

I glanced back to see if we had privacy. "I feel like I'm being set up, but I can't prove it," I whispered. "There's this new broker named Connor in my unit and we can't stand each other. I was his trainer initially, and I knew he had problems with a sista giving him instructions. When I got a performance bonus and he didn't, he got pissed." I leaned against the elevator partition. "One day he told me I wasn't qualified for my job, and I told him off. Ever since our argument, I've noticed reports missing from my desk. I didn't get certain e-mails that were mass distributed. One e-mail pertained to an important unit meeting. I never got it, so when my secretary reminded me, I was already a half hour late. You know that didn't look good."

Andy took a duster out of his cart. He dusted around the baseboard perimeter of our space. "You think it's the new guy messing with you?" he asked.

I nodded. "It has to be," I said. "I'm pretty cool with everybody else. I told my boss about the missing reports, but he sorta brushed it off. He said Connor had given him advance copies of the reports, and not to worry about it." I put my hands on my head. "One day I went to my desk to find my laptop gone. I started trippin' and rushed over to Garvey's office, only to return to my desk and find it there."

He put the duster away. "Wow girl, something does sound a little shady," he said.

I walked over to the window. "That's not it," I said looking at the cityscape. "Each intern transmits an electronic status report to their boss. One time I had processed a ton of new account applications, so I knew my stats were good. I sent Garvey my numbers for that week. He confronted me with a hardcopy that was different from what I'd sent over the computer. Instead of an app count of 402, it showed 204. I knew I hadn't transposed the numbers by mistake, because I double checked the report before I transmitted."

Andy came and stood beside me. "Why don't you go to HR

if you feel your boss won't listen?"

I looked at him. "Andy, please. What color do you think Connor is? A certified broker, who is also a computer programmer, compared to a college intern?"

He held his chin. "You got a point."

I folded my arms. "Plus, when you file a complaint with HR on another employee you better damn well have enough proof. Connor is clever, and what it boils down to is I don't have jack to pin on him. Just my instinct."

Andy rubbed my back. "Girl, watch him. Lock up your shit. Take it home if you have to."

I looked at my watch. "Yeah, I've been doing that lately. Well, I gotta get back," I said. I smiled as I touched Andy's arm. "I didn't mean to talk your ear off."

"Paris, anytime you need to talk, you know where to find me," he said.

"Okay, Andy. Thanks for listening."

He kissed my cheek. "It's what I do best."

I pushed the elevator button and the doors opened. "Come upstairs and see me sometime," I said stepping inside. "I got some new pictures of Maceo."

He waved. "I'll see you soon."

Get On The Bus

The cotton armpits of my oxford shirt were drenched, I was so mad. That Andrew stole my thunder. Paris was my assignment, and he tried to take over. Well, he should've thought twice about switching his butt into her business, because now he was gonna have to deal with me. It was seven-thirty and he stood on the bus stop at Connecticut and M Streets. His head bobbed to whatever jump-jump music he had playing through those headphones. I marched right over to him and smacked the back of his head.

"Ow!" he shrieked as he jerked the headphones off. He swung around with his fists balled up.

"What you gonna do Andrew, yelling in that high voice?" I hissed. "You ain't scaring nobody. I should be the one ready to fight, seeing as you done cut my finger with that Brillo weave you got on your head."

He smirked, looking me up and down. "Don't hate Miss Anela. You might wanna get you some hair, 'cause that gray halo you got is too tired."

"I'm old and I'm gray, so I don't see the need to be Lola Falana, unlike some people I know," I said frowning. "You may think you cute, but you still a young scrub to me."

"Why you always on my case, huh?" he said with his hands on his hips. "What have I ever done to you? I speak, you turn the other way. I gave you that manicure set and you shoved it in the trash." Andrew sniffed hard into the air then moved closer to me. He reared back abruptly. "Humph, I need to spread some brotherly love and go across the street to CVS to get you a two pack of Sure deodorant." He fanned his nose.

"Watch your mouth, Andrew," I snapped, pointing my finger in his face.

"Watch them arms," he said laughing. He moved to the curb.

"You ain't a brother of mine," I said turning my back to him.

"We all God's children," he hummed.

"Yeah, and God sure does love children and fools," I said as I shot a scornful look in his direction.

"Boss, you hear that?" Andrew said looking up to Heaven. "We got a situation. Better sprinkle some estrogen down here."

"Why, so you can steal it like you stole Paris," I said folding my arms.

"Paris? What are you talking about?" he said.

"Boss gave that assignment to me, so why are you conversing with Paris?"

Andrew smiled then came over to me, touching my shoulder. "I'm sorry Miss Anela. Boss told me to mention something to you but I've been so busy, it slipped my mind. Boss switched a couple of our cases when he remembered that Paris and I were friends. We go way back. We lost touch when she quit bartending and I left *The Savoy* to dance at another lounge. She never even knew about the car accident. Boss thought her drama on the job was a good opportunity for me to re-connect with her."

"Well, tell me about the assignment I inherited from you," I said.

He took out his compact mirror and removed some mahogany gloss from his jacket pocket to apply on his manly lips. Who did Andrew think he was fooling? He read my mind from my lackluster stare and laughed.

"Come sit down with me," he said touching my shoulder.

I rolled my eyes at him as we walked over to the bus stop shelter. We sat on the recycled plastic bench that was now chilled due to the cold night air. I rubbed my hands together as my teeth chattered. Andrew took off his bone colored, leather bolero jacket and put it around my shoulders.

"Your next case is a woman named Effie Mae Peters. Real nice from what I understand. Boss said he'd fill you in with the details later," he said.

"Okay," I said breathing warm air onto my hands. I miss the weather back home."

"Me too." Andrew cleared his throat, then looked at me apologetically. "I'm sorry if you felt slighted with the Paris case. I should've told you as soon as Boss made the change."

"You should have," I said slanting my eyes at him.

"Sometimes Rookies get stuff twisted, my bad," he said.

I shook my head as I looked at his leopard print Lycra bodysuit. Lord, have mercy. A body like Leroy from *Fame* and a wig like Ru Paul. Twisted was right. "Where are you going, anyway?" I asked.

"I gotta check on my client real quick before I head home," he said shivering.

"You want your jacket back?"

"No Miss Anela, you keep warm," he said looking up the street. "Here comes the bus now."

The bus exhaust whistled as the bus slowly stopped in front of us. I got on and surveyed the area for available seats. The middle and back rows were filled with a mixture of old timers and a few youngsters. Andrew and I decided to sit in the very first row, parallel to the aisle.

"I'm sittin' up here so I won't kill nobody with my scent," I whispered.

"Miss Anela, relax. You among friends on this bus. Besides, we in the heart of D.C. where the people love some funk. Funky music like Chuck Brown, funky fashions and funky hair, like Free from BET. They call funk, Neo Soul."

"Oh really," I said peering at him.

"Yep. Ain't that right, Saul?" Andrew said to the bus driver.

"That's right," Saul said winking back at us in the rearview mirror.

"Well, I still would like to get home so I can freshen up," I said as I leaned my head against the Plexiglas window. "It's been a long day."

Andrew patted my knee. "So, what's got you so stressed, Miss Anela? Is it just me?"

I lifted my head a little and touched Andrew's arm. "It's not you, I got a lot on my mind, that's all," I said.

He smiled and nudged closer to me. "I'm a good listener," he said.

I breathed heavily as I straightened up in the seat. I took Andrew's jacket off and placed it around his shoulders. He waited for me to talk. His sympathetic eyes let me know I could trust him. "Can I ask you something?" I said looking down at my hands.

"Anything," he said.

"Do you like the way you are, Andrew? I mean . . . Are you comfortable with yourself?"

"You mean, am I comfortable with being gay and dressing in drag?"

I shrugged nervously. "Yes, I guess that's what I mean."

"Totally. I've been this way since birth. When you know you're different, it's torture trying to conform to what everybody else thinks is normal. You got more straight people out here raising HIV statistics than homosexuals. I'm tired of hearing about all that Down Low nonsense. You are what you are. My brother was straight up homophobic. We couldn't stand each other. I died from a DUI accident and he died from the AIDS virus he contracted from frontin' with his male trucking buddy. Ain't that a trip?"

I hugged myself and stared out the window. "Andrew, let's not talk about this anymore."

He grabbed my hand. "We need to talk about it, Miss Anela. You got a heavy heart."

"I want to understand why. . . . "

"Gabriel acted the way he did?" he asked.

I winced from hearing my husband's name. "Yes," I said biting down on my lip.

Andrew sighed. "I tell you what Boss told me once when we were talking. He said some things aren't for us to comprehend, we just accept them."

I rested my head against the window as I looked out again. Andrew squeezed my hand. "I saw what you did for Pashen," he said smiling.

I glanced over at him. "Yeah?" I said raising my brow.

"Uh huh. Nice work," he said folding his arms.

"Thanks," I said proudly as I lifted my head.

"One suggestion, though. Learn to follow the advice you gave Pashen," he said.

"What advice?" I said.

"Let go. Let the past go, Miss Anela."

"I'm trying, but I can't seem to forget," I said looking down. "There was someone that I used to love and his. . . . "

"Name was Cyrus," he said.

"You know all my business, don't you?" I said shoving his arm playfully.

"Small world, Miss Anela," Andrew said laughing.

I got serious again as I looked around at all the passengers on the bus. "Not small enough," I said, disappointed. "Why isn't he on this bus?"

Andrew gently lifted my hand and kissed it. "Maybe you should talk to Boss about that."

"Maybe," I said as I held Andrew's hand securely in mine.

"What's goin' on with all these sad faces up here?" a high cackling voice asked.

Andrew and I looked up to see Pearl standing beside us. Her blue, peacock feathered hat was tilted to the side, almost covering one eye. The violet silk dress she had on was becoming, but those saggy suntan colored knee highs were not. They clashed with her taupe colored skin. I chuckled at the wide, toothless grin on her face. Pearl was around eighty-five years old, and obviously forgetful. Where were her dentures?

"I look good, don't I?" she asked, already knowing the answer.

"Yes you do, girlfriend," Andrew shouted. "You got a hot date tonight or something?"

"Yes indeed, Andy," she said puffing out her small chest.

"I'm going to the nursing home to visit my husband, Ralph. He's been calling out to me in his sleep lately."

She walked down to the beginning of the aisle and squint-ed out the window. "Saul, slow down some," she said. "My stop is coming up."

"Don't worry Miss Pearl, I won't miss your stop," Saul said chuckling.

"Yeah, 'cause I gotta see my man, bless his old heart," she sighed. "Ralph's been so lonely since I passed. Boss told me to go ahead and take him out of his misery. I'ma run in here real quick and put somethin' on him."

Saul opened the front door as Pearl straightened her hat and smoothed a wrinkle out of her dress.

"Now Saul, you set right here," Pearl said tapping him on the shoulder. "It's only gonna take a minute, two at the most, knowing Ralph. Once he get a taste of this sweet puddin' he gonna go into cardiac arrest. So y'all just hold tight. The two of us will be back on the bus soon." Before she departed, she walked up the aisle, close to Andrew and me. She shook her finger at us. "You two need to stop cryin' over spilled milk and go out and get your groove on, like Stella in that book."

Andrew tried to respond, but was caught off guard by the sight of Miss Pearl's bloomers falling down to her ankles. Pearl frowned, baffled as to why everybody laughed hysterically.

"What is so funny?" she asked with her lips pursed.

"Uh, Miss Pearl, do you suddenly feel a draft?" I asked pointing to the floor.

Pearl looked down and didn't bat an eye when she stepped out of her panties and sashayed to the bus door. "Don't mind them," she said winking back at us. "I'm not gonna need draws, anyway. I wanted to wear my Victoria thong, but Ralph's arthritic hands can't handle the string too well." She blew a kiss as Saul took hold of her arm and helped her down the steps. As he escorted her to the front of the building, I shook my head.

"That Pearl is something else," I said smiling.

"All the time," Andrew said. "Well, I hope she hurry up so she can get these panties . . . wait a minute?"

He looked at me and I looked down to see the underwear gone. I turned to see Otis limping back to his seat, stuffing Pearl's secret in his pocket.

"Otis!" I yelled, standing with my hands on my hips.

"Anela, ain't nothin' to see here, go on," Otis said, waving me off as he sat back down to read his newspaper.

I rolled my eyes at him and sat back down. Saul got on the bus and closed the door. "Saul, how long you gonna wait for Pearl. This could take all night!" I shouted.

"Patience, Miss Anela," Saul said grinning at me.

I was not amused. "I'm ready to go home," I said resting my head against Andrew's arm.

"I'm gonna be late for my appointment," Andrew said as he crossed his legs. "See, that's the problem with public transportation. Unreliable." He glanced at Saul, who deliberately ignored him.

"Boss should at least give us some company cars when we're down here," I said.

"I know. I asked Boss for a Lexus, but I'm not gonna hold my breath," Andrew said.

I pouted. "I want a white convertible. Della Reese has a convertible," I said.

"Miss Anela, she got a convertible on TV. When her time come, she gonna be walking and riding the bus like the rest of us."

"I guess you're right," I said sighing. "Even Jesus walked."

"Jesus wept, too. Probably from walking all over the place," Andrew said. We had a good laugh as we waited for Pearl to bring her frisky self back on the bus.

Oh No He Didn't

I placed the client folders on the conference table, preparing for a meeting the next morning when Garvey walked in and closed the door.

"I want to talk," he said.

"About what, Garvey?" I asked. "I'd rather remain professional."

He clasped his hands. "Please, I need some advice," he said. "I think my wife is cheating on me."

I sat down across from him. "What gives you reason to think she's being unfaithful?"

"I have a gut feeling," he said. "She's been real distant lately. I cut down on some of my hours. Reduced my traveling schedule to spend more time with her, yet she still seems unhappy."

"Have you told her how you feel?" I asked.

"Yes, but she says I'm being ridiculous. Paris, I know something's up."

I took off my glasses to wipe my tired eyes. "Well, I don't know what to tell you, Garvey. Maybe you should seek professional help."

"Perhaps," he said tapping his fingers on the table. "My marriage has to work. It simply has to."

I sighed. "Garvey, do you love Alicia?"

"I do love her," he said. "We've been together six years. For the past two years we've been trying to have kids, but have been unsuccessful. There are infertility issues on both sides." He looked down. "For one, I found out that I have a low sperm count."

I raised my eyebrows, shocked. "Uh, too much information. I really didn't need to know that, Garvey."

"Why?" he asked. "We've had candid conversations before? Anyway, Alicia had gained some weight, and bugged me to get her a membership at the new Bally's, near Montgomery Mall."

"I thought about joining there," I said. "It was out of the budget for both me and my fiancé, so I let him get a membership. He's more into lifting weights, anyway. I'm fine with doing my little Reebok Step aerobics at home."

"Yeah well, she seems really impressed with the facility, and the staff," he huffed.

"What do you mean?" I asked.

"I caught her getting into a car with the personal trainer that gave us a tour of the place. I think his name is Jesse. Should I confront her?"

I folded my hands. "Did you tell her you tried to seduce me?"

"No," he said moving a folder from side to side.

I threw up my hands. "That's your answer then."

He put his head in his hands. "I'm afraid she's gonna leave me," he said.

"You think she would leave you, just because you may not be able to give her a child?"

He slowly looked at me. "I don't know."

"Well, maybe you need to re-evaluate your perspective on marriage," I said. "Staying with someone who doesn't love you unconditionally is selling yourself short, in my opinion."

He frowned. "Paris, I really don't want to dissolve my marriage. It wouldn't be right."

I glared at him. "Only in your perfect world, Garvey," I snapped. "I admire your business savvy, but you say simple stuff at times. You remind me of my fiancé, Russell. Everything has to look or be a certain way for him. He can only work at places where he's the center of attention. He thinks I'm snobby, yet he turns his nose up to manual labor, unless it's muscling somebody as a bouncer. That's probably why alcoholism and suicide rates are high in this society. People are so caught up in stuff lookin' right. They fail to recognize what is really important in life." I got up from the chair and walked out.

❖ ❖ ❖ ❖ ❖

I opened the door to find Russ banging some long haired bitch like there was no tomorrow. It took both of them a few seconds to realize someone was staring at their trifling asses. Russ noticed me first. He opened his mouth, looking like he'd seen a ghost. "Fuck!" he shouted.

"Huh?" the woman said as she turned her head around to look at him.

Guilt made Russ bow his head. I guess the rage in my eyes burned his eyes when he looked at me. "Russ, why did you stop?" The woman finally looked up and saw me.

"Shit!" she said as she pulled away from Russell's body. She dove under the sheets. He stayed frozen on his knees. I did a good job of holding back the tears. I shook my head, looking at the woman. I knew her. Tears rolled down her face. She knew me.

"Hello Alicia," I said.

"Hell . . . Hello Paris."

Russell frowned. "You two know each other?" he asked.

I bit my bottom lip as I tried to stay calm. "Yes" I said. "But not as intimately as you do." I walked out of the room.

"Paris!" he yelled. I heard Russ jump out of the bed. His naked ass had the nerve to follow behind me. "Paris, wait!" He tried to grab me, but I pushed him.

"Russ, you better stay the hell away from me before my foot causes your dick to stop bouncin'!"

He backed off. I walked out, slamming the door behind me. Russ cheating on me was one thing. Fucking my boss's wife was another story. He had definitely gone too far this time.

❖ ❖ ❖ ❖ ❖

My fight with Russell prompted me to move in with my cousin Janise. Luckily, she lived in the same apartment building. Janise and I were cooking dinner when someone knocked at the door. She answered it. "What you want Russ!" she yelled. "You broke ass bum!"

"I want to talk to Paris," he said. "She here?"

"Why don't you go talk to that skank you screwin'?"

I walked out of the kitchen towards the both of them. I held out my hand. "Don't start, Janise," I said. "Let him in."

She jerked her head back. "You sure?" she asked.

I sighed. "Yeah. He and I need to talk. Go check on the catfish."

"All right." She rolled her eyes at him and walked back to the kitchen.

"Come in Russ," I said. "Have a seat." He walked into the living room as I closed the door. I sat on the other side of the sofa sectional. He wrung his hands, trying to think of the right excuse.

"You tryin' to get me fired, Russ?" I asked.

He shook his head. "I swear to God, Paris. I didn't know she was married to your boss."

I folded my arms. "How long have you been seeing her?"

"About a month. We met at the gym. I'm sorry Paris."

"Sorry for what?" I said. "What are you sorry for? Please tell me."

He put his head in his hands. "Sorry for disrespecting our home."

"The only thing you're sorry about is getting caught." I moved close to him and jabbed his shoulder. "I wanna ask you something. Do you feel sorry for me, Russell? Are you holding onto this relationship, because you promised you'd be better to me than Maurice?" I bit my lip. "I mean, you seem to have no problem in creeping on my ass. Why is that? If I don't make you happy, why don't you just leave me?"

He reached for my hand. "I don't feel sorry for you, and I don't want to leave you Paris. I love you."

I released my hand. "You musta picked up your love customs from somewhere in Africa, 'cause you sure are a polygamist when it comes to the pussy!"

I heard a giggle behind us. I turned to see Janise's eavesdropping butt rush back into the kitchen. Like nobody noticed she was being nosey.

He took my hand again. "Paris, I do love you," he said. "You know that. You got me so damn frustrated." His jaw tightened. "I can't even talk to you anymore. I feel like I'm competing against you. You always on my case about the apartment, my job search, and sex. When I'm making love to you, I don't wanna hear no instructions."

I narrowed my eyes at him. "I instruct you because you don't listen. I'm tired of letting you do whatever. I'm tired of being patient with you. You're a grown man. Grow up and use your balls to drive you someplace besides the bedroom."

"You went to college and changed, Paris. For real."

I stood up and put my hands on my hips. "You are correct," I said. "I did change. I want to be the best I can be, which is why I've decided to get rid of your stagnant ass."

He jumped up. "What? I can't believe you're saying this," he said. "Paris, we got three years together. Bartender and bouncer meetin' and holdin' it down. You gonna let that go down the drain?"

"Russ, the first year was cool, 'cause you got me out of a bad situation. I will always be thankful to you for saving me from Maurice. But what have we accomplished together within those three years?" He had no answer. "I think it's time to stop feeling like I owe you." I played with a button on his Polo shirt. "Honestly, I think I got with you, because you were the first man that didn't try to control me. You protected me. Moved me into a nice place, closer to school. However, chivalry and geography are not good reasons to stay with someone."

He massaged my shoulders. "You don't love me?" he asked.

I looked down. "I tried to convince myself that I loved you to justify us living together. Once I became an intern at Stockard and Gray, and you became unemployed, I realized I wasn't in love with you. I bust my ass to get good grades in school. I'm a parent, and I manage to work full-time. The only thing you manage well is your playing schedule. I care for you Russ, but I've lost respect for you. That's why we got to cut this thing off."

"Give me a little more time," he pleaded. "I'll get it together."

I stepped away from him. "I can't do that Russell."

He threw his arms up. "You get a job at a buppie factory, and now you think you better than me?" he said.

I shrugged. "I don't think I'm better than you. We're just not on the same page."

I could tell Russ was pissed. He walked to the front door. "You wanna end it, that's fine with me," he huffed. "I ain't gonna kiss your ass to take me back."

I walked over to him. "I didn't ask you to, Russell. Besides, there's plenty of ass out there to kiss, right?"

"You're right," he said puffing out his chest for a second. He stood there, trying to look tough. Deep down inside he was still a teddy bear. He knew it, and I knew it.

Despite his flagrant wrong doing, I decided to let bygones be bygones. I embraced him. "Russ, I'm not mad at you. I just gotta get from under your wing. I'm straight now. It's time for you to look out for you."

I tried to pull away, but Russ held me tight. He lifted my head to kiss me. I didn't see any harm in a goodbye kiss. Afterwards, we held hands. Russ got teary eyed. He looked for wetness in my eyes. There was none.

"I wanna still be in Maceo's life," he said.

I looked away. "I don't think that's a good idea."

"Don't be cruel, Paris. I love that boy."

"He loves you, but blood is thicker than water. He wants his mother happy. I told him that you and I were not getting married, because we weren't getting along like we should. He accepts that, and he's okay with us leaving you."

Russ put his hands in his pockets and looked down as he opened the door. As he turned the doorknob, he glanced back at me. "You can always come back, you know," he said.

I slowly shook my head. "No, I can't Russell. Not this time."

❖❖❖❖❖

Garvey rushed over to my cubicle. He sat down on the edge of my desk, smiling.

"What's gotten into you?" I asked closing a folder. "You

sure are happy about something."

"Guess what?" he said.

I raised my shoulders. "What?"

"Alicia's pregnant."

I felt my stomach suddenly twist in a knot, but I maintained my composure. "Really?" I said in an unsteady voice.

He had a proud grin when he folded his arms. "Yep. We suspected she was a couple of days ago, but I didn't want to say anything until we knew for sure," he said. "The doctor confirmed it this morning. She's about six weeks."

That's about right, I thought. I gave him a smile. He deserved one, considering. "Congratulations, Garvey," I said tapping his arm. "I know this is what you wanted. Seems like things are looking up for you."

"I think this is just what we needed to get our relationship back on track." He got up and gave me a pat on the shoulder. "I didn't mean to disturb you," he said. "I just couldn't wait to share my good news!"

I tried to look sincere. "I appreciate you sharing," I said.

"Miracles do happen, eh?" he said as he walked out of my cubicle.

I looked at him walking away. "Yes, they do Garvey," I said softly. "I'll pray for a miracle for you."

Fired

The "Diversity and Leadership" gala hosted by my company was in full effect. It was one of those parties you had to go to if you wanted to be promotion material. When the brown nosing and fake conversations got the best of me, I made a dash for the Ladies Room. I exited the bathroom stall, face to face with the community hoe . . . Alicia. We were alone, so I decided to step to her. Her eyes got wide as saucers. She had the audacity to speak.

"Paris, I want to. . . . "

I pointed in her face. "Don't say a word to me," I hissed. "You get what you fuckin' deserve. Garvey won't think you're so lovely when I tell him you were in my bed screwing my former fiancé. I know the jury's still out on that baby you're carrying."

She held her stomach with her nose in the air. "This is Garvey's baby," she said.

I shook my head. "You know you're a slut, so don't stand here and think I'm gonna believe what you just said. Hell, I'm sure you're still trying to convince yourself. At least be woman enough to tell Garvey he's not the one that moves you, so he can move on to someone worthwhile."

She looked me up and down. "Like you?" she asked.

I put my hands on my hips. "No, like your mother," I said. "I'm sure she has better morals and more discretion than you. She should have repeated herself when she told you to save yourself for marriage."

"You hussy. How dare you speak of my family!"

"I'll say it to her face. Right after I tell her there's a chance her grandchild is gonna look like his bulldog daddy, instead of fine ass Garvey. What were you thinkin' girl? A brotha with an estate home, Jaguar Coupe, and mediocre dick versus a brotha with no house, no job, and dick so good, it sends sistas itching to the clinic about once a quarter."

She wrinkled her nose. "You're disgusting," she said.

I grimaced. "No you are," I said. "I'm sure you sucked on that Chlamydia stick. One doze of Metronidazole was all I needed to stock up on the condoms and keep my lips off that poison. So bitch, beware."

I walked over to the vanity station to apply some more lipstick. Alicia followed me. "By the way, Russ has the sickle cell trait," I said rubbing my lips together in the mirror. "I got it too. That's why I never got weak and let that fool impregnate me. I suggest you get tested. Unfortunately for you, my son didn't know about the sickle cell thing. He thought his mommy and future step daddy were taking too long to give him a baby brother. So, he tried to speed up the process. He got a hold of the condoms and did a Pokemon on them. I caught him, and took the box from him. I left the condoms on the nightstand and forgot to throw them out. Damn, I can be absent minded sometimes. I guess you and my ex got so hot and heavy, you never noticed the holes. Oh well."

Alicia fidgeted with her hair.

"Nervous?" I asked. She stared blankly into the mirror. "I would be. Enjoy your pregnancy, girlfriend. Life is gonna get a little hectic after that. Poor baby . . . A bastard for a father and a liar for a mother." I walked out to rejoin the party.

❖❖❖❖❖

I saw Connor in Garvey's office and got nervous. Perhaps he complained about the fact that I refused to speak to him unless it pertained to business matters.

Around five o'clock this afternoon, Garvey called me into his office. His expression was soured. No smile. No pleasant conversation. I looked over and saw his boss, Mr. Mosby standing by the window. Bad news was coming for certain.

"Paris, there has been some disturbing evidence found pertaining to the recent theft of checks from the service registry," Garvey said. "Please sit down." I sat down and watched him spread several checks on his desk, pointing to one in particular. He put his finger on a signature. "Do you know anything about this?" My name was on the endorsement line. "This check shows your authorization, but Stockard & Gray never received the proceeds from this transaction."

I was in total disbelief. I had never authorized payment on any checks. Furthermore, I was insulted by the implication that I was a thief. I spoke up. "Garvey, this is not my signature," I said holding up the check. "I've never taken checks from the registry. That's out of the scope of my duties. Penny processes incoming money on new accounts. That may be my name, but I did not steal a check and cash it."

"Paris, the signature matches the one we have on file for you in Human Resources," he said.

I folded my arms. "I don't care what it matches, Garvey. I'm telling you the truth. Don't you believe me?" I asked.

He said nothing. My heart sank, knowing that I could've fallen for a man who was now looking at me like a common criminal. A man who obviously would've slept with me, then discarded me like a piece of trash. Looking at Garvey right now, I was confident that I'd made the right choice by not weakening to his temptation. My reputation was on the line. I wasn't going to let him or any of these fake ass executives get away with accusing me of wrong doing.

Mr. Mosby walked towards me. "Miss Parker, we have also been monitoring your computer for the past two months. Our survey revealed improper use of the Internet on your part."

"What!" I shouted. I jumped out of my seat I was so angry. "What did you find?"

Mr. Mosby frowned. "You exploring pornography sites," he said. "Entering illicit chat rooms."

I shook my head as I forced the tears back. "I am innocent of these allegations! Did you interrogate every one else in the unit like you're doing me?"

"Miss Parker we did a thorough investigation," he said raising his nose up to me.

Thorough my ass. They didn't question anyone else. I was a target. I'd fight to the end to prove that Connor framed me.

"Mr. Mosby, I can prove that I am innocent," I said.

"Miss Parker, what evidence do you have to prove that you didn't do these things?" he asked.

I threw up my hands. "My word, first of all," I cried.

"Your word isn't good enough," he said going towards the door. "You are lucky we didn't press charges against you. Garvey, please handle this situation as we discussed."

"Yes Sir," Garvey said in a hushed tone. Mr. Mosby walked out.

Garvey came over to face me. He sighed. "Paris, I'm going to have to let you go."

I didn't care about the tears running down my face. "I can't believe you are firing me," I muffled.

He clasped his hands. "It wasn't my decision," he whispered.

"Then fight for my job back!" I screamed. I grabbed his arm. "I'm innocent."

He looked down. "I'm sorry, but I cannot do that."

I scowled. "You can't seem to do a lot lately."

"What do you mean?" he asked looking back at me.

"Ask your wife," I snapped.

Those were my last words to him. I walked down the aisle, amidst peeping Uncle Toms. I almost let my emotions get the best of me, but then I got it together. I dried my tears, knowing that Stockard & Gray had not seen the last of Paris Parker. They didn't have to believe me. My attorney would be more than willing to prove that my word was always my bond.

❖ ❖ ❖ ❖ ❖

My termination had me so upset, I was crying in the bedroom as Maceo walked in. "Hey Ma!" he said.

"Why are you so dirty, young man?" I asked looking at his clothes.

He wiped his hands on his jeans. "I was down in the grass

out front . . . Trying to get you some flowers. Then, I saw Mr. Meyers coming at me with the broom. He said he was gonna beat my butt if he caught me taking flowers again. I dropped the flowers and ran. I slipped on the grass. Mr. Meyers still didn't catch me."

I frowned as I reached over to the nightstand for a tissue. "Mr. Meyers better not lay a hand on you, or he'll have to deal with me. I should go tell the rental office that I caught him sleeping by the pool." Maceo laughed.

Mr. Meyers was the apartment grounds keeper. I saw him take more naps than he cleaned up. I also saw him come out of Miss Claudette's apartment during business hours, grinning and fixing his trousers. You didn't hear that from me, though.

"Mace, I told you I appreciated the flowers, but I don't want you to get into trouble," I said. "I'll raise your allowance a little so you can buy me some every now and then."

He nodded as he sat beside me on the bed. "Cool," he said. He touched my wet cheek. "Were you crying, Ma?"

I sniffled. "A little."

"You thinkin' about Russ?" he asked.

I shook my head. "No. I was thinking about you," I said touching his nose. "Thinking that I wish you had your space shuttle already built, so you and I could get in and fly away for a while."

He groaned. "Ma, be patient. I gotta learn Algebra first. Give a brotha a break."

I laughed as I pulled him towards me. "You're too grown to be seven years old," I said playing with the curls on his head.

He smiled. "No, I'm not," he said. "I'm just smart like you."

I blushed. "Gimme a kiss," I said. He did. "Yes you are, baby. Smart just like your mom."

"I'll be back," he said.

"Where are you going?" I asked.

I didn't hear anything, but Maceo came back with two candy bars. I slanted my eyes at him. "How did you get those, young man?"

"Miss Miles downstairs gave them to me. She said the dentist took out all her teeth, and she couldn't eat them." He held his belly as he laughed. "Ma, you should see her! She only has two little teeth left. She looks like baby Dani!"

He referred to Janise's daughter Danielle, who was ten months old. I cracked up when he started doing gumming motions with his mouth. Maceo always knew how to cheer me up.

"Well, you know Mace, when people get old, they lose their teeth and start to look like babies again."

He shrugged. "Can't she buy some more teeth?"

"She probably doesn't have enough insurance."

"What's that?" he asked.

I sat him on my lap. "It's like money," I said. "If you don't have it, it'll make you cry."

He kissed me on the cheek. "I don't want you to be sad."

I smiled. "I'll be fine," I said. "I'm smart, right?"

He nodded *yes*. I took one of the candy bars from his hand. I opened mine, and he opened his.

"A Snickers bar is much better than flowers, Mace."

He already had a mouth full. "Yep," he mumbled.

I nudged him. "You make sure you brush your teeth good after you finish," I said.

He swallowed. "Okay, Ma."

We stood up. "I'll fix dinner. Go into your room and start your homework. Make sure you review your words for your spelling test on Wednesday. I'm gonna quiz you."

He gave me a hug. "I will." He started walking, but turned towards me before he left the room. "Ma?"

"Yes, Maceo?"

"Before I go to sleep, I'll ask God to help you."

"Thank you, son."

❖ ❖ ❖ ❖ ❖

I ate lasagna while I watched Judge Mathis tell some fool he was guilty on TV. I heard a knock at the door and got up to answer it.

"Who is it?" I asked.

"Paris, it's Andy."

I opened the door. "Andy?" He smiled as I gave him a hug. "What brings you here?"

"Mama you said come see you, so here I am," he said walking in.

"Well, it's good to see you," I said closing the door. "Have a seat. Can I get you anything? I was just finishing up lunch."

"No chile, I can't stay long," he said. He sat on the sofa. "I got a lot of errands to run. I was in the neighborhood, so I thought I'd swing by."

I sat beside him. "I wish I would've known you were coming." I looked around my living room. "I would've straightened up a little."

He scowled. "Girlfriend, the only thing you need to straighten up is that head. Paris what is going on with that bush? You borderline M'fu-fu!"

I shook my head. "I know. My girlfriend's gonna trim it down for me tonight. I've been in a funk lately. I don't know whether you heard or not, but I got fired."

He crossed his legs. "I did hear that. I went upstairs three days ago to see Maceo's pictures and they told me you didn't work there no more."

I frowned as I fell back on the sofa cushion. "That's because those bastards let me go without even giving me a chance to prove my innocence!" I screamed. "Do you know they accused me of stealing checks from new accounts and cashing them? What's worse is they tried to say I entered sex chat rooms on the Internet and went into pornography websites. Can you believe that shit? All the stuff they blamed on me has Connor's name written all over it."

He grabbed my hand. "Did you tell your boss about Connor?" he asked.

"I told him I thought I knew who was responsible, and he asked me to present the evidence right then and there," I said. "Of course, I didn't have anything. He didn't want to hear anything else I had to say. He let me go the beginning of last week." I wrung my hands as I looked down. "Andy, I'm so depressed. I've been beat on, cheated on and lied to, but to have somebody I don't know drag my name through the gutter? How am I supposed to get another good job now that this has happened?"

He smiled. "You'll get another good job." He opened up his backpack and handed me a VHS tape. "Because the proof's in the puddin', sugar."

I raised a brow. "What?"

He folded his arms. "This Connor dude, I know him. Know him real well."

I shrugged. "How?"

"When I went upstairs to your department to see you last week, I saw him. He didn't recognize me, though."

"Huh?" I asked as I sat up straight.

He looked at his freshly polished nails. "Connor knows me as Angel. I've only been around him in drag." He smirked. "He's one of my ponies, Paris. He's gay."

My mouth opened. "Are you serious?"

He nodded. "He hangs out at my spots in Georgetown all the time," he said. "He went to Boston U, right?"

I covered my mouth. "Oh my God! Yes he did," I said.

He licked his lips. "Blond hair, blue eyes? Walks like he got me up his butt?"

I laughed. "Yeah!"

He slapped me five. "Chile, that's him. He doesn't use the name Connor with me. He uses Devin. We hook up on the regular and let me tell you, he is a kinky little thang. Drinks like a fish, too."

"So Andy, what's on this tape?" I asked.

"Your lawsuit evidence, girl," he said. He winked. "You know me, I'm wild. I like to see myself in action sometimes. One night Devin was over, and we were both lit. After we did our thang, the tape was still rolling. He started rambling about how he got over on his company. Got him some revenge, because they stabbed him in the back. Told me how he stole checks and had them cashed. Made it look like a girl in his unit did it. He went on about the computer hacking, and how he was glad he brought this girl down, because she was nothing. He said you were sleeping with the boss, and getting all the fringe benefits."

I smacked my thigh. "That's a lie!" I shouted.

He touched my back. "I know."

"Did he say my name?" I asked.

"Not right away, but I'm good. I refilled our wine glasses and told him let's make a toast to your sorry butt. I said, *Devin, here's to* . . . And he said, *Paris!*"

I hugged Andy. "I love you!" I cried.

"I love you, darling," he said. "You know I wouldn't let my girl go out like that. I want you to be the next Oprah, Star, or whoever, just as long as you rakin' in that dough. You deserve it. I'm glad I was able to help."

I wiped my eyes. "Andy, I owe you big time."

He kissed my cheek. "Girl, you don't owe me a thing. The bill's already paid. You just gotta do what you promised."

"What's that?" I said.

"Get that degree and take care of Maceo," he said.

"Oh, you know that," I said.

Andy got up. "Listen, I gotta fly. You look at the tape, and put it in a safe place."

I stood up. "Shouldn't I take it to my attorney?" I asked.

He shook his head. "Not right away. I got two other copies. My friend Anela has one. You can trust her. I have the other. My supervisor moved my cleaning area upstairs to your old unit. I'm scheduled to clean the big conference room for a meeting on Tuesday. I found out that your Connor is the speaker. A request was put in for a TV and VCR. Let's give the folks some entertainment, shall we?"

Victory Is Mine

I filed suit against Stockard & Gray for wrongful termination. The case never made it to trial. The parties agreed to
Mediation, and I won. I wasn't seeking a fortune from this case.
I just wanted my former employer to pay for their mistake, and
pay for Maceo's college education.

The ordeal was trying, but I definitely found strength from
someone bigger than all of this bull. Andy's tape proved to be
a crucial piece of evidence. Embarrassed, Stockard & Gray
offered to settle the case. I made them eat humble pie for a few
days. In the interim, they increased the settlement offer. Before
I gave my decision on the offer, I asked my attorney to confirm
that Connor Drust had been fired. He had been. I accepted the
terms, which brought closure to yet another dramatic chapter
in my life.

❖❖❖❖❖

I was so proud of myself. I'd bought my first house. I
packed up my last box in the apartment when I heard a knock
at the door. "I'll get it Ma," Maceo said as he put his Gameboy
down and ran to the door.

"It's probably the movers," I said wrapping a wine glass in
bubble wrap. "Make sure you ask first before opening the
door."

"Okay. Who is it?" he yelled.

"It's Garvey Daniels. Is Paris Parker there?"

"Ma, you want me to open it?"

My face soured. "No. Let me take care of it. This is a business
matter. Why don't you go into your room for a little while, okay?"

"All right Ma," he said frowning at me as he picked up his toy and went down the hall. I abruptly answered the door.

"Yes?" I snapped with my hand on my hip.

Garvey looked pathetic. "Uh . . . Hello Paris," he said.

I shook my head. "Why are you here?"

He looked at his hands. "I was hoping that I could talk to you for a few minutes."

I scowled at him. "I was hoping that I'd never see you again. You made yourself painfully clear when you fired me."

He held up his hands. "Paris, please try to understand," he pleaded. "I was just following orders, I. . . . "

I smirked. "Just like a good boy should. You know that saying, *If you don't stand for something, you'll fall for anything*?" I asked.

He nodded slowly. "I do."

"You fit the bill," I said.

He folded his arms. "I resigned from Stockard & Gray," he said.

"You should have. You were much too talented to fetch for Massa forever."

He sighed. "I've started my own financial company. I have a proposition for you."

I raised a brow. "Yeah?"

Garvey handed me a portfolio with his company name etched on the front. "I'd like for you to join my firm. I need your talent." He clasped his hands together. "I'd like for us to start over."

His proposition amused me. My laugh let him know so. I tossed the portfolio outside the door, beside his feet. "Did you hear my answer to your proposition, or should I turn the volume up?" I hissed. I flipped Garvey my middle finger and slammed the door in his face. I patted myself on the back for not fucking him when I had the opportunity. No regrets.

❖❖❖❖❖

I promised Andy once I got settled into my new house I'd have him over for dinner. It was the least I could do for him hooking me up with the tape. Two weeks before Christmas I tried to call, but there was never an answer. When I arrived at his apartment, I saw his friend Anela. She stood on the porch, talking to a police officer.

She smiled as I approached. "Paris," she said touching my shoulder.

"Yes Anela," I said as I hugged her. "What happened?"

She dabbed her eye with her handkerchief. "Andrew was killed two nights ago in Georgetown."

"What!" I cried holding my head. The police officer quietly excused himself and walked into Andrew's apartment.

She rubbed my back and sighed. "I thought something was wrong when I hadn't heard from him," she said. "A biker found his body in the woods, not too far from the university. Investigators arrived on the scene and found another body a few yards away. I'm surprised you didn't hear about this in the news."

"I've been so busy unpacking these last few days, I haven't paid much attention to what's going on," I said. "Was the other body of a guy?"

She nodded. "Yes, a white guy. Andrew was shot in the chest and the other man was shot in the head. The killings may be related, but they won't confirm anything until the autopsies are done. One detective said they may have been victims of a hate crime."

I had my doubts about that theory, but I didn't say anything. My theory was that the other body was that devil, Connor . . . And he killed Andy for setting the truth free.

Virtuous Woman

2004

Missing You

My husband looked like a complete fool when he came into the kitchen where I was washing dishes. He stared at me, moving a toothpick from side to side in his mouth. I took my hands out of the soapy water and snatched that thing out of his mouth. He knew I hated to see him grinding a toothpick. If he'd played with dental floss as much as he toyed with those picks, he'd still have some good teeth left. I grunted when I noticed his pants zipper was halfway down.

Clarence cleared his throat. "Effie Mae, I got somethin' to tell ya." He sniffed, rubbing his nose with the back of his hand. "I'm leaving home. I can't stay here no more."

"Clarence have you lost your mind?" I asked drying my hands on my apron. "You're leaving home? Leaving to go where?"

He coughed and scratched his wooly hair before putting his hands deep into his pockets. "Now, now Effie . . . Li, listen here," he said stuttering. "I've had some things I wanted to say to you for a while, but haven't had the gumption."

"What things?"

"You smotherin' me, Effie Mae. You nag all the time."

"Like when?" I said putting my hands on my hips.

Clarence threw his hands up in desperation. "Like everyday!" he screamed. "Like today. Orderin' me around like some child."

I sighed as I shook my head at him. I was tired from cooking, and I wasn't about to raise my pressure over this nonsense. "Clarence, I asked you to go to the grocery store," I said in a neutral manner. "I can count on one hand how many times I've asked you to do that. The only reason I asked you today is because I was in the middle of cooking turkey legs and black eyed peas. The menu you had to have this morning."

"Don't 'spute me woman!" he said tightfisted.

"Don't what?" I said, surprised by his combative stance and incoherent words. I stepped closer to my new stainless steel stove, just in case his foolish mind confused our peaceful home with a pool hall. Clarence never did anything stupid when it came to handling me, but we're all human. Everybody got to be humbled now and then. He looked over at those thick beans boiling; then he noticed my scowl. I saw his puffed out chest deflate. One wrong move, and somebody would be wearing beans, singing Al Green's *Love and Happiness*—and it would not be me.

"Clarence, I can't understand what you're saying. Why don't you go upstairs and put your teeth in," I said.

"Se..see that's what I'm talkin' bout," he said storming down the hall into the living room. "You talk down to me. Lost some pounds off your behind from Weight Watchers, and now you think you something."

I followed him into the living room. I heard bass from a car radio, shaking the foundation. I pulled back the curtain to see an unfamiliar vehicle in our driveway. A young, light skinned woman with braids sat in the passenger's seat. She chewed gum and bobbed her head to the music coming from the speakers. The same rap crap my grandson Corey played when he came over here.

I sucked my teeth. "Well, I must not be too much, seeing as you got that young gal sitting out there in our driveway. Who is she Clarence?"

"My friend," he said.

"Your friend? I sent you to the store for some milk and honey and you bring back some child you callin' your friend?"

I asked. "What's this friend's name?"

"Madalyn . . . I mean Madison," he whispered.

I chuckled. *Lord, have mercy*, I thought. Her name might as well be Alicia Keys, since he can't remember it. "What did you do, Clarence? Rob the daycare center down the street?"

"Shut up, woman! Don't disrespect her."

"I don't know her to disrespect her," I said. "I do know I'm standing in front of a man that is acting silly. The car Missy is sittin' in? Where'd you get it? Where's the Buick?"

"I traded it in," he said with a goofy grin. "It was time for a change. Got me a new Lincoln Navigator."

"A bat mobile. Just what we needed," I said shaking my head. "No wonder you've been gone six hours."

"Madison helped me pick it out."

I grabbed his shoulder. "Let me lay hands on you, 'cause you definitely let the devil in today."

He pushed my hand away. "Don't touch me woman! You can't do nothin' for me no more. I want a new life."

"A new life? Clarence, what are you talking about? You're my husband. We've been together since we were kids. We're supposed to move to North Beach next year to build us a rancher. That was our dream."

"No, that was your dream," he said. "Spending my money on a new house."

"You don't think that child wanna spend your money, Clarence? Did you tell her about your insurance settlement from the job?" He was silent as he poked out his lips and turned his head away.

"I know you did because you can't keep a secret from a fly," I said. "She switched her behind your way, and she's been seeing dollar signs ever since."

"She's not a gold digger, Effie Mae. She's a lady," he said adjusting his lipstick stained collar.

"Why don't you adjust that zipper down there while you at it?" I snapped. He looked down at his pants and zipped up quickly. "Clarence, you found a fast ass girl that would step right over you if you were some broke, old man lying in the gutter. You better be glad Clarence Junior didn't stop past the house for breakfast this morning, or you would've been left in the dust. He likes hot tail."

"Junior got a woman," he said as he walked through the foyer to open the front door.

"And you got a wife," I said. I briefly closed my eyes as I massaged my scalp. My freshly pressed hair was starting to frizz from the sweat on my forehead. "Clarence, you've let those droopy eyes wander at women before, but this is ridiculous. What are you going through, a late life crisis? Were almost sixty-one years old. Our golden years are right on the horizon. Building a house in Southern Maryland was your dream, too. You wanted to move out of the D.C. Area, to the country to be closer to your brothers."

"Well, that was before my hand got burned off three years ago," he said. He stared solemnly out the storm door window. "I work thirty years for District Steel, and they bring some new computer machinery in to wipe out half my job. They don't test the dumb machine right and it drops ore on my hand." He glanced down at his injured limb. "That's the thanks I get for thirty years," he huffed. "Now, I can't work anymore. Can't fix things around the house right. A million dollar insurance check don't make me no man."

Clarence wasn't loud talking anymore, and his expression was serious when he looked over his shoulder at me. I got scared when he unlocked the screen door. I slowly walked up to him, hugging him from behind. "Clarence baby, I understand," I said.

He moved away from me. I could see tears in his eyes. "No you don't, Effie Mae," he said. "How you gonna understand what I go through? You're not disabled. You don't have people staring at you when you reach for something, or when you try to give a friendly handshake. All you do is boss: *Clarence, take your medicine. Clarence, don't eat that. Clarence, wrap your hand. Do your exercises.*" He held up his hand. "What's the use of exercising something that don't do what you want it to do?"

I wiped my tears. "I'm sorry Clarence. I didn't mean no

harm."

I held his hand and stared in his eyes. My eyes begged him to lock the storm door and come back into my arms. He kissed my forehead. I smiled, convinced that he had changed his mind. When he slowly opened the door, I knew his kiss had only been to pacify me. A gesture to make me feel better about his decision to leave forty years of marriage to lie with a stranger. I clenched my teeth as I looked at the woman in the car. She covered her eyes with her hands, wringing phony tears. She mocked me. I rolled my eyes and cursed her under my breath.

Clarence sucked in his lip as he looked at me. "Effie, I'll get my belongings later. Good-bye," he whispered as he hurried down the steps.

I didn't say anything as he got into the car and pulled out of the driveway. I sighed and locked the storm door. Something told me that he would be back. No one would tolerate his tantrums and wash his dirty draws like I did. He'd left me before, right after Junior was born. Once he realized his other woman couldn't hold a candle to Effie Mae's sweet ham, collard greens, and buttermilk biscuits, he came right on home. Miss Madison needed to watch out, 'cause Clarence might've been fooled, but I wasn't. That insurance check had both of our names on it. I took care of Clarence when he couldn't do for himself after the accident. My power of attorney was still active.

"Clarence can spend his pension fund all he wants, but his girlfriend won't see a dime of that settlement money," I said removing my apron.

I called First Federal to report my family's checks and ATM cards as stolen. Junior responded to the voice mail I left and picked me up to handle my business at the bank.

❖❖❖❖❖

I missed him. Clarence had only been gone a month, but I was worried. He had sugar and high cholesterol. I prayed he took his medicine. I didn't understand what I'd done wrong. I spent my entire life loving Clarence.

We met in 1963 at a New Year's Eve dance at Andrews Air Force Base in Landover, Maryland. I was a scrawny, country gal from a small town outside of Frederick. Clarence was a tall, broad shouldered serviceman originally from Leonardtown. I sat at the table with my friend Betty when Clarence and his buddy, Douglas came over to us. I fell in love with Clarence from the first time I laid eyes on that brown sugar smile. He was so suave in his military uniform, he made me weak in the knees. He could be cocky, but he was never overbearing or annoying to me. His big mouth distanced some folks, but I loved his "take charge" nature. He was outspoken, but he was also a good listener, which was a quality I wanted in a man. Clarence and I brought in the new year, slow dancing to a Sam Cooke song. We recited wedding vows with Betty and Douglas in a double ceremony on base the following summer.

Several years later, the Air Force took both men away from their brides, sending them into combat at Vietnam. Unfortunately, Doug was killed during an air strike. I was thankful that Clarence came home, but he acted differently after the war. He didn't smile or tell jokes often. He kept to himself, except when he would go to the tavern with his cousin Larry. I don't think Clarence fully recovered from Doug's death. They were very close. Betty and I remained friends, until she told my son he wasn't good enough to date her daughter while they were in high school. I guess she lost the good sense God gave her when she lost Doug. Junior grew up and became a Defense Purchaser for Lockheed Martin. Betty's pristine Bonita was unemployed, chasing after three men for child support checks.

❖ ❖ ❖ ❖ ❖

Clarence and I tried to live life as best we could. I was always a homemaker, and Clarence got a job with District Steel a few months after he was discharged from the military. We were homebodies, expect when we attended church or an occasional function at the Veterans Hall. I was content with cooking and keeping a nice home for my husband. Clarence took pride in making furniture for people as a side job. I must admit,

I did most of the talking in the relationship. I wore Clarence out at times, but I couldn't help it. I was an only child growing up. Back then, children were supposed to be seen, not heard. Mama and Pop didn't fool too much with me until I was grown. Meeting Clarence when I was a young woman was my escape from country life and boredom. He became my best friend. We've lived in the same house for almost forty years. We were finally at the point in life where a simple nod or grunt was well understood. No exchange of words was necessary to know what the other was feeling—at least that's what I thought. I got comfortable hearing Clarence's grunts, or hearing him bang wood down in the basement. Maybe I got too comfortable. There have been no grunts or banging since he's been gone, and it's killing me.

❖ ❖ ❖ ❖ ❖

Clarence called me every week. The first few calls after he left were short and to the point. He'd say, "Hi. How's the house? You need anything?" I told him I didn't need anything but him. He got quiet when I told him that. I did mention that Junior and I put the Christmas lights up. Clarence would never admit it, but I think he missed decorating the tree, and building something to add to our Nativity scene on the front lawn.

During one of our talks, Clarence told me that Madison was a flight attendant, and that she was from Chicago. He said he loved shopping for her and taking her out to fancy restaurants. I couldn't believe this was the same man that I had married. He took her to Atlantic City and the Poconos. He said he loved her, but it seemed to me she only loved him when he flipped out the credit card.

Clarence shared with me that he'd been taking Viagra. I advised him to save his money. He barely kept his penis out of park when he was with me. Now his libido was in overdrive? All of his hot air during our conversations sounded too good to be true.

❖ ❖ ❖ ❖ ❖

The last few times I talked to Clarence he didn't have much pep to his voice. I was in the kitchen baking a pie for the

Christmas bazaar at the church when he called. "Hello?" I said.

"Effie Mae," he said in a raspy voice.

"Clarence, what's the matter?" I said sitting down at the breakfast bar. "I can barely hear you."

"There was a pause. "I . . . I'm a little under the weather today," he said.

"What's botherin' you?" I asked.

"Don't really know," he said. "I got bad stomach pains and a fever. My bowels ain't right."

"Have you been to the doctor?"

"I'm not spending time with no doctor for him to tell me I got a cold."

"Stubborn mule. You need to see a doctor, Clarence. You know you got health problems."

"There you go telling me what to do, Effie Mae," he said.

"I'm telling you to take care of yourself," I snapped. "Madison must not be doing too good of a job."

"Madison is taking care of me just fine."

"Oh Clarence, stop this craziness. Having an affair is one thing, but do you really believe this gal loves you?"

"None of your business!" He coughed violently.

"Clarence!" I screamed. He didn't respond. "Clarence! Sweet Jesus!" I yelled as I jumped to my feet, yanking the apron off my waist.

"Oh, I'm all right," he said in labored whisper. "You worry too much."

"I need to worry when you sound the way you do," I said. "Is Madison there?"

He sighed. "No. I don't know where she is," he said.

"Give me the address where you're staying. I wanna see for myself that you're all right."

"No Effie!" he said in a raised voice. "I don't need your help."

"Fine," I said pacing the floor. "You won't let me help you. You don't want me no more. Why are you calling, then?"

"I don't . . . I don't know, Effie Mae. I don't know much no more."

"Well, stop calling!" I cried. "I can't take this!" I slammed the phone down.

❖❖❖❖❖

I prayed for Clarence every night, hoping he was okay. I kept busy with church work, which helped to ease some of the loneliness. No calls came from Clarence for about two weeks. One morning, the phone woke me up. I thought it was my neighbor Carol's daily call telling me Creflo Dollar was on TV. I picked up the receiver. "Mornin' Carol," I said with a yawn.

"Mrs. Peters?" a pleasant voice said.

"Yes. Who's calling?" I asked.

"Good morning. My name is Anela Grace."

"Who?"

"Anela Grace. I'm calling on behalf of your husband, Mr. Peters."

"What's wrong?" I said as I turned my nightstand lamp on and sat up in bed. "Did something happen?"

"Mr. Peters hasn't been feeling too well," she said. "He hired me last week to do some cleaning around the townhouse while Ms. Bell was away."

"Ms. Bell?" I said. "You mean, Madison?"

"Yes. Mr. Peters said she is. . . . "

"I know what she is," I hissed.

She cleared her throat. "Ms. Bell isn't home too much. Mr. Peters said she works a lot. Last few days, she has been home, fixin' his meals. Mr. Peters can't seem to keep nothing down, though. He just can't seem to get over that cold. This morning when I arrived, he was alone in the bed, vomiting. I called Ms. Bell a couple of times, but she didn't return my calls."

"My Lord," I said, putting my head in my hand.

"I knew your son Junior was supposed to come over later to set up a new TV, so I called him," she said. "He came over right away. Mr. Peters was so weak, we called an ambulance. Paramedics left here about ten minutes ago to transport him to Washington Medical Center."

I jumped out of bed and ran to my closet. I balanced the phone on my shoulder as I pulled down a fleece sweatsuit to put on. "Why didn't Junior call me?" I asked as I pulled a navy T-shirt over my head.

"He tried, but the line just rang," she said. "I told him I would call you. He went with your father in the ambulance."

"Sometimes I don't hear the phone if I'm real tired, " I said, grabbing my socks and Easy Spirits. "I stayed up past midnight, downloading recipes from the Internet. Well, I'm on my way. I gotta wake my neighbor Carol, so she can take me to the hospital."

"All right," she said. "Mrs. Peters, there's something else."

"What?" I asked zipping up my jacket.

"I took the trash out back when the paramedics left, and I discovered something very peculiar," she said. "There was a dead cat lying next to a torn garbage bag. I guess the poor fella had busted the bag to search for scraps."

I walked downstairs into the kitchen. I opened the bottle to my pressure medication, and emptied two tablets in my hand.

"Anela, I really don't care to hear about some stray cat right now," I said, putting the medicine bottle back on the counter. I grabbed a small glass from the cabinet and walked over to the water dispenser.

"There were several empty bottles of rat poison inside the bag, along with an open container of spaghetti sauce and apple sauce. Mr. Peters told me that Madison had given him spaghetti for dinner last night, before she left for work."

I almost choked on the water I'd gulped to wash down my pills.

"Mrs. Peters?" she said. "Are you okay?"

"Anela, don't worry about calling me Mrs. Peters," I said. "I'm Effie."

"All right, I'll remember that," she said.

"I do need you to call the police," I said. "The dead cat and Clarence's upset stomach got something in common, and Madison's gonna have some explaining to do."

Reunited

Junior kissed his father gently on the forehead then gave me sugar on the cheek. "I'm going down to the cafeteria to get some lunch," Junior said as he opened the window blinds slightly in Clarence's hospital room. "Can I bring you something, Ma?"

"No, son. I'm fine for now," I said. "You just feed that growling belly."

"Okay," he said smiling. "I hope Dad wakes up before I have to go to work tonight."

I swept my finger across Clarence's cheek. Despite the breathing tubes, IV's, and fluid bags attached to him, he was still a handsome man. I sighed. "Your father is so drugged up from the pain medicine and anesthesia, he may not wake up until tomorrow morning. Doctor said he's still critical."

"Yeah, but we don't put all our trust in doctors, do we?" he said hugging me.

I patted his back. "That's right, Junior. I'm so glad God gave me you."

"I'm glad he gave me a mama who could make sweet potato pie," he said laughing.

I gave him a playful push. "Get outta here boy."

"All right, I'll see ya in a little bit," he said walking towards the door. "Call me on my cell phone if you need anything."

"I will," I said as I moved my chair closer to the hospital bed to adjust Clarence's blankets.

Junior left out and I turned on the TV. I looked at the remote, trying to adjust the volume when I heard Clarence make a soft wheezing sound. His eyes slowly opened. "Hey Sleeping Beauty," I said touching his shoulder. I glanced over at the TV. "You're just in time for Cosby." Watching *The Cosby Show* was one of our favorite past times. Clarence briefly looked at the TV mounted to the wall. He winced and held his chest.

"Clarence, you want me to call the nurse?" I asked rising from my chair. He mouthed an inaudible *no* as I reached for the call button.

"I think the nurse needs to check on you," I said. He motioned for me to sit back down as he struggled to lift his head. "Relax, Clarence. Don't try to do too much. You wanna be raised a little?" He nodded slowly. I noticed a tear creep out of the corner of his eye.

"I'm sorry, Effie Mae," he whispered as he reached for my hand.

"Shh . . . Save your energy," I said.

"I gotta say something," he said. "I knew Madison was using me, but I guess my pride wouldn't let me admit to you that I was wrong. When I found out your attorney blocked the settlement funds, I got angry. I told myself I didn't need you. She wanted me to fight you in court, but I knew all along I wasn't gonna do it. Deep down inside, I believed you were still protecting me."

"I was protecting you, Clarence," I said as I held his hand firmly in mine. "I froze those accounts, because I realized that gal was a leech from the moment I saw her in our driveway."

"She took out insurance policies on me," he said.

"Well, she wasn't smart enough to clean up her mess before she deserted you," I said. "The police found her fingerprints everywhere. She gonna be dealt with and justice will be served, you mark my words."

"You forgive me, Effie Mae?" he asked in a meek tone.

I smiled. "I'm here with you, aren't I?" I said. "Of course I forgive you, sweetie."

Clarence breathed a sigh of relief. He looked over at the monitors beeping. "I feel death setting in, Effie Mae," he said in a hoarse voice. "I had a heart attack and barely made it through. That poison ate half my stomach. I taste decay in my mouth. Ain't nothing sweet about me no more. It's been that way for a while now."

I squeezed his hand. "Don't talk like that," I said. "I prayed for healing from the Lord, and that's all you gonna need to get well."

"You talking crazy, woman," he said, closing his eyes for a second. "You and I both know I'm not gonna make it out of this hospital."

I nudged him. "You're the one talking crazy, Clarence," I said. "You'll be home eating a fresh pot of turkey legs and beans before you know it!"

He shook his head. "I was such a fool," he said. "I can't believe I messed with a woman who would do such a thing. I guess I got what I deserved for hurting you."

I exhaled. "Clarence, you made a mistake," I said. "You hurt me, but I wasn't playing when I recited our wedding vows. Love bears all things. I may not be Madison, but I'm a faithful wife. The Bible says in First Peter, Chapter Three: "Wives be submissive to your husbands, so that some, though they do not obey the word, may be won without a word by the behavior of their wives, when they see your reverent and chaste behavior."

"You've always hung in there with me, Effie Mae," he said. "Putting up with my foolishness."

"Clarence, you can call yourself a fool all you want, but you're my fool—and I'm just as in love with you as the day we met in '63 on New Years Eve."

His fingertips tenderly rubbed the back of my hand. "I love you too," he said. There was a cough mixed in with his chuckle. "We had some good times back then, didn't we? Sometimes, I wish I could go back to those days."

"You can, baby," I said. "Just close your eyes and let those memories take you back. I ain't going nowhere."

Clarence smiled as he closed his eyes. The warmth in his palm began to fade. I placed his hand on my breast for comfort. My husband was leaving me again. Though, this time I knew he would be in good hands.

Saving Grace

Anela helped me prepare for visitors after the funeral. She understood my pain, because her husband Gabriel had passed recently. The repast went fine and surprisingly, guests didn't linger long. Anela and I finished cleaning up the kitchen. "Anela, you gonna have to take some of this food home with you. I got enough to feed an army!" I said.

"I appreciate that Effie," she said. "I can eat leftovers for the rest of the week."

"That's right," I said getting some containers out of the pantry. Clarence came to mind and I began to chuckle.

"Effie? What are you laughing about?" she asked.

"I know Clarence is turning in his grave with his lips poked out," I said. "He never missed a meal of fried fish and collard greens 'til now!"

She laughed. "Those filets were good, especially with a little dab of hot sauce."

"You know we got to have our hot sauce," I said.

"That's true," she said. "There's nothing like a good meal to calm the weary."

"Anela, you've been so helpful these past few days. Seems like I didn't have the energy to clean this old house and cook for visitors."

"It was no trouble, Effie. I wanted to help. I know what it's like to lose someone whose been special to you for so long."

"Well, God bless you, because you've been a comfort to me," I said. "My mama always said there were angels on earth."

Her face glowed when she smiled. "Really. I believe that

too," she said.

We walked into the dining room. I pointed to the platters on the table. "Help yourself," I said. "I'm gonna taste some of this apple pie Mervyn brought from the church. Everything should be real good, except that chicken casserole in the red dish over there. Cousin Dot made it. That woman swears she sayin' somethin' in the kitchen, but I don't mess with nothing she makes. I wouldn't even feed her food to a stray cat. Talk about something that will make you croak?" Anela and I had a good laugh as we sat down to the dining room table.

Anela told me she would come back to get her card tables the next day, but I never heard from her. I called the house and the phone just rang. Later on that evening, I went by her house. A neighbor Cyrus came from across the street to tell me Anela had been killed in a car accident on the Baltimore-Washington Parkway. I couldn't believe it.

Life Is But A Dream

Rain To Roses

Sometimes weeping endured for more than a night. God seemed to be taking his angels fast, like a thief in the night. Anela Grace was her name, but I called her still waters. She was gentle by nature and knew how to talk to you without saying a word. My friend, still waters.

Anela's funeral was at Case Funeral Home. Now I knew the Case family for years. They gave true meaning to the saying, "gone on to glory". Folk weren't even cold yet before they closed the box and wheeled them out the place. Ronnie Case started the business, but he got too senile. After being sued a couple of times for mixin' folk up, he decided to let his sons Ronnie Jr. And Randy take over. Those boys smiled and took people's money at the same time. A casket the price of a Mercedes and a drive-thru service to match.

I ignored the Las Vegas style carpets and pillars as I walked through the funeral home. I ran into Ronnie Jr. "Miss Effie," he said with open arms.

I extended my hand for a handshake. "How are you Ronnie? You look well."

"Oh, Miss Effie. God is so good."

"All the time Ronnie. Well, seems like you're doing all right," I said scanning his suit. "Business okay?"

"Yes, our ministry has been such a blessing. You don't know how rewarding it is to comfort those in the hour of bereavement, Miss Effie."

Yeah right, I thought as I smiled.

"You knew Miss Anela?" he asked.

"Yes, she was such a lovely woman," I said.

"She was indeed. The Selah Room will be open in a few minutes. Why don't you sit in the parlor? I'll be sure to come and get you."

"Fine Ronnie." I took a handkerchief out of my purse as he turned to leave. I had to wipe my tears from his cologne. He must have used the whole bottle. As I got myself together, a pretty young woman came into the parlor. She gave me a pleasant smile. "Good morning," I said.

"Good morning," she said sitting beside me. "I'm Hailee. Hailee Shaw."

"It's nice to meet you Hailee. I'm Effie Mae Peters." We shook hands.

"You here for Anela's service?" she asked.

"Yes, I'm here to say goodbye," I said. "Her death was just so sudden, you know?"

"Yes. I didn't get a chance to spend a lot of time with her. She helped me through some family issues. She convinced me to stay in college." Hailee looked down at her hands. I could see a tear running down her cheek. I touched her on the shoulder.

"Sweetheart, I'm sure Anela understood. You need a tissue?" I asked reaching for my purse.

"No thanks," she said. "I'll be all right."

Another young lady walked in. "Hello," she said smiling.

"Oh my God," Hailee said covering her mouth. "You're Onyx Devoe!" Hailee was so excited, but she calmed down once she remembered she was in a funeral parlor. "I'm sorry. I didn't mean to get loud. I love your CD. You're one of my favorite singers."

"What's your name?" Onyx asked sitting on the chaise lounge.

"Hailee."

"Thanks Hailee," she said. "People have been very supportive. I can't tell you how much that means to me."

I was clueless as to who this child was. I'm sure she could tell by the expression on my face. "How are you Ma'am?" she said standing up to greet me. "I'm Onyx Devoe."

I shook her hand. "A very famous Onyx Devoe from the way Miss Hailee carried on." We all laughed. "My name is Effie Mae Peters, Onyx."

"Pleased to meet you," she said.

"Did Anela work for you, Onyx?" Hailee asked.

"No, she was a friend of the family," she said. "I lost a baby recently. Anela was such a great help to me during that time. I probably wouldn't have pursued my singing career if it wasn't for her encouragement."

"Lord, to lose a child. Can't get no worse than that," I said. "Sorry for your loss, sweetheart."

"Thanks Effie," Onyx said. "Anela taught me how to be strong. She will be greatly missed."

We sat in silence for a while. Another woman came in. "Hello," she said. "I'm Paris."

"I'm Effie," I said.

"Paris?" Hailee said.

Paris looked over at Hailee. "Hailee?"

"Yeah girl." They hugged.

"Hailee, how you doin'?" Paris asked. "I haven't seen you since two years ago at The Black Family Reunion in D.C."

"I know," Hailee said. "How are you?"

"I'm hanging in there," Paris said. "Still in school."

"Me too," Hailee said. "You here for service?"

"Yeah, Andy and I used to work together."

"Oh, you called her Andy?" I said.

"Yes Ma'am," Paris said.

"That's nice, I called her Ann sometimes. Were you and Hailee classmates?" I asked.

"No, we used to work at the same nightclub, back when I lived in Baltimore," Paris said.

"Nightclub?" I said. "Y'all don't look a day over eighteen!" They laughed.

"Paris, you know who this is," Hailee said pointing to Onyx.

"For sure," Paris said. "Hey Onyx."

"Your hair cut is sharp girl," Onyx said to Paris.

"Thanks. That chinchilla fur you're wearing is nice. And I loved the duet you did with Jazz from Dru Hill," Paris said.

"I appreciate that," Onyx said. "You all right over there, Effie?"

"Yes," I said wiping my eyes. "It's nice to see our young black women doing well."

We all started to get a little misty when funky boy walked in.

"Ladies, the room is open," Ronnie said. "Take as much time as you like." He led the way as we entered. I was the first to reach the casket. My mouth went wide open when I saw the body. The other ladies looked shocked as well.

"Miss Effie?" he said. "Is something wrong?"

"Yes Ronnie there is," I said. "This ain't Anela."

"Excuse me?" Ronnie said.

"Is your father working here part time because this is not the right body," I said.

"Now Miss Effie," he said tapping my shoulder. "You try to calm down. Your grief has you hallucinating."

"Boy, don't disrespect me," I said pushing his hand away. "You got some nerve calling me crazy when your daddy used to lose people's kinfolk. I think he done struck again."

"Effie is right," Onyx said. "This is definitely not Anela."

Paris's mouth was opened as she shook her head. "Anela?" she whispered. "Anela passed? I didn't know . . . I'm here for Andy." She hugged herself, trying to make sense out of this mess.

I squeezed her hand. "Don't worry baby," I said. "I'm gonna get some answers, because this woman is not Anela, and obviously not your friend, either."

"Anela was older than this," Hailee said peering into the casket.

"And she was full figured with short hair," Onyx said.

"Huh?" Hailee and I said in unison.

"Excuse me," Paris said to Ronnie Jr. "Is this your only

funeral today, because I think I'm in the wrong place."

"Me too," Hailee said shaking her head.

I pointed to the door. "Ladies I think we should discuss this with Ronnie in another room," I said. "Let's leave this woman in peace."

"I agree," Paris said. We walked out to the hall.

"Ladies, what seems to be the problem?" Ronnie asked.

"Your cologne got you high Ronnie?" I asked. "That woman is not Anela!"

"Miss Effie, the woman in that room is Anela Grace," he insisted.

"Ronnie, where's your brother?" I said. "I'm gonna get to the bottom of this. Ladies I'll be right back. Oh, I left my purse in the room. Ronnie, you come with me."

We walked back into the room and I screamed. The body was missing from the casket. The ladies rushed in.

"This is too freaky for me!" Ronnie yelled. He back peddled towards the door.

"Ronnie, you come back here!" I shouted. "How you gonna be scared of souls, and you own a funeral home? Ain't that something?"

Ronnie didn't pay me no mind. He ran out the door, calling to his brother. Onyx got light headed at the first pew and Paris ran over to fan her. Either she couldn't take the confusion, or that fur coat got too warm. I was headed to the office when Hailee called out to me. "Miss Effie?" she said. "Wait. There's a note inside the casket." She handed it to me. I opened the white envelope and began to read the message:

Hailee, Onyx, Paris, and Effie,

You came to pay homage to the dead but no one has died. Please don't mourn. Now is not the time to embrace sadness. It is time to celebrate life. A new life each of you was given. You asked for help, and help was granted. Don't fret over an empty casket. Once you understand why it is empty, you will understand His love. Peace be with you, always.

-Anela

I looked over at the ladies. Looked at each of their faces. Looked through the tears.

We all got stories. Some bitter, some sweet. Anela brought us together for a reason. I suspect she wanted to turn troubled waters into still waters. I smiled and put my arm around Hailee as we walked over to Onyx and Paris huddled at the pew. "Ladies, it's time to go," I said. "There's a coffee shop right down the street. Why don't we go sit for a while? Have a little talk."

"All right, Miss Effie," Hailee said as we all joined hands. We walked out of the room, never looking back.

Forgiven

The notion of confronting my husband's killer made me uneasy. I placed a hand on my gurgling stomach as I walked into the women's correctional facility in Lorton, Virginia. I was nervous as I walked down the dimly lit visitor corridor, but I'd promised God that I wouldn't hold bitterness in my heart towards Madison. She was His child, and I was woman enough to make peace with her.

I waited in my cubicle, staring through the Plexiglas window into an empty room. After a couple of minutes of waiting, the female correctional officer brought Madison through the door. The officer removed her handcuffs and pointed to the booth where I was located. Madison took a few steps over to the window, then stopped. Her jaw locked, as she stood frozen in disbelief. The officer instructed her to sit down to face me. Although a dirty and scratched piece of Plexiglas separated us, I clearly saw the woman who had ended my marriage.

Madison sat down at the booth with her eyes fixed on me. We picked up our phone receivers at the same time. "What do you want with me, Effie?" she said with a frown. "I heard enough from you at the hearing. What else do you have to say?"

"I'm not here out of anger, Madison," I said. "I could hate you, but I don't. I'm a Christian woman, and the Bible says I gotta love my enemies. That's why I'm here." I swallowed hard and closed my eyes momentarily. "To tell you, I love you."

Madison reared her head back, laughing hysterically as she dropped the phone on the counter. My palm was covered in sweat as I gripped the phone, wishing I could break the glass to shake that girl. I saw the correctional officer shout at Madison and she settled back down. She rolled her eyes as she picked the receiver back up.

"Why don't you get out of my face, old lady," she said with her teeth clenched. "You don't know me."

I pitied the child who scowled at me for no reason. I moved closer to the glass, staring into her spiteful eyes. "Madison, I don't know you, but you better pray somebody knows you at the pearly gates on Judgment Day."

"Whatever," she said, putting her hand on the glass to cover my face.

Convinced that there was nothing I could do for this confused spirit, I held a Bible up in the air. "I had this book for you and an angel pin, but Security said I wasn't allowed to give them to you, " I said. "They did tell me that all prisoners had access to Bibles."

Madison sat stone-faced as I slowly rose to my feet, holding the receiver snug at my ear. "Maybe one day you'll be in the mood for this," I said as I looked at the Bible under my arm. "Learn to love something other than money."

I gently placed the phone down and walked away, praising God for saving me from the hopeless life I saw behind the window.

Black Butterfly

Time flew by. I started my professional singing career a year ago and my first album, *Black Satin*, went platinum. I did a successful U.S. Concert tour, and I was nominated for a Grammy. Sometimes I still pinched myself to make sure I wasn't dreaming. Imagine being down on your luck for so many years, then in what seemed like an instant, everything was right again. Like a rainbow rushed in to stop a flood gate of tears. God showed me life doesn't always have to be bitter.

My publicist Stacey walked in my office as I reviewed promotional campaigns for the next album. "For you, Ms. Devoe," she said smiling.

I frowned as I took the huge bouquet of red roses from her hands. "From who?" I asked.

She shrugged. "I don't know. Here's the card."

I took the card from her and opened it. It read: *You'll get that Grammy, my diva sista. I wanted you to know I'm fine, and trust me when I say . . . your health is fine. The surgery was a dream. Your blessings are a reality. Peace and love from Anela, and Melody—who looks more like you each day.*

The flowers fell to my desk as I broke down in tears. Stacey ran over to me. "Onyx, what is it? What can I do?" she asked as she handed me a tissue.

I wiped my face and exhaled. I grabbed Stacey's hand. "I'm fine, Stacey. The flowers are from a dear friend that I haven't seen in a while."

She leaned on my desk. "Must be a *very* special friend to have you teary eyed."

I nodded. "You're right."

"Well, I'm getting ready to leave," she said as she got up. "You need anything before I go?"

I picked up the bouquet and smelled the flowers. "No, I'm okay. Go home to that fine firefighter of yours."

Stacey blushed and swayed her hip. "You know, he has an older brother who is a firefighter in New York. Very nice, and very fine." She gave me a sly grin. "Interested?"

I laughed. "Not now, but I may need my sprinklers checked one day, so keep his number handy!"

She shook her head, "All right, see ya tomorrow." She walked to the door then snapped her finger as she turned around quickly. "I almost forgot. You had three messages while you were on the phone with Clive," she said handing me the pink message slips.

"Thanks Stacey. Take care." She left. I looked at the messages. One was from my mother, one was from my choreographer, and one was from Wayne. I crumpled his message into my fist. I did an Air Jordan, and the ball successfully went into the waste basket. Then I realized that trash would not be picked up again until the next evening. I got up from my chair and walked over to retrieve the message from the basket. I unraveled the ball as I walked to the paper shredder. I didn't trust myself to keep it in the waste basket. I dropped the paper in the slot, and turned the shredder on. I sighed. "Better," I said as I dusted off my hands and walked back to my desk. "Much better."

Ribbons In The Sky

You Are Cordially Invited

White doves ascended into the sky as Hailee and Isaac sealed their union with a kiss. I breathed a sigh of relief, knowing God had to move mountains for this day to happen.

"You crying again, Miss Effie?" Paris asked handing me a tissue.

"I never stopped," I said dabbing my eyes. "I'm so happy for those two."

"They were meant for each other," Paris said, raising her camera to capture Mr. And Mrs. Isaac Graham jumping the broom.

Onyx sang *Lord Lift Us Up Where We Belong* as liturgical dancers gracefully waved pastel ribbons in the air. The happy couple strolled down the aisle, waving at the guests. I held my chest, overwhelmed with emotion. Paris put her arm around me as we watched the wedding party depart to the water garden for wedding pictures.

"I never knew getting married in a cemetery could be so beautiful," Paris said.

"Yes Lord, this glorious day should've been taped for Oprah," I said. "Definitely the prettiest wedding I've ever seen."

We looked back at Onyx who smiled at us. She was regal in her blue chiffon dress. "Onyx outdid herself, singing 'The Lord's Prayer' during the ceremony," Paris said.

"Yes indeed," I said. "That girl made my soul shake she

sounded so good." I kissed Paris's cheek. "All y'all somethin' else. My sweet little babies. You, Hailee, and Onyx have become the daughters I never had."

"And you know we got love for ya, Miss Effie," Paris said hugging me.

I blushed. "I can't wait for our luncheon date next month so Hailee can tell us all about the honeymoon. I heard Aruba is lovely."

Paris smiled as she smoothed down one of my spiral curls. "Miss Effie, I was wondering if we could move the location for our next luncheon date?"

"Why?" I asked.

"I know you've enjoyed hosting it at your place since we stopped meeting at the coffeehouse, but I wanted to have everybody over to my new house. I'm finally unpacked and settled, and you deserve a break. We can't get you to sit down once you start clanking pots and pans in the kitchen. You should let your girls handle the cooking this time."

I raised an eyebrow at Paris. "Did you get that Rottweiler?"

"You know I did," Paris said sucking her teeth. "I promised Maceo."

"Well, keep him close to you, because I don't wanna have to spice him up with a little pepper, you know what I mean?" I said as I playfully bumped her hip.

"Miss Effie, you need to stop," Paris said. "He's only a puppy."

"Yeah, with puppy sharp teeth," I said.

"I'm surprised at you. You got a new doggie."

"Uh huh. A dog who thinks he's a cat, jumping all over my furniture. That Jack Russell watches his belly expand more than he watches my house."

"Stop feeding him pork chops with onion gravy and maybe he'll be all right," she said. We laughed. "Paris, I think I will take you up on your offer," I said. "Doctor said my pressure is high." I looked down. "I need to rest these swollen ankles."

"Great. Now, who is that handsome gentleman admiring you from the groom's side," she said leaning her head towards the pew directly across from us.

I giggled when the gentleman's eyes caught mine. "Oh, that's Mr. Harris," I said. "I met him at the rehearsal dinner last night. He's Isaac's uncle."

"He sure seems interested in you," she said. "Is there another wedding in the works?"

I simply shrugged as I kept my focus on the chocolate man with the curly gray hair.

Paris laughed. "I'm gonna tell Hailee to throw the wedding bouquet to you!"

"If I catch it, I'm not gonna complain," I said winking at Paris. "It's about time I had some fresh roses."

At Last

God, how could something so wonderful come from me? I thought as I watched my daughter dance with her father.

"How you feel, Pashen?" Anela asked, rubbing my back. We stood inside a hilltop gazebo at Woodmoor Gardens Cemetery, watching wedding guests party inside a ballroom tent.

"I got mixed emotions," I said wiping my eyes. "Hailee's happy, and she has a good man to take care of her. I just wish I could've given her peace when I was with her. I've changed so much."

Anela smiled as she dabbed my eyes with her handkerchief. "Hailee's changed too," she said. "She's wiser and more confident. I believe it's from loving you."

"You always know what to say, Anela," I said as we sat in the gazebo rocker.

"Pashen, you are that child's greatest inspiration. She fought for you because of love. What you feelin' in your soul is the same thing she's feelin' today."

I smiled. "I can't wait to see more grandbabies. That Lena is a cutie pie."

"She sure is," Anela said as we enjoyed Lena twirling in front of Isaac on the dance floor.

"Hailee looks fabulous in that wedding dress," I said. "That thing never fit me right." I shook my head. "Jeff finally got the big wedding he wanted. He and Connie eloped, but he's celebrating in style with his little girl."

"Are you relieved that Hailee knows the truth?" Anela asked.

"Yeah," I said. "She's always loved Jeff. Jeff and I were young and dumb, making a baby. He'd moved out of the city to Towson before I even knew I was pregnant. Once I found out, I didn't want to cause controversy. His father was the first black Fire Chief in Baltimore. When we became cops, I thought about telling him, but he was newly married to Connie." I sighed. "Maybe I was wrong, but I thought keeping it to myself was the best thing to do."

"Jeff and Hailee are together now, and that's all that matters," Anela said.

"I agree," I said. "Hailee put two and two together when she found that old picture of Jeff and me at the State Fair when we were fourteen."

"I guess that was God's special way of turning back the hands of time," Anela said.

"I guess so," I said squeezing her soft hand.

A car horn honked from behind, startling Anela. "Who is that?" she said, squinting at the man who waved from a distance.

"That's our ride," I said.

"Our ride?" Anela frowned. "I thought we were taking the bus?"

"Not anymore," I said, grinning. I stood up in the gazebo and blew a kiss to Hailee. It was time to go. "Come on, Anela." I pulled her up from the rocker. She held my arm as we approached the road, scrutinizing the man who leaned against the car door.

"You know him?" she asked.

"Uh huh," I said.

"What are you up to?" she said.

Anela watched me suspiciously as we reached the asphalt road. I held my breath, trying to conceal happiness and jitters. I had to get this introduction right. I stood beside Anela and the man, prepared to speak when his jazzy voice took over.

"*Anela Jewel,*" he sang.

No words from my mouth could match that hypnotizing tone. He showed an impeccable smile as he moved closer to Anela.

"I've missed your love poems," he said.

Anela examined him closely. "Cyrus!" she cried. Anela almost collapsed like a rag doll but he grabbed her waist. She rested her head on his chest, sobbing as he kissed her cheek. Her shaky hands reached up touch his smooth face. "Cyrus Williams, where have you been?"

"I've been waiting for you," he said.

"I thought I'd never see you again," Anela whimpered, looking into his eyes.

"Oh, I knew it was only a matter of time before I'd see your pretty face again," he said wiping her cheek. "Just as fine as the last day I saw you."

Anela blushed. "A little silver on top," she said.

"Same here," he said patting his head.

I smiled as I got in the car and turned up the radio. Nat King Cole sang, *Unforgettable*. Anela and Cyrus didn't miss a beat, crooning and catching up on old times.

"You like your gift?" Cyrus asked, nodding at the shiny white convertible with rose leather seats. "Boss said you been waitin' a long time for this. Della Reese ain't got nothin' on you now, baby."

Anela sighed. "I don't care about the car," she said. "As long as I have you."

"You're never gonna lose me again, Anela Jewel," he said.

I folded my arms proudly as they continued to reminisce. This reunion was definitely a match made in Heaven. "All right you two," I said. "I'm gonna be late for my first assignment. If Boss has something to say, I'm telling Him it was your fault."

"Hush, chile," Anela huffed. "I've waited longer for this man than your time on Earth, and in Heaven put together."

I winked at her. "I can't argue with that," I said as I started the engine. The two lovebirds stopped being sentimental long enough to get into the back seat. I checked out my Chanel shades in the rearview mirror and released the hair clip holding my ponytail.

"I need some real convertible music," I mumbled. I snuck a Biggie CD in the player and peeked behind me. As Anela and

Cyrus smooched, I grooved to *Big Poppa. I* pumped up the volume and hit the gas pedal. The car zoomed off into the sunset, putting all of our wings to the test.

About The Author

Shawan Lewis received a Bachelor of Science degree in Sociology from James Madison University. She worked as an insurance professional for eleven years before she became a Realtor and novelist. Shawan lives in Baltimore with her family. She loves to hear from readers. You can email her at <u>shawanlewis@aol.com</u> or visit her website at www.shawanlewis.com.

Help Wanted

ORDER TODAY!
(photo copy)
Jaya Lane Publishing
PO Box 1236, Owings Mills, MD 21117

Purchaser Information:

Please send me the book:
Help Wanted

_____ @ 15.00 (U.S.) = _____ (quantity)

Shipping/Handling* =   _____

Total Enclosed = _____

Please Print:

Name_____

Address_____

City_____ State_____ Zip Code_____

Phone Number_____Email_____

Please make sure Purchaser information is complete
prior to submitting order.
*Enclose $3.50 to cover shipping/handling
($6.00 for orders totaling more than $30.00).

Methods of Payment: Money Orders payable to Jaya Lane Publishing
or purchase books directly from author's website www.shawanlewis.com.

NO CASH or PERSONAL CHECKS accepted.

Send your payment with the order form to the above address, or order
on the web. Please allow 3-4 weeks for delivery. Thank You!